'**I am** ~~~~

His reaction was immediate. A brief widening of his eyes followed by a frown.

Beatrice's stomach fluttered uneasily. 'Is something the matter?'

Gregor wasn't at all certain how to react. He was on his way to take possession of Warehaven Keep—*and* its heiress. Of course fate would ensure that he should run into the heiress along the way.

To make matters worse, she didn't appear to fear him in the least. For the first time since the disastrous event that had passed as his marriage he feared that he might eventually come to care for a woman.

Not just any woman, but this woman…

Author Note

Over twenty years ago, in 'story' time, Randall FitzHenry and Brigit of Warehaven began their journey in *Wedding at Warehaven* from the Halloween Temptations anthology. Over the years they thrived and prospered, fortifying Warehaven, building a successful shipping empire and raising a family. That family consisted of three children: Jared the eldest who, after much grief, married his childhood love Lea of Montreau—the same woman who once left him at the altar and wed another— in *Pregnant by the Warrior*. Then there was Isabella who, while kidnapped and carted far from her home by Richard of Dunstan, discovered the love of her heart in *The Warrior's Winter Bride*.

Now it's time for Beatrice, the youngest of the family, to find her love in the least likely of places in the last Warehaven story *At the Warrior's Mercy*. I hope you've enjoyed reading about the Warehaven family even half as much as I've enjoyed creating their stories. Perhaps in this final tale we'll discover the answer to the question that's long bedevilled Beatrice—will her lover be strong enough to hold her should she swoon from his kisses?

Happy reading!

AT THE
WARRIOR'S MERCY

Denise Lynn

Published in Great Britain 2017
by Mills & Boon, an imprint of HarperCollins*Publishers*
1 London Bridge Street, London, SE1 9GF

© 2017 Denise L. Koch

ISBN: 978-0-263-92567-8

Award-winning author **Denise Lynn** lives in the USA
with her husband, son and numerous four-legged 'kids'.
Between the pages of romance novels she has travelled
to lands and times filled with brave knights, courageous
ladies and never-ending love. Now she can share with
others her dream of telling tales of adventure and romance.
You can write to her at PO Box 17, Monclova, OH 43542,
USA, or visit her website: denise-lynn.com.

Visit the Author Profile page
at millsandboon.co.uk for more titles.

To my family and husband with love, always.

Prologue

'It has come to our attention that Warehaven has been left too long without a lord.'

Gregor, second son of Roul Isle's former lord, held the questions hopping around on the tip of his tongue. Instead, he focused on the sound of workers fortifying Carlisle Castle, making it bigger and stronger. Hopefully, sooner or later King David would get to the point of this discussion before the ceaseless drone of construction drove him mad with impatience—Gregor had been too long away from his own building project and the sounds of hammering and sawing made his hands itch to wield an adze or axe. Either tool would suit him fine since he'd rather be shaping or cutting lumber than standing here in the King's court.

King David's frowning countenance during his prolonged hesitation gave Gregor the sinking feeling that not only would it be a while before he could return to his half-built ship, but that this time he wasn't going to like the task about to be placed on his shoulders.

Not that his liking would matter in the least. After nearly ten years he was still paying for his father's sins in attacking the foreigner who had been given control over some mainland property just south of Roul Isle. Gregor failed to understand why his father had never been able to accept the fact that the King's word was law, or why it mattered who held the mainland property. His father had been lucky to die an old man at home in his own bed instead of in a less pleasant manner for treason.

However, Gregor and his brothers hadn't been quite as lucky. They'd found themselves paying the price for their father's actions. Even now, his older brother Elrik, the current Lord of Roul, was off on some secret mission for the King. For the moment both Edan and Rory, his younger brothers, were at home. None of them had a choice in the matter. The alternative had been to hand over Roul Isle and leave Scotland for good. Since the only place they could go would be to Roul Keep, an unknown cousin's fortress in Normandy, all four had agreed that leaving wasn't a desirable option and had placed their lives in King David's hands.

'It was also brought to our attention that you've somehow reached your twenty-eighth year of life without a wife.' King David paused to stare at him before adding in a less accusing tone, 'Lad, a wedding ceremony which ends in death does not count as a marriage.'

Again Gregor held his tongue. What could he

say? Everyone knew what had happened that day. A marriage arranged by the King had come to a bloody end mere moments after the new bride had discovered to whom she'd been wed.

Gregor had had so many hopes for the marriage. While he'd been warned that it wouldn't curtail his service for King David, it would have provided him a welcome respite between the tasks. He'd been certain that, given time, he and Sarah would come to care for each other, create a home and a family together. He had envisioned cold winter nights spent in front of the fire, his wife at his side, while their children played at their feet.

He had looked forward to this marriage, never imagining how wrong he'd been. The day had started filled with hope and whispered promises of dreams soon to be fulfilled. It had ended moments after one of the guests had congratulated *the Wolf* for having snared a mate.

In that single heartbeat, time had slowed and he'd watched as his new bride's eyes had widened, all colour leaving her face as if she'd been drained of blood. He'd reached for her, his fingertips barely brushing the sleeve of her gown as she'd gasped, turned and then run from the Great Hall.

He'd followed, but had been unable to catch up to her until she'd reached the battlements and climbed up on to a crenel. With her arms outstretched, Sarah stood with her palms flat against a merlon on either side. The wind had whipped the long skirt of her gown, as it had her hair—both billowing around her. She'd looked over her shoulder at him. Fear and dread had shimmered in her stare. A frown of what he liked to think was regret had wrinkled her brow. Perhaps she'd had a second thought as she'd perched so high above the ground. But then, in the next heartbeat, she was gone. Nothing but air filled the space between the merlons.

The accusations had started immediately—the Wolf had pushed his new bride to her death—he'd thrown her from the wall in a fit of rage. At first he'd defended himself and the accusations had tapered off to rumours circling behind his back. But nothing would ever rid him of the memory, or the guilt. As far as he was concerned he was guilty—of not being able to stop her from jumping, of not knowing her well enough to realise what she might do and of being so terrifying to her that she chose death.

For a long time after that horrifying life-changing event, he'd thrown himself whole heartedly into the role of being King David's Wolf in a wasted effort to avoid the nightmares haunting him. If a task required any measure of ruthlessness, the King seemed well pleased to call on Gregor. He'd answered those calls without question, leaving him with an enhanced reputation that made most people, especially women, give him a wide berth.

Sometimes late at night, or when the icy winds of winter threatened to freeze him to the bone, the useless dreams of a wife and family teased at his heart. Those fanciful thoughts were short lived and easily pushed aside, as being alone was for the best. He had too much blood on his hands, too many stains upon his soul. No woman deserved to be burdened with a husband who frightened her to death, or worse prompted her to choose death at her own hands over becoming his wife.

'Are you listening to me, Wolf?'

Gregor turned his attention fully to his King. 'Aye, my lord. Warehaven's lord Randall FitzHenry seems to be absent and I have no wife.'

'My niece is certain that she has a solution for both…difficulties.'

Considering how irritated the Empress Matilda was with him at the moment for nearly ruining a marriage between two of her noble families, Gregor couldn't begin to imagine how dreadful her *solution* might prove. It was doubtful the Empress would ever forgive him for causing strife between Lady Emelina of Mortraine and Comte Souhomme. Obviously she was also irritated with her bastard brother, otherwise Warehaven wouldn't be considered a *difficulty*.

Almost as an afterthought, the King added, 'If you solve these difficulties, your service to me will be fulfilled.'

That promise picked up his spirits. Just the

thought of no longer having to pay for his father's crime was a relief that seemed nearly heaven sent. Gregor asked, 'What of my brothers?'

'It is time you think of yourself, Gregor, let them worry about their own service. However, the successful completion of this task might prove beneficial even to them.'

The weight that had been lifted at the mere mention of freedom from this service settled heavily back on to his shoulders. Gregor silently vowed that regardless of how irritated the Empress was with him, or how difficult the task put to him, he would do whatever was necessary to see this mission through to completion.

'What would you have me do?'

Chapter One

South of Derbyshire—July 1145

'Do not fight me on this. You will not win.'

Beatrice of Warehaven stared in shock at the man confronting her so boldly in the privacy of his tent.

Charles of Wardham had been the love of her life. With his lean limbs, unblemished face unscarred by any wounds of war, fair hair and oh, so deceptively kind and caring manners, he'd easily won her heart.

How was it possible that this was the same man with whom she'd fallen so desperately in love nearly three years ago?

She stared harder into his pale blue eyes, trying to see through the fog of dismay clouding her vision. Once upon a time she'd wondered if it were possible to drown in his gaze. Now she would be amazed if she did not freeze to death beneath his unwavering icy glare.

Her heart hurt—physically hurt as if it had been splintered by a battering ram as she realised that her parents had been right in their assessment of this man. They trusted him not and were certain something darkly sinister lay beneath his mild exterior. She'd so foolishly been certain of their error in judgement. Certain enough that she'd given little thought to permitting him to escort her back to Warehaven without her family's knowledge.

'Come, Beatrice.'

Neither his steady, calm tone of voice, nor the smile that never reached his eyes, fooled her. Never again would she be so fooled by a man, any man—but especially not by this one. She knew there would be nothing gentle about his touch. Even had there been any hint at gentleness, she was not about to give herself to him before they were married and since now she was certain they would never be wed, sharing his bed was not an option.

A bitter coldness of betrayal flowed down her spine. She backed away from his outstretched arm and called out, 'Edythe!'

Charles laughed at her cry, saying, 'You waste your breath. Your handmaiden's attention is occupied elsewhere.'

He parted the flap to the tent, letting the deep boisterous laughs of his two companions float into the stifling confines. Their seductive chuckles were joined by Edythe's teasing response. Now she knew why Charles had insisted the younger Edythe accompany her instead of Agatha, her former nursemaid. He'd wanted someone who would turn a blind eye to his underhanded plans.

The heat of anger chased away the chill. Beatrice glared at him. Her show of displeasure only drew another laugh from him. 'Did you just now realise your mistake?'

'My family will kill you.'

He shrugged, replying, 'While they may wish to do so, I highly doubt they will.'

'They are not afraid of you.'

'I never said they were.' Charles slowly approached, his intent plain in his lecherous gaze. 'However, they aren't about to leave their pregnant daughter without a husband.'

'I am not carrying your child.'

He wrapped a hand around her upper arm and leaned down to whisper, 'Not yet, perhaps, but rest assured you will be by the time we leave here.'

She silently cursed her stupidity for giving him a reason to voice such a threat. 'Why are you doing this? Why can't you wait until we have a chance to convince my parents of our...devotion to each other?'

Devotion. She nearly choked on the term, but it was the only word she could think of at the moment that wouldn't draw a humourless laugh—or a cry from her.

His brows rose as his smile turned into a smirk. 'You think I haven't noticed your displeasure these last two nights?'

There was much truth in his question. She'd been so disgusted by his drunken comments and those of his two companions that she was certain even one who was blind would have sensed her anger. The men spoke as if they'd been in the company of hardened soldiers on the battlefield. She'd heard milder words from her father's shipboard crew.

'I held my tongue because I had expected to be free of your friends' influence once we arrived at Warehaven.'

'Your expectations were sadly mistaken. I know you, Beatrice. I am aware of your headstrong nature and childish temper. I am not foolish enough to believe your patience would have lasted that long.' He slid a hand down her arm, brushing his thumb against the side of her breast, causing a shiver that had nothing to do with desire and everything to do with distaste and building fear. 'Hence the quickening of our relationship.'

Without giving herself away, Beatrice scanned the contents of the tent while asking, 'You would choose them over me?'

He pulled her tightly against his chest before moving towards his pallet. 'For most things, yes. But not this. I am certain burying myself in the warmth of your body will prove far more enjoyable than anything they could offer.'

His obscene answer stung, but she wasn't about to let him know that his foul words had hurt her as much as they had disgusted her. When they reached his bed, she pushed against his chest to no avail. 'Charles, you are not going to have your way with me. Release me.'

His laugh grated against her ears. 'Oh, my lovely Beatrice, save your demands. I see not how you can stop me.'

She reached down and grasped the handle of a metal ewer of water that sat on a wooden chest next to his bed and quickly, before he could determine her move, swung it against the side of his head.

His hands fell away from her, his eyes widening before he hit the floor of the tent with a thud. Beatrice leaned over him to make sure he still breathed, then whispered, 'I will stop you just like that, Charles.'

Knowing that the others would soon realise no sound came from inside the tent, Beatrice grabbed the dagger from the scabbard at his side and slid it through the fabric at the back of the tent. She grimaced at the sound, but didn't cease her actions. As soon as the tear was big enough to step through she stuck the dagger securely behind the belt wrapped low about her waist. At least she'd have some type of weapon at hand.

Beatrice exited the tent, then paused to determine which way to run. While the road they'd made camp alongside would be the easiest way back to Montreau, her brother's keep two days north, it would also prove the easiest way for Charles and his companions to capture her.

She stared into the darkness of the woods, wondering what terrors would lie in that direction. The dagger at her side wouldn't prove very useful if she truly needed to defend her life, but it gave her an odd sense of bravery.

'Charles?' Bruce, one of his companions, called from the front of the tent.

Knowing her time to decide was past, Beatrice grasped hold of her slender thread of bravery tightly and ran into the dark woods before anyone could notice Charles's prone body or her absence.

Without looking back, she ran until her legs ached and her heart raced from the effort. The brightness of the full moon had provided some light for her desperate escape through the dense brush bordering the forest, but under this thicker canopy of trees she was unable to see clearly and tripped over yet another gnarled root. Her knees throbbed from the repeated times she'd fallen on to the hard ground and her shoulder burned from where she'd scraped against a tree trunk as she fell.

'I must get away.' She beat her fists against her legs, nearly crying in frustration.

A noise too close behind her prompted Beatrice to jump to her feet, gather the long skirt of her gown in one hand and once again resume her stumbling climb up the side of the hill. She knew not who was behind her. It could be Charles and his companions, an animal hunting for food, or it could be a roaming band of thieves and murderers who meant ill will to any they came across. Either way, she couldn't let them catch her, as they were all equally dangerous to her safety.

Shivering from the cold, she choked back a sob as she scrambled up a steeper section and cursed the impractical clothing she'd donned at Charles's insistence. He'd wanted her to dress nicely for their evening meal. Since she'd packed little for her dash to what was supposed to have been the beginning of a new life with her love, other than the clothes on her back, she'd had only the clothing she was to have worn for their marriage. While beautifully bedecked with embroidered, gem-studded flowers and leaves, the thin linen layer of her gown and even thinner layer of the chemise beneath provided little protection against the inclement weather.

She wrapped her fingers tightly around the grip of the dagger with one hand and lifted the skirt of her gown with the other, wondering if cutting the length might make her journey easier. But the snapping of branches echoing through the darkness let her know there was no time for hacking at her gown. Oh, how she longed to be back at Montreau, sitting before a blazing fire where she'd be dry, warm and safe.

Gladly would she suffer her brother Jared's demanding rules and the endless lectures from his wife, Lea. Beatrice knew that had she paid the least bit of attention to the rules or the lectures she'd not have found herself in this dire predicament.

Her parents had sent her to Montreau for her protection after her older sister Isabella had been kidnapped. Nobody had expected her to remain at her brother's keep for so long, but at the same time of the kidnapping, her mother's family in Wales had fallen on hard times, then they'd been beset by illness. So her parents had spent their time travelling between Warehaven and Wales while also searching for Isabella.

When the kidnapping had turned into a marriage that produced a child, their parents had left Wales and sailed to Dunstan—Isabella's new home—for the birthing. After that, they'd immediately returned to Wales, leaving Beatrice with Jared and Lea.

The natural son of a former king, her father possessed the wealth and right to not only build, but also amass, a fleet of ships, so travelling with little notice was never an issue. Even though doing so was fraught with danger from the unforgiving sea and unpredictable weather, both of her parents preferred journeying by sea rather than over land.

However, their penchant for travelling to and fro had left her essentially stranded at Montreau. The lengthy stay had shortened her patience, which in turn had made Jared and Lea less accommodating. For the most part, they'd suffered in silence because they knew how much she longed to return home, but of late their suffering hadn't been quite as silent.

Another crack of a branch prompted her to set

aside her musings and pick up her pace. If she didn't escape the monsters trailing her, listening to her brother and sister-by-marriage would be the least of her concerns.

A thorny bush snagged the back edge of Beatrice's gown, nearly ripping it from her as she stumbled once again to the ground. Biting her lips to keep from crying out in pain and giving away her location, she staggered to her feet, using the dagger to free herself from the prickly bush before sliding it back in place. One step forward sent her over the edge of a steep embankment.

Certain this would be the moment of her demise, Beatrice prayed. 'Please, Lord, let my death be swift.'

If now was her time to die, she'd prefer a quick end rather than one that would take days—or perhaps even weeks—of suffering.

Her rolling tumble came to a sudden stop at the grassy bank of a stream. Face down in the soft grass she groaned, grateful that she hadn't stabbed herself with the unsheathed blade, then she stretched her arms and legs to ensure nothing was broken before dragging herself towards the sound of the rushing water.

Hoping the cool water would help to revive her exhausted body and muddled mind, she plunged her hands into the stream only to slide on the bank's wet grass and splash face first into the shallow water. Unprepared for the frigid coldness drenching her clothing, she gasped in shock and staggered to her feet.

A man's mumbled curse set her heart to race even faster and drew another gasp from her lips. She backed away from his voice, slipped on the rocky bottom of the stream and, with a splash, landed once again in the icy cold water.

His curse this time was louder and decidedly less mumbled. She winced at the ungodly words spewing from his mouth as he strode into the water and reached a hand down towards her.

Uncertain of his intent, she pointed her weapon at him and stared, tipping her head back to look up at his face. The full moon provided enough light to see most of his features—at least enough to see that his returning gaze was more one of impatience and surprise than a threatening glare.

With his arm still extended, he tilted his head and cocked one dark eyebrow before asking, 'Do you not find that water a little cold for a bath?'

Beatrice grasped his hand and before she could take a breath found herself held tightly against his chest as he spun her, along with her sodden clothing, out of the stream and on to the safety of the bank.

Beatrice closed her eyes and struggled to breathe. She wasn't certain whether it was the hard, rapid pounding of her heart, the fact that her nose was pressed against his breastbone, or that said breastbone belonged to a man—a stranger

who might prove more dangerous than Charles—
that made breathing nearly impossible.

He released her, then tore the useless weapon
she still held from her hand and secured it beneath
the thick sword belt round his waist before cupping the back of her head with a large hand. 'You
are shivering.'

Of course she was shivering. The water had
been frigid and the cool night air did little to lend
any warmth.

He studied her, then asked, 'Are you otherwise
uninjured?'

She found his strangely accented, deep voice
incredibly…soothing. A barely perceptible twitch
low in her belly gave her pause. His voice was
more than just soothing. With the speed and accuracy of an arrow sent flying silently through the
night his voice calmed her to the point where she
would willingly do whatever he bid.

Beatrice swallowed. This would not do. She
would not be swayed by a deep, calming voice.

'I am whole.' She pushed against his chest, demanding, 'Release me.'

He did so instantly, but the look of regret on his
face matched the sudden twinge of loss flitting in
her gut. Oh, yes, he was dangerous in more ways
than she'd first feared.

He spread his arms before her with his hands—
his very large, strong, capable-looking hands—

palms up. Beatrice blinked and then dragged her gaze away.

He tore off his cloak and settled it about her shoulders, saying, 'I'll not harm you.'

At this very moment his *harming* her wasn't what had her concerned. At least not in the manner he'd meant.

She gathered the skirt of her sodden gown and wrung out some of the water, as if that would help it dry faster, or make it more presentable, when in truth the garment would never dry in the dampness of the night and was beyond saving. What she'd truly sought was a moment to collect her thoughts. 'I thank you for your assistance, but if you'll kindly return my knife, I'll be on my way now.'

He glanced around before asking, 'Alone?'

'Yes.'

As she turned to leave, he said, 'I can't let you do that.'

'You can't stop me.'

'Stopping you would be easy.'

He had a valid point, one she didn't want to put to the test knowing full well she'd lose any physical tussle with him. She turned back to look at him. 'I am not your responsibility. I know you not and I've no wish to remain in your company.'

'True. But you are a lady alone in the middle of the night.' He glanced down at the bedraggled skirt of her gown and added, 'A very wet lady.'

Beatrice held out the skirt of her gown. 'That is rather obvious.'

He dragged his pointed gaze from the top of her head to her toes and back up again, making her realise that holding her gown out from the side had only served to tighten the skirt against her legs. She frowned at him and plucked the fabric away from her body. 'If you are finished staring, this lady needs to be on her way.'

His eyes widened in what she could only assume was shock and she groaned at her lack of manners. *Dear heaven above, had she truly just admonished a grown man who was not related to her?*

'I apologise.'

He ignored her apology to ask, 'Where are you going?'

The sound of a pebble or stone bouncing down the hill behind them drew her attention away from his question. That hadn't dislodged by itself. Something—or someone—had kicked it loose.

He stepped closer to her and rephrased his question. 'Who are you running from?'

'A mangy cur who needs to be put down.' Beatrice closed her eyes. What was happening to her? Why did this man's nearness make her feel safe enough to speak her mind? He was a stranger and from his rugged looks more warrior than simple man.

'Your husband?'

She swung her head to look up at him. 'God be praised, no.'

His soft laugh made her smile. Clearly he'd heard the overwhelming relief in her breathless tone and found it amusing, not off-putting.

'I sense a tale worth telling.' He nodded downstream. 'There is an inn in the village. You can hide there while sitting near the fire to dry and tell me your story. In the meantime, I can decide what to do with you.'

While he might think his plan sensible, Beatrice thought otherwise. 'I can't walk into an inn with you. We are not related, nor wed. You know what people will think.'

He slung a large, muscular arm about her shoulders, turned her towards the village and started walking, giving her little choice but to walk beside him. His thigh brushed her hip and she tried to sidestep, hoping that putting a little distance between them would ease the restless fluttering of her heart. Unfortunately, the small space was far too little.

'Do you know the people in this village?'

Beatrice shrugged. 'I am not even certain what village this is, so it's doubtful if I'll know anyone.'

'Then what do you care what they might think?'

'I have a reputation to think of and I already look quite dreadful.'

'Ah, a rich heiress, no doubt.'

In truth she was. But she wasn't about to admit

something that could possibly put her in even more danger. It would be an easy task for him to take her hostage and then bleed her father of gold in exchange for her return. 'Heiress or not, I still have to protect my reputation and future.'

He shook his head and made a noise that sounded suspiciously like a chortle of disbelief. 'Which is why you are running about at night alone.'

She bristled at his chastising tone and tried to pull away, but he only tightened his fingers over her shoulder, keeping her in place. She frowned at the warmth seeping into her at his touch before stating, 'You are neither my father nor my brother and thus have no right to remind me of my shortcomings.'

He stared down at her. 'You put your life and your precious reputation at great risk and you call that nothing more than a shortcoming? You need count yourself lucky I am not your father or brother, for if I were, I would use more than simple words to remind you of your place.'

She knew exactly what he meant, but little did he know that it wasn't her brother or father who would be tempted to take a switch to her backside if they found out what she'd done. It was her mother who would be sore pressed not to do so. Beatrice knew that regardless of whether any punishment was meted out or not, her parents would be unable to trust her and, short of locking her in a cell, their only other choice would be to marry her off to the first man who showed up at their walls.

A fate she could have avoided had she acted with more caution, like her sister Isabella would have done, instead of being so impulsive. It was imperative that she learn to think things through before dashing off to follow her heart's desire.

'I know full well the foolishness of the risk I took. I've no need to be reminded of it.'

'If you knew it was foolhardy, what made you take such a risk?'

Beatrice sighed. 'I thought I did so for love.'

To her amazement, he didn't laugh at her childish notion. Instead he simply shook his head, then said, 'Since this shouldn't be too difficult a mystery to solve, let me guess. Once alone he decided to take what he thought was his whether you agreed or not.'

She nodded in reply.

'Did no one ever warn you about the wicked ways of men?'

'Of course they did.'

'But you thought he was different.'

'Yes,' she admitted.

'Then perhaps you learned a hard lesson. All men are the same.'

'Even though this wastrel proved to be a beast, I would say you are wrong. While I did learn a lesson that I'll not likely forget, not all men are the same. Neither my father nor brother are vile animals.'

'They are related to you, so of course they do not act like fools in your presence.'

Beatrice smiled at his statement. Sometimes her brother acted like the worst of fools, but she knew what this stranger meant. Still, what about him? 'I disagree. You have not offered me harm when you could have easily done so.'

'You do not fear me?'

'Do I act afraid?' Although, by all rights she should be afraid. Terrified, in fact, and she didn't understand why she wasn't. Her lack of fear confused her—it made no sense. She was alone in the company of what appeared to her to be a seasoned warrior.

The only explanation she had was that all of her fear was directed at Charles and his companions, leaving none for this man. Perhaps once her senses cleared and she regained the ability to do more than worry about those chasing her, she would find herself beset with the proper amount of fear.

'Perhaps you should be afraid.'

'And perhaps once I am safe and dry I will be afraid.'

'How can you be so certain I am leading you to safety?'

'I cannot. But if I am to die I would much rather it be at the hands of someone I know not, instead of one I thought I knew well.'

She felt his questioning stare and hoped he didn't ask her to explain what probably seemed like a strange notion. She wasn't certain she could find the right words to tell him that being harmed by a near stranger would only hurt physically and while it might take time to heal, she eventually would. Whereas any harm Charles inflicted would also linger in her heart, preventing her from ever healing fully.

'There are worse things that could happen to you than being killed.'

Beatrice shivered harder, knowing he was right. 'Is that your intention? To do things worse than death to me?'

He withdrew his arm from about her shoulders, pulled her dagger from behind his sword belt, then grasped her wrist, pressing his thumb into the soft flesh until she spread her fingers open, and then he slapped the grip of the weapon into her hand. 'The only plan I have for you is to see you safely delivered to your home and family.'

The angry frown etched on his face seemed to hide something else. She parted her lips to apologise, but before she could utter a single word he marched off towards the village, leaving her to follow or not.

Beatrice hesitated, uncertain what to do. She had her dagger in hand and could head for Warehaven as she'd originally planned—on her own. A shiver of cold raced down her spine beneath the dripping clothing. Or she could accept his offer of a warm fire to sit beside while she decided what to do next.

Either option was a better choice than having remained with Charles.

Chapter Two

While the noisy, smoke-filled inn had been an unexpected find, Gregor of Roul had been glad for the warmth and shelter it had provided him earlier when he'd sought to escape the company of his men for a few hours of time alone and had no aversion to being once again beneath its thatched roof.

He raised his cup, only to find it empty, and signalled one of the maids over to his rough-hewn table in the far corner near the fire.

She placed a jug of ale before him, then lingered to give him an assessing gaze—a look signalling that she didn't know anything about his reputation or his identity.

He wondered idly what women saw when they looked at him before they realised who he was—when they gazed upon him as if he were just a man instead of a treacherous beast. Did they see that his once coal-black hair had started turning silver too early, making him look far older than his twenty-eight years? Or did the strand of silvery-white hair hanging across his forehead make them think of the wolves that populated his ancestor's demesne lands in Normandy, giving them the name Roul?

Did they notice that his nose was crooked from

one too many fights? Or the jagged scar that ran the length of his jawbone, accentuated now by the stubble from not shaving these last three days on the road. Did these imperfections make him appear a warrior to be pitied, or one to be feared?

He knew the very second she realised who she might be serving. Men would instinctively reach for their weapon and willingly choose avoidance if possible. But as happened more often than not with women, her smile vanished and the tell-tale shimmer of fear brightened her widening eyes and enlarged her pupils.

'Will you be needing anything else?' Her previous warmth cooled, leaving her tone curt and distracted as if she couldn't get away quickly enough.

Gregor sighed. Had he been anyone else, she'd have followed her query with a saucy wink and lingering touch on his shoulder to let him know that if he was so tempted, she'd be more than willing to keep him company this night.

She was a fine-looking young woman, with blond hair that tumbled in loose waves down her back and a gown laced so snugly that nothing of her curvaceous form was left to his imagination.

But it wasn't a blonde serving wench who filled his thoughts at the moment. Instead a dark-haired, headstrong, wayward lady flitted around in his mind. One with the take-charge spirit of a warrior, flashing green eyes full of curiosity, an impertinent mouth that begged to be kissed and a lack of fear that both fascinated and intrigued him.

He'd been intrigued from the moment she'd grasped his hand. Had she felt the same shocking spark of warmth flow through her at the contact as he'd experienced? Or during that brief moment when she'd rested against his chest, had she been struck by the rightness of it, as if that was where she belonged?

Even though it would make no difference, he couldn't help but wonder what would happen when she discovered who had come to her rescue. A small part of him wished that, just for a moment perhaps, her impertinence could be far stronger than any fear.

He blinked. What was he thinking? The last thing he needed was a woman, especially one who had caught his interest, distracting him from the task at hand. It was bad enough that when he'd seen her tumble down the hill, then slip into the water he'd felt strangely compelled to lend assistance. It had gone from bad to worse when he'd grasped her hand to pull her from the water and had looked into her eyes—something inside him had sparked to life—something that was best left alone. He didn't need to make things impossible by imagining things that could never be.

Forcing his attention back to the waiting maid, he added a couple of pennies to the charge for the ale, something extra for her, and shook his head. 'No, there's nothing else I require.'

She reached down with a trembling hand, scooped up the coins quickly and nearly ran from his table.

'Please, someone, help me.'

Ah, he recognised that voice. She'd chosen to accept his protection after all. Not that she'd really had a choice as his intention had been to let her stew for a short time, then go and find her.

He shouldered his way through the now-gathering throng of men surrounding her and grasped her elbow. 'Come with me.'

She followed him without hesitation, until he paused before his table and waved her to take a seat on the bench.

'No. I cannot. There is no time.' She paused to cast a furtive glance towards the door, adding, 'I need to hide.'

Gregor adjusted his cloak that was still about her shoulders and pulled up the hood to conceal her features. He waved the maid over again to ask, 'Is there an available room above?' At her nod, he placed more than enough coins in her palm and said, 'You've not seen either of us.'

Her eyes bulged at the amount in her hand, but finally she replied, 'I'll let the others know.'

Thankful for that bit of assistance from one so reluctant, he added more coins to what he'd already given her. 'I thank you. See to it that everyone has a full cup.' He paused for a quick glance down at the woman he sought to hide, then handed the maid even more coins, saying, 'If you have any dry clothing available, it would be more than welcome.'

The woman's eyes once again grew wide, but this time with shock instead of fear. She closed her fingers tightly over what must seem to her riches in her palm and nodded.

Gregor turned his focus back on the woman shivering at his side and placed a hand on the small of her back. 'Come. You can hide above.'

She hesitated. He read the uncertainty in her piercing green gaze. He understood her indecision—even though they'd spoken by the stream, she truly didn't know him and couldn't be certain that he didn't pose an even greater threat than those she wanted so desperately to avoid.

The door to the inn opened once again, letting a cold gust of wind enter and whip through to swirl around his ankles. Her stare jumped towards the door. Gregor leaned slightly closer to ask, 'The wolves at the door, or the one at your side who has yet to have offered you harm?'

And her gaze darted once again, this time, as he knew it would, to the shock of silver now hanging low over his forehead. For whatever reason, she hadn't been afraid of him before, but now he saw the flicker of fear in her eyes. He caught her uncertain stare with his own and held it, promising, 'You can trust me, my lady.'

As three men entered the inn, she bolted for the stairs. Not wanting her to draw attention, Gregor draped an arm across her shoulders. 'Slowly, as if we're simply two lovers headed above.'

She stiffened momentarily at the insinuation, but slowed her steps.

Once they reached the upper landing, he lowered his arm and pushed open the first door. Ushering her inside, he closed the door behind them and then dropped the thick locking bar in place.

Beatrice's breath caught in her throat at the sound of the timber falling securely into the iron holders. What had she done? While it was true that for this moment she was safe from Charles and his companions, she was now locked into a bedchamber with a man she did not know.

Outside of this inn he'd been oddly easy to talk to, but now the fear she'd not felt then welled to life.

He had jumped to her aid so quickly. Too willingly, perhaps? Had he done so out of chivalry? Had he done so for his own nefarious reasons? Reasons that would leave her in greater peril than she'd faced from Charles?

It mattered little now. Her fate was sealed. Whatever was going to happen was out of her hands as she had no way to escape. The only window in this room was nothing more than an unshuttered narrow slit that she'd never be able to fit through and the timber bar across the door was thicker than her forearm. It would prove far too heavy for her to remove alone.

After once again mentally cursing her rashness in leaving Montreau, she took a breath and watched the man closely.

He walked around the edge of the room, keeping as far away from her as space would permit in this small bedchamber.

For that she was grateful, but she knew that it would take no more than a quick lunge from him to reach her.

He picked up the pitcher from the small table against the wall on the other side of the bed and poured water into the ready cup. After taking a swallow, he extended the cup, asking, 'Thirsty?'

Even though her body was wet and cold, she was parched. While the water would quench her thirst, she worried that by accepting his offer she would put herself too close, enabling him to grab her. Beatrice shook her head, eyeing the water with longing. 'No, thank you.'

He raised a dark eyebrow and set the drinking vessel back down on the table. 'It is here if you want it later.' And then walked back along the walls to take a seat on the small bench next to the door.

Beatrice's glance returned to the water. Her mouth was so dry that she wondered if her tongue would stick to the roof of it permanently.

'By the sound of it, your pursuer seems to be

in no hurry to leave, so we're going to be here a while. Drink the water. Remove that heavy cloak and sit near the brazier to dry before you catch your death of cold.'

Beatrice moved to the other side of the bed and raised the cup to her lips. The cool water quenched the dryness of her mouth. She shot the man a glance. He'd leaned the back of his head against the wall and closed his eyes. She let the cloak slip from her shoulders, trying not to sigh aloud at the absence of its over-warm weight and spread it out on the end of the bed where she could feel the heat of the coals. Careful to keep her soiled gown wrapped close about her, she sat on top of the cloak and stared down at her lap.

In the still quiet of the room even her breathing seemed loud to her. Suddenly the hairs on the back of her neck rose. That prickly sensation of someone staring at her, watching her, studying her, stalking her like prey chased warning shivers down her spine.

Beatrice hazarded a quick glance over her shoulder and met his intent blue-grey stare.

'So now your fear has caught up with you.'

He hadn't phrased it as a question, but she felt compelled to answer. 'It seems that way, yes.'

'Earlier outside with nothing but the moon as a witness you were not afraid. But here, with an inn full of people who would hear any scream for help, you are suddenly overcome with fear? Where is the sense in that?'

Beatrice shrugged a shoulder. How was she supposed to make enough sense of her emotions to be able to explain them to him when she could barely understand them herself? So much had happened this day that her thoughts and senses were all awhirl with confusion.

Finally, knowing he waited for an answer, she nodded towards the barred door. 'Outside I had somewhere to run if needed. In here I am trapped by solid walls and a door I could not unbar no matter how hard I tried.'

She then patted the lumpy mattress beneath her. 'And it is obvious that the place to do the deed if you chose is at hand.'

His bark of laughter surprised her. To her relief he remained seated on the small bench.

'You truly are an innocent. Trust me when I tell you that while a bed might be more comfortable for you, I could just as easily make do with the ground.' His gaze narrowed. 'Or press your back against a tree, lift your gown and do the *deed*, as you call it, standing up.'

His eyes shimmered and a crooked half-smile curved his lips as if the thought of doing just what he'd described pleased him.

Unable to swallow or catch her breath, Beatrice tore her gaze from his and again stared down at her lap. The tremors racing along her spine now had nothing to do with fear or cold and her imaginative thoughts were making her much warmer than had the heavy cloak.

His deep, soft chuckle before he fell blessedly silent didn't help at all. It only made her bite her lower lip to hold back a gasp at the heat now burning her cheeks.

It took more than a few moments, but finally her breathing returned to normal and she noticed the voices below filtering up through the floor. Charles was still below, his voice was loud enough to be heard clearly as he demanded she come out of hiding. A demand that would go unmet.

'Why is he so intent on finding you?'

She jumped at the sudden break in the quiet of this room. Uncertain how to respond, she remained silent.

'You didn't lie to me, did you? You aren't a runaway wife?'

'No, I did not lie. Thankfully, I am not his wife. But I could have been.'

Beatrice frowned. Why had she added that last bit? Maybe the gentleness of the stranger's gravelly voice had lulled her into giving away information best left unspoken.

'Perhaps now is the time to discover your story. How is it you could have been, but aren't? Is he your betrothed?'

She shifted on the bed, so she could look at

him, then shook her head. 'My parents wouldn't permit it.'

'Mayhap they had their reasons?'

'I am certain now that they did.' She wished that they had shared their reasons with her, instead of just insisting he was not suitable.

'Ah, but yet here you are without any chaperon at hand, being chased by him. Did he kidnap you and somehow you escaped?'

'It was no kidnapping.'

'So you went with him willingly and when he tried to take what was not his, you ran.'

'Yes.'

'Obviously you'd known this man for a while.'

'Nearly three years.'

'I suppose you thought that having conversed with him in the company of others made you believe you could trust him in private.'

She felt the flush rush up her neck to cover her face.

His soft laugh drew her attention, prompting her to ask, 'What do you find so amusing?'

'You,' he answered simply.

'Why me?' As far as Beatrice was aware, she'd done nothing anyone could consider amusing in the least. Nothing about this day had been *amusing*.

'I trust you do not gamble, for if you did, your face would give you away.'

What an odd thing to say. 'How so?'

'Your flushed cheeks tell me plainly that you

and your would-be suitor were not always chaperoned.'

To her horror, her cheeks flamed again. 'That is none of your concern.'

'Concern is not my intent. I thought only to point out your inability to lie.'

'Since I was not raised to do so, then perhaps my lack of skill is a good thing.'

'Certainly. At least until you find the need to do so.'

'Hopefully, I will never find myself in dire enough straits where I need to lie.'

He nodded, but she saw the corner of his mouth twitch in what she assumed would be another laugh at her expense.

However, he didn't laugh, or even smile, instead he said, 'I would guess it is now your intention to return to the safety of your family.'

Since he was basically stating the obvious, she only nodded in reply.

'And when they ask where you've been without the oversight and guidance of your lady's maid or at the very least a guard, you'll tell them what? That you slipped away under the cover of darkness with your lover?'

Beatrice closed her eyes. He had a point. Since everything had gone awry so suddenly, leaving her more worried about her safety, she'd given no thought to tomorrow or the days after, let alone the day she'd arrive at Warehaven.

She most certainly wasn't going to tell her parents that she'd run away from Montreau with Charles. With her luck they would force the two of them to wed just to save her reputation. She'd rather die than become Charles's wife.

When she didn't respond, he suggested, 'You will lie to save face.'

She twisted the edges of her once-fine sleeve in her hand. 'Yes, you are correct. I will lie to them. But not to save face.'

'Oh? Then why? Surely not to save the man who so obviously caused you such distress that you ran away in the middle of the night.'

'No!' she nearly shouted. She swallowed, hoping to soften her tone before adding, 'He can rot in Hades for all I care.'

At that comment, the man did laugh and, to her amazement, Beatrice found that she rather liked the sound of his mirth. It was deep and full, an honest laugh that seemed unforced.

'Well, at least you hold no misguided hope that he'll change his underhanded ways.'

'That is not likely to happen.'

The man frowned and leaned forward to slowly study her before asking, 'Did he harm you? Is there any reason I should go below and show him the error of his ways?'

'You sound like my brother.'

'I doubt that. I'm sure your family would go

down there and soundly trounce the fiend long before they thought to ask your blessing.'

That much was true. She shook her head. 'No, he did not harm me. I knocked him out with a water pitcher before he could do more than pull me into his tent and threaten me.' Thankfully the rounded metal bottom of the ewer had made just the right contact with his head.

'Ah, so he does need to learn the benefit of manners.'

When he rose, Beatrice frowned. What was he up to?

He headed towards the door and she gasped, guessing his intent. 'No. Do not. He is accompanied by two other companions who are just as vile if not more so and I wish them not to know for certain that I am here.'

'I heard him just as plainly as you did.' He rolled his eyes before removing the timber bar from the door. 'He already knows you are here. Either he saw you enter, or someone below told him about a woman seeking help. He and his companions aren't going to leave without you in tow.' He turned back to face her, adding, 'I am not about to let that happen. Besides, three men who see fit to terrorise a defenceless woman will prove little threat to my well-being. Once I have finished with them they'll think twice about not keeping their distance from you.'

His words only served to increase her confusion. 'Why would you do that for me? I am not a member of your family. You know me not.'

'You are a lady alone in need of help. Should I turn my back and leave you to your fate when I know how unpleasant that fate will prove? No. I have enough stains upon my soul without adding another that I could have easily prevented.'

Beatrice sprang from the bed and rushed to grab his arm. 'No. Please. Do nothing. I've caused you enough trouble already.'

He easily shook off her hold. 'Quiet yourself. I have every intention of returning you to your family and I'll not have them question your safety while under my care.'

'No. I—'

But before she could beg him not to confront Charles, he'd stripped off his tunic, tossed it on to the bench and was gone.

She wrung her hands. What was she to do now? She didn't want him to put himself out for her, no matter how much she appreciated his kind offer of help. However, she didn't want him to return her to her family, because then she'd have to explain everything to them and she wished to avoid that at all costs. On the other hand, she most certainly didn't want to risk him losing a fight with Charles and his friends because that would only leave her at their not-so-tender mercy.

She raced back to the small table, grabbed the pitcher and then emptied the water out of the window. Instead of standing here fretting, the least thing she could do was be there to lend a hand if needed.

By the time she made it to the bottom step the fight was all but over. Charles and one of his friends were prone on the floor of the inn. The third man was winded and backing towards the door as her rescuer pummelled him with fists to the stomach and face. She blinked and nearly missed the punch to the man's jaw that sent him flying from his feet, backwards out the door to the boisterous delight of those watching.

Beatrice didn't know whether to be impressed with his strength, skill, the fact that he'd so easily defended her honour, or the muscles evident in his arms and shoulders beneath his thin shirt.

No! Not again. Had she not just learned that lesson? Judging a man by his looks was more than foolish—it was dangerous and it was something she'd vowed never to repeat.

She'd once asked her sister Isabella if her betrothed's arms were strong enough to hold her if she swooned from his kisses, as if that was any trait on which to base a marriage. Isabella's embarrassment when discussing the form of men had made her laugh. No more.

It was time she grew up. And it was far past time that she started thinking about her future like a woman, not a child. She needed to be more like her sister and consider something besides looks—

things like strength, honour, truthfulness, a sense of humour and perhaps even kindness for a start. When had Charles ever shown her any of those qualities? Never.

Yet, this stranger walking towards her with his face devoid of any expression—not prideful ego at how he'd soundly trounced the other three men, nor regret that he'd done so—had shown not only strength, but he'd pulled her from the stream and offered her a place to get dry and warm. He could have walked away when he'd seen her in the water and she would never have known.

Not a word was spoken when he stopped before her, he simply extended his arm, motioning her to return upstairs. When she remained rooted to the bottom step, he walked past her up the stairs.

Beatrice turned and followed him, feeling oddly hesitant. Her pulse quickened with a nervous tension she couldn't quite define. She shook her head at her sudden bout of uncertainty. My, my, wasn't she just full of indecision at the moment.

This inability to decide was foreign to her. Before this night she'd easily made up her mind and acted, whether said decision—or action—was in her best interest or not.

What was it about this man that made her so… confused and off balance?

He once again closed the door behind them after she'd entered the bedchamber and then turned to stare at her, a single eyebrow arched in obvious question.

She looked down, in the direction of his stare and shrugged before waving the empty pitcher. 'I thought perhaps you might need assistance.'

'And you planned to toss water on us?'

'Heavens, no.' She tipped the pitcher on end. 'I'd emptied it to use as a head smasher.'

'Ah.' The corners of his lips quirked. 'I take it smashing heads is your preferred way of protecting yourself?'

Since he seemed in the mood to tease her, Beatrice lifted her chin and shot him what she hoped was a threatening glare. 'Yes.' She shook the pitcher at him. 'And I'm very handy at it, too.'

'I'll keep that in mind.'

She walked around the bed and set the pitcher back on the small table before once again taking a seat on the cloak. 'When the sun rises, I will take my leave.'

'No. That's not a good idea.'

'But I need to return to my home.' Without someone who could tell her parents what she'd done. Their last missive to Jared had said they'd be returning to Warehaven soon. She wasn't certain if they'd returned yet or not, but it was a risk she didn't wish to take.

'I may have warned off those threatening you, but that doesn't make it safe for you to head off on your own. I can't in good conscience let a woman go traipsing about alone and unprotected. I will escort you.'

'No. That's not necessary. I'm certain they've learned their lesson and will bother me no further.' Although, knowing how doggedly determined Charles could be at times, there was still a chance he hadn't given up for good. It would not surprise her in the least if he showed up at Warehaven intent on telling her parents that she'd left Montreau alone with him, hoping to force her into a marriage to save her reputation. She could only pray that she arrived at Warehaven well ahead of him.

He shrugged. 'They may or may not have learned their lesson. So, travelling alone is not wise.'

Somehow she had to dissuade him. 'My home is a long way from here, I wouldn't want to squander your time. I am certain I can hire someone to serve as a safe escort, someone with free time to spare.' Actually, at the moment she had little idea how far away Warehaven was, other than it was still south, since yesterday the sun had passed over them from her left to her right.

He sat down on the bench and started to remove his boots. 'I have nothing pressing at the moment, so you need not worry about squandering my time.'

This would not do. 'And what do you think would happen should I show up at the gates escorted by you? How would I explain that?'

'Fear not, I am under royal orders, your parents will believe whatever I tell them.'

That took her by surprise. She'd assumed he was a warrior, but a royal knight on business for his liege? She didn't care to ask which royal because both King Stephen and the Empress Matilda were related to her family through her father, so one of their men escorting her home could prove disastrous—it would only encourage her parents to ask more questions than normal.

Regardless of which royal held this man's allegiance, his travelling alone on some official business didn't make sense to her. Normally he'd have a squad of soldiers and guards in his party.

She stared hard at him then asked, 'Who are you?'

He toed off one boot, letting it thud to the floor. 'Gregor of Roul.'

Beatrice closed her eyes in disbelief. This man was King David's Wolf? Somehow, he wasn't at all what she would have expected. He was too young, too comely and far too kind to be the dreaded warrior spoken of in tales of horror. She would have thought he'd be someone much older, more scar riddled, surly, completely without mercy and fearsome. But then wolves were a sly lot, were they not?

She opened her eyes to look at him and then sighed at the odd question that immediately sprang to her mind, since after all Roul meant wolf.

He narrowed his gaze at her briefly before loosening the ties of his remaining boot. 'I can see the questions causing frown lines on your face. What do you wish to ask?'

She glanced at him to judge his mood. When he didn't seem distressed in the least, she let the question roll off her tongue. 'And how many times have you been called the Wolf of Roul?'

'Too many times to count. It has been my name for my entire life.' He let his other boot fall. 'The silver in my hair doesn't help in avoiding the question. And this bit—' he flicked the finger-wide swath of silver hanging over his forehead '—has been there for as long as I can remember.'

'Ah.' He sounded as if he didn't like the odd colouring. Did he not realise how strikingly pleasing it made him appear?

'And still you don't fear me?'

Beatrice frowned. Of course she'd heard the tales told of this man. If King David needed some distasteful or difficult task completed, he sent his Wolf. It mattered little how the deed was handled, once the order was given, no one escaped the Wolf's grasp.

So, yes, she should be terrified of him. She should probably quake and wail in fear that he was about to add her to his long list of those he'd dispatched to their maker.

And while his reputation made her leery, there was no reason for King David to have ordered her death. Besides, this man had offered her no harm thus far. In truth, he'd lent more help than she would have expected from any warrior. Finally, she shook her head and admitted, 'You are not what rushes to my mind when I overhear hushed whispers of King David's Wolf.'

'Did you expect blood to be dripping from my teeth?'

'There is no cause to be so gruesome.' She glanced around the room before stating the obvious. 'I am completely at your mercy, yet you have offered me no harm.'

'That doesn't mean I won't.'

Her judgement of men had been sorely taxed this day and had come up wanting. She was in no position to pass any judgement on him, a man she knew only by reputation. A reputation that claimed he was more than just ruthless. Yet she had seen no evidence offered to prove she was in any danger. 'Are you seeking to intentionally frighten me?'

When he didn't answer, she said, 'I just watched you soundly thrash three men, all of whom lived. I would not have shed a single tear for any of them had they died. Yet contrary to the tales told of King David's Wolf, you left them alive and breathing. But now I am to believe you will take my life without any cause whatsoever?'

'You are a strange woman.'

'Perhaps. But I have sorely misjudged a man I

thought I knew well this day. Would it make sense for me to judge you based on hearsay alone?'

When he once again didn't answer her question, she said, 'I told you before that I would rather die at a stranger's hand than one I thought I knew well. I cannot stop you, so if it is my blood you wish to shed, then do so and be done with it.'

He rose slowly, filling the space in the small chamber, towering over her even from across the room. Then he furrowed his brow and glared at her, giving the impression of targeted rage.

Beatrice felt her eyes widen as her heart kicked hard inside her chest before settling back down into a more normal rhythm. Oh, yes, she imagined that he could be very intimidating when he wished.

From his harsh expression, she also imagined he could be quite deadly when the situation required. She'd already witnessed his accuracy and speed with his fists when he'd fought with Charles and his companions, so she doubted if he'd be any less accurate with a sword, mace or a battle axe.

However, if he thought his stance and glowering countenance would make her quake in fear of her pending death, he was wrong.

She was a warrior's daughter and another warrior's sister. She'd grown up playing at the docks and shipyard. She'd seen men lose their tempers, become enraged more than once and had witnessed the grisly outcome of many a fight. Even so she knew if he were to make a move to attack her she'd quickly find herself shaking from fright. However, the events of this day, combined with the simple fact that his eyes glimmered far too much for one seeking to instil fear, made it impossible to take him seriously.

When he deepened his scowl, she burst out laughing.

He sat back down on the bench. 'Not quite the reaction I had expected.'

'I…am sorry…truly sorry…please…' Beatrice managed to choke out what she hoped sounded like an apology before she gave up to wave a hand in the air, then wiped the tears from her eyes as she fought to catch her breath. 'I do apologise, nothing this day has been expected. I assure you, I am normally not this…this…'

'Brazen?' Gregor supplied.

She did her best to temper her mirth before it once again escaped. Never before had she actually laughed so rudely at someone. Her mother would be horrified by her behaviour. Beatrice knew that in truth both of her parents would be horrified by everything she'd done the last few days.

Thankfully, Gregor didn't appear horrified, or angry at her outburst. She really did need to treat him with a bit more respect. It would also be wise if she was a little more wary around him considering who he was and how she'd placed herself at his mercy.

That thought helped lessen her humour. She

folded her hands in her lap, took a deep steadying breath and once again said, 'I am sorry for laughing at you.'

He sighed, his shoulders heaving as if in defeat. 'You've no need to apologise. I was intentionally seeking to make you feel at ease by acting like a fool. Apparently I underestimated my abilities.'

She felt her lip quiver and turned her head away, praying she'd not burst into laughter once again.

Certain she could retain control over her emotions, she turned back to look at him.

He leaned against the wall. 'Now that you know who I am, it's your turn.'

'I suppose it's only right that you know who you defended so handily.' She found herself oddly nervous at the idea of divulging something as personal as her name. Shaking off her sudden qualms, she said, 'I am Beatrice of Warehaven.'

His reaction was immediate. And strange.

A brief widening of his eyes was followed by a frown which he tried to cover by rubbing a hand across his forehead.

Beatrice's stomach fluttered uneasily. 'Is something the matter?'

Chapter Three

Gregor wasn't at all certain how to react, so he rubbed his temples in an attempt to gain enough time to respond.

If this wasn't some sort of jest devised by Satan himself, he didn't know what was. The complete irony of this situation would make his two younger brothers hoot like drunken fools. His older brother Elrik would shake his head and claim that it was Roul's curse coming to life once again.

He and Elrik had both lost wives in horrific manners, but his brother had also lost a child along with his wife. So when Sarah had chosen to end her life rather than be his wife, Elrik had claimed they were cursed never to have wives or families.

Gregor didn't know if he believed they were cursed or not—he'd chosen not to believe. What he did know was that no one could ever accuse him of relying on luck, since it had never run to his favour. Because he was on his way to take possession of Warehaven Keep and its remaining heiress, of course luck would ensure that he would run into the heiress along the way.

To make matters worse, the fiery lass didn't appear to fear him in the least. For the first time since the disastrous event that passed as his marriage, he feared that he could eventually come to care for a woman.

Not just any woman, but this woman.

She was too easy to be near. Far too easy to look at and talking to her was quickly becoming something he could get used to doing—especially when they could make each other laugh.

More than that, he'd seen her nervous tension around him. The lady was far too innocent yet to realise it, but that tension had nothing to do with fear, but with interest. He'd recognised it because he felt it, too. And knowing that within a matter of days her world would come crashing down around her, ending with her marriage to him, did nothing to quell the budding desire—in fact, it only made it worse.

This was not good—for either of them.

If he was only going to Warehaven to force her hand in marriage, she might somehow be willing to eventually forgive his actions. But that wasn't at all the case. He was going to intentionally harm this young woman's family, perhaps bring about the death of someone she loved. At the very least he would take everything her family had worked for, steal her future and break her heart.

There was no way of knowing what she would do—no way for him to tell if she would resort to the same actions as Sarah had. He couldn't afford to care about her. More importantly, she could not be given the chance to care about him.

It would do neither of them any good.

The one mission where his ability to feel nothing would be his strongest armour was in jeopardy. No, he corrected that thought. The success of the mission was not in any danger, it would just be harder to complete. His focus would need to be more well defined.

It would have to be more finely honed than his sharpest blade, all because this slip of a woman wasn't afraid of him, but found him desirable, and because he was oddly attracted to the sound of her laughter—even when it was directed *at* him. It had raced across his heart warm and inviting. The sound had soothed him while at the same time left him wanting more.

More was something he couldn't have—not from her. The only thing he would gain from her was hatred.

'Gregor?'

He took a deep breath and rose on suddenly shaking legs.

She tipped her head and studied him with obvious concern, causing him to clench his teeth at the sharp prick to his heart.

A soft knock on the chamber door stopped him from having to say anything. 'My lord? I am putting the things you requested right outside the door.'

He opened the door to find the waiting pile. Gregor picked up the stack and after quickly sorting through what seemed serviceable enough clothing, he tossed them on to the bed. 'Not as fine as you are used to, but they'll be dry. I'll step out while you put them on.'

Before she could once again question his obvious change in mood, he grabbed his boots, walked out of the chamber, slamming the door closed behind him, and headed below. It was doubtful any amount of ale would make tomorrow bearable, but a throbbing head would provide a good excuse to avoid her, or to be surly enough in her presence that she'd wish to avoid any conversation.

For now, that seemed the best course of action.

Beatrice flinched at the coldness in his tone which he'd punctuated by slamming the door closed on his hasty exit.

What was wrong with the man?

She frowned, mentally going over everything they had said since coming back up to this bedchamber. And yet, rehashing their conversation repeatedly provided her with no answer.

True, she'd laughed at his display of aggression, but he'd not seemed angered by her lack of composure, a little surprised perhaps, just as he had when she hadn't quivered in terror at knowing his identity. Neither of those things had brought about a change in his demeanour.

That hadn't happened until she'd told him her name.

Why?

Somehow she was going to have to reason this out on her own, because it was doubtful he was going to tell her.

She pulled the pile of clothing closer to her and shook her head. The wool gown and serviceable shift were every bit as fine as what she wore at Warehaven. Did he think she always dressed in fine-spun linen and silk bedecked with embroidery and gems?

If so, then he obviously didn't know the workings of a large keep, or the women who saw to its day-to-day operation. If she'd shown up in the kitchens dressed in such finery, Cook would have sent for her lady mother long before Beatrice could stir a pot or knead a loaf of bread.

To her great relief, she found a large towel mixed in with the garments. She stripped off her ruined slippers and stockings, then glanced at the door. It was doubtful that Gregor would barge in on her, but there were others about. Knowing she'd never be able to fit the bar into place, she dragged the bench in front of the door. It wouldn't stop anyone from entering, but the noise it would make as the door shoved it across the wooden floor would warn her of the intruder's presence.

Anxious to once again be dry and warm, Beatrice struggled with the laces of her gown. The wet knots refused to give and she knew she'd never be able to gather the skirt and pull it over her head.

She cursed through gritted teeth, then spied

the small dagger. With no one to help her, there wasn't any choice in the matter of removing her wet clothes.

And it wasn't as if she was ever going to wear this gown again—she wanted nothing that would remind her of Charles. Perhaps, once it was washed and dried, there would be enough decent fabric left for someone to use. If nothing else, they could pick the gems free from the embroidery. Surely that would be payment enough for the clothing the maid had brought.

Beatrice stuck the tip of the blade through the neck edge of the gown and cringed. She'd spent a goodly amount of time on not just the sewing of the gown, but on the trim work, too. With a determined stroke, she sliced the gown down to her waist.

It took some doing, but after slitting the shoulders and tops of the sleeves, she managed to pull her arms free of the wet, clingy fabric and let the gown fall to the floor at her feet.

However, she wasn't as willing to destroy the fine pleated chemise. It was her best one and she wasn't leaving it behind for someone to salvage. Gathering the long skirt in her hands, she leaned over and peeled it from her body. It was thin enough that it would dry quickly by the brazier.

While drying herself off, she kept glancing towards the door. Other than her name she'd said nothing that could account for the swift change of

Gregor's mood. What was it about her name that had put him off so quickly?

As one of King David's men, he had to recognise the name Warehaven, since King David and her grandfather King Henry were brothers by marriage and King Henry had never hidden her father's identity as one of his natural-born sons.

King David was also Matilda's uncle and the Empress, her father's half-sister, had recently been demanding more ships from Warehaven. Demands that Beatrice knew her father had ignored. It was highly likely that David thought to defend his niece by sending his own demands to Warehaven, using Gregor as the messenger.

Perhaps once King David learned the reason for her father's refusal he would understand Warehaven's reluctance. Matilda and her husband Geoffrey's ill use of the ships and men had resulted in the loss of three vessels along with the souls of all the men aboard. A horrible blunder that her father hadn't taken lightly, one he refused to chance repeating. Those men had had families. Wives and children for whom he now felt responsible. Besides, he had worked too hard for what he had and wasn't about to hand it all over to Matilda for her ongoing fight to wrest the throne from King Stephen.

If Gregor was acting as a messenger for King David, it would explain why he was travelling without an armed escort, since he would travel faster on his own.

Beatrice slipped into the dry clothing and then sat down on the bed with a soft gasp of exasperation. All of this was only speculation on her part, but if he was headed to Warehaven it was going to be difficult to slip away from him. She was not going to risk showing up at Warehaven's gate in the company of a man not related to her.

He might consider that a minor obstacle easily overcome with words, but she knew better. Her parents wouldn't care who he was, or why he was there. They wouldn't listen to his explanation. The only thing they would see was that their daughter had been alone with him, unprotected, unguarded for days.

By the time her father finished blustering and her mother ceased harping, she and Gregor would find themselves together in their marriage bed trying to determine how they got there.

A flush warmed her cheeks. Just the thought of being in any bed with Gregor made her dizzy. She couldn't begin to imagine what she'd do if it were to ever happen.

Beatrice patted the mattress beneath her. It was soft, not too lumpy and the covers appeared to be clean. She glanced out of the narrow window. The sun wouldn't rise for a couple of hours yet and she had no desire to head off in the dark again.

She slid further back on the bed to stretch out and froze. King David wouldn't squander his Wolf on simply delivering a message. If Gregor was headed to Warehaven, and from his reaction upon hearing her name she was convinced that was his destination, it was to deliver more than a message.

Perhaps his presence was meant to ensure that whatever request, or demand, made was met.

And what would happen if it wasn't?

Her stomach knotted. She knew how badly her aunt the Empress wanted those ships. How far would King David go to ensure their delivery?

If her father once again declined to supply them, would Gregor simply try to take them?

Her father would see him dead first.

An icy finger of dread skipped down her spine. That was a fight she didn't want to happen. She didn't want to witness her father risk his life to defy his half-sister. This war between King Stephen and Matilda had been going on for nearly ten years without an end in sight. Her father would rather set sail to parts unknown before taking sides. He'd come of age with Stephen at Henry's court and Matilda was family. As the old King's son, even a natural-born one, he was able to make such a choice that another lord would not be permitted.

She loved her father dearly, but she didn't want to see anything happen to Gregor either. He had been kind and he'd stood up to Charles for her when he didn't have to do so. Outside of her family, Gregor had been the only man who'd ever shown her the meaning of honour. He was honourable—to a fault. He'd sworn to see her safely home whether she wanted him to or not.

She needed to make haste for home—preferably arriving before Gregor. Beatrice swung her legs around to sit on the side of the bed. How was she going to accomplish that feat?

According to the last missive her father had sent to Jared at Montreau her parents weren't back at Warehaven yet—but they would be soon. She needed to warn them about the possible visit from King David's Wolf.

Sneaking away from her unwanted escort wouldn't be easy. Nor would it be wise. As much as she hated to admit it, he was correct. Travelling by herself was dangerous, not to mention foolhardy, especially since she wasn't certain what Charles's next move might be.

Earlier she'd told Gregor that she could hire an escort. Could she find someone else willing to escort her to Warehaven? There might be someone below she could bribe. Beatrice glanced down at her gown and smiled. While flawed, surely the numerous gems sewn on to her gown still had some value. There were enough to leave some for the maid and hopefully to pay a willing escort.

She picked up the gown from the floor, rose to get her knife from the table and then took a seat near the brazier. By the time she finished slicing through the thread work on the edges of the neck, sleeves and hem, she had enough stones to fill both of her hands, but nothing to carry them in safely. With a sigh of regret, she cut a square from the bottom of her chemise large enough to hold the gems securely. Now, to find someone who appeared trustworthy enough to act as her guard for the journey, but with Gregor below it would be impossible to do so.

She rose to look out of the narrow window opening. The moon was high in the night sky. The sight made her yawn as she realised she'd had no sleep yet this night—a lack that would leave her dull-witted on the morrow.

A glance towards the bed was enough to convince her to head in that direction. She lay upon the bed and stared up at the ceiling, wishing she'd never left Montreau in the first place.

Gregor pushed his half-full cup across the table and waved the owner of this establishment away when the man thought to bring him more ale. His earlier idea of drinking until he could stand no more had quickly evaporated at the thought of riding with an aching head.

There were only a couple of men left in the inn besides him and he kept them at bay with a hard scowl. The last thing he wanted was company of any sort. He'd taken a seat at the far table to be away from those still gathered so he could reason out what to do.

Another draught of cool, damp night air raced

across him and he turned to look at the newcomer who'd just entered. He groaned. Of course Simon would find him. The man was like a dog on the trail of a hare. A nod in Simon's direction brought him to his table.

'This is the last place I expected to find you.'

Gregor glanced up at his captain. 'The role of nursemaid doesn't suit you.'

'I think I would make quite a handy nursemaid.' Simon took a seat across the table. 'Especially for charges who think to slip away unnoticed.'

'If this is the last place you thought to find me, why are you here?' Gregor motioned the owner to pour another cup of ale that Simon retrieved, then brought back to the table.

'Because it was the only place we hadn't looked.'

'We?'

Simon took a long drink of the ale, before explaining, 'I have two of the men out scouring the countryside for word of their lord.'

'Ah, well, here I am, safe and sound. You can gather the others and go back to camp now.'

'Safe and sound for now, perhaps. But I hear tell from the three battered men who passed through our camp earlier you are breathing your last.'

Gregor snorted. 'You believed them?'

'No, but I couldn't wait to hear this tale so I came looking for you.'

That made more sense since Simon, like the rest of his guard, loved nothing more than a good tale.

Especially one they could embellish and then share with others. Gregor's reputation was partly owed to their retelling of tales. A fact he'd discovered too late to do anything about.

'There isn't much to tell. I rescued the woman those three men had thought to abuse.'

Simon's eyebrows rose. 'Do tell.'

'I just did.'

His man looked around the inn. 'Where is she?'

'Above, in a chamber.'

'And you are down here?' Simon leaned forward, to ask in a near whisper, 'Did you let the Wolf frighten her so quickly?'

'Quite the opposite. The maiden above is Beatrice of Warehaven.'

Simon's cup hit the table. It teetered, then fell, letting the remaining contents spill across the wooden plank. 'You are jesting.'

Gregor waited until the owner finished cleaning up the mess Simon had made. Once he replaced his man's drink with another and left, Gregor said, 'I wish I were.'

'Which Warehaven lass would this be?'

'The young, as yet unmarried one.'

'Dear Lord above. How did this happen?' Before Gregor could respond, Simon raised his hand. 'Never mind. Only you could have such ill-fated luck.'

Not able to disagree with the obvious, Gregor shrugged. 'I know. Sometimes it is truly amazing.'

'Does she know?'

'Well, of course upon discovering who she was the first thing I did was to tell her that right after I kill her father and take command of his keep and ships, she is going to become my wife.'

'So, you left the chamber without saying anything?'

'Yes.' There was no need to lie about it, not to Simon. The older man had been his father's captain-at-arms and his older brother's captain until Elrik decided he could no longer deal with the man's tendency to play nursemaid. The man might be old, he might also be a frightening-looking nursemaid, but he had been with the Roul family since before Gregor could walk and there was no one more worthy of his trust.

'This one is going to make a fine retelling.'

'The only retelling that is going to happen is that you are going to go back to camp and tell the men to keep their mouths shut about this entire mission. I am escorting her to Warehaven and I don't want her to discover what is going to happen ahead of time.'

'And how are you going to handle that?'

'I don't know as yet. But I have until the sun rises to make a plan.'

'Well, then, you'd best hurry, because—'

'Yes, I know.' Gregor cut him off. 'The night is half over.'

Simon stared down into his ale. His forehead

creased, his eyebrows pulled together making a long grey caterpillar above his eyes.

Gregor sighed. 'I recognise that look well. What are you wondering about?'

'What is she like, this Beatrice of Warehaven?'

The memory of her laughter ran through Gregor, leaving him warm and wanting. Finally, he admitted, 'Someone who would probably make a fine wife for someone in want of one.'

'Ah. So she didn't cringe and cower at discovering your name?'

'No. She bluntly told me that I wasn't who she expected to be David's Wolf.' Before he could stop himself, he added, 'And she laughed at me.'

Simon frowned for a long few moments, then asked, 'My lord, is it necessary to kill Warehaven?'

'Do you think he's going to let me take his keep and ships from him without a fight?'

'No.'

'Then, no, I see no way around it. Given the order came from his family, it would be a waste to take him hostage as I doubt they would pay ransom.'

He didn't add the simple fact that he had no choice in completing this mission. His future and that of his brothers depended on him doing precisely as King David and the Empress wanted.

'She will hate you, lad.'

'Tell me something I don't already know. But there is nothing I can do about it except to sleep with one eye open the short time I'll be at Warehaven.'

Simon frowned, then asked, 'The short time?'

'King David ordered me to take Warehaven and marry the heiress. He said nothing about living there with her. Once the island is under my control it shouldn't take long to install enough of my men to keep order, marry the woman and get her with child.'

'And then what? You'll just leave?'

Gregor shrugged. 'I can either take up residence at the shipyard on Warehaven, or at the one back home. It doesn't matter to me.'

'Are you sure it will be that easy?'

Easy? No, he wasn't sure, but it was the only plan he could devise. 'The only thing I am sure about is that the night is wasting. You need to gather the men back at camp and give them the order to keep their mouths closed. The first one who so much as whispers a word about our mission will find himself lacking a tongue.'

Simon rose. 'And you?'

'Need to devise some lie to cover why I bolted upon learning her name.'

After his man left the inn, Gregor talked the owner into supplying him with some lukewarm stew, bread, cheese and a pitcher of water for a price. He then headed back up to the bedchamber with the food.

He pushed against the door with his shoulder,

only to find it blocked by something weighty from the other side. Apparently she'd already found reason to mistrust him and had used the bench, since it was the only thing in the chamber with any weight besides the bed to keep him from entering.

Setting down the food, he shoved the door open, hearing the sound of wooden legs scraping against wood floor. Once the opening was wide enough, he slipped through, moved the bench back to its original spot alongside the wall, retrieved the food and came back into the chamber.

Gregor placed the food on the bench and then secured the door. He turned to glance at the woman on the bed. She must have been exhausted, because she still slept even after he'd made so much noise getting into the chamber.

He walked further into the room. She'd been busy during his absence. Her wet gown was a lump on the floor near the brazier and he noticed a hastily made pouch on the small table near the bed that hadn't been there before.

Reaching out, he touched the chemise she'd hung over the bedpost nearest the brazier. He removed the now dry garment, noting the square hole cut from the hem, folded it and placed it on the foot of the bed. Retrieving his still-damp cloak from a peg by the door, he hung that from the bedpost. She would need something to keep her warm and dry during their journey over the next two or three days and his cloak would have to do.

Warehaven's maiden mumbled something he could barely make out. A step brought him to the side of the bed. She still slept, but her shivers would soon have her awake. He leaned over her, reaching across to pull the free side of the covers she slept upon over to cover her body.

She turned in her sleep. The warmth of her breath brushed lightly across his cheek, sending a tremor of nearly forgotten longing racing down his spine. Suddenly he wanted nothing more than to gather her in his arms and hold her close until he chased the cold away.

Gregor tucked the edge of the cover beneath her shoulder and quickly stepped away, silently cursing his stupidity. What was he thinking? Had one missed night of sleep left him so dull-witted that he believed things best left alone could come true on a whim? What made him think just because this woman was interested that she would allow him such liberties?

He needed to face the facts. He was never going to have the marriage or future he'd long desired. Especially not with Warehaven's heiress. Once all was said and done, not only would she never permit him such closeness, he'd be surprised if she sought anything other than his death.

While he didn't know her well, he was fairly certain that she would devise some slow and painful way to send him to his grave.

Chapter Four

Beatrice blinked her eyes open, squinting against the shaft of sunlight streaming in through the narrow window across her face.

She sprang upright on the bed, fighting off the lingering traces of sleep that left her uncertain of her whereabouts.

'Good morning.'

The deep timbre of the voice greeting her to the day brought it all flooding back. She sank back down on to the bed, silently cursing her lengthy slumber. The intent had been to rise early so she could sneak away and find someone else to escort her to Warehaven.

Now with that chance lost, she would have to devise another plan that would permit her to arrive at Warehaven without his escort. In the meantime being rude would not serve her well.

'And a good morning to you, too. I see you returned.'

'Yes. You were asleep when I came back and I had no wish to wake you. So, let me now apologise for leaving so abruptly. It was troubling to find myself responsible for such a high-born heiress.'

Something about his explanation didn't sit right, but she wasn't going to argue with him about it. Instead she forced a laugh and sat back up. 'Oh, yes, I am certain you find King David's court lacking in high-born ladies.'

'Ah, but I rarely find myself personally responsible for any of them.'

Beatrice swung her legs over the side of the bed away from him. 'You are not responsible for me.'

Hadn't she just decided not to be rude, or argue with him? Yet here she found herself eagerly fanning the flames of an argument. Why? If she were to be honest with herself, she was doing it for no reason other than the fact that she liked the sound of his voice, especially now when it had a gravelly tone as if he, too, had just been roused from sleep.

'Oh, but I am. I would be remiss in my duties if I were to knowingly permit a granddaughter of old King Henry's to travel without so much as a guard.'

Beatrice rolled her eyes, and stood to shake out her gown. 'A grandfather I met but twice.'

'I would imagine your grandfather had a few more important things to tend to than playing with his grandchildren.'

She couldn't help smiling at the memory his comment drew forth.

'What do you find amusing now?'

'Amusing? Nothing really. I was just remembering the first time he came to Warehaven.'

'It must have been an enjoyable visit to produce such a smile.'

'I think I was three or four at the time. The only

thing I actually remember is sitting on his lap and playing with a small wooden horse he'd given me. He was the brave knight on the horse coming to rescue the Princess Beatrice.'

Gregor frowned. 'Not exactly an image I can fathom.'

She shrugged. 'He wasn't at court and, besides the ship's crew, he had only brought a few guards with him, so I'm certain the time spent at Warehaven had been more of a break from his usual responsibilities than any official visit.'

'While that is a nice memory for you, King Henry is not here to take responsibility for you. As unworthy as I may be, I am all you have and I will see to my duty.'

Obviously he was as eager to argue as she. Turning to face him more directly, she put her hands on her hips and shook her head. 'As a warrior for King David you are far from unworthy and I cannot have someone in such an exalted position act as a mere servant. Surely you have more important matters to attend for your King. I can find someone more suited to the position of guard. Someone of less…importance.'

He rose from his seat on the bench, not bothering to smother his laugh as he had last night. 'Perhaps someone less apt to inform your parents of what you've done?'

Oh, this Wolf was quite cunning. 'Well, yes, there is that.'

'Since doing so would only direct their focus to me, fear not as I have no intention of informing your parents of this little…journey. And as I am more than suited to guard the safety of Warehaven's daughter, I am…' he paused to bow before finishing '…willingly at your service, my lady.'

'I wish not to deter you from your duty to your King, as this journey would do.'

'Since I am already on my way to Roul Keep in Normandy to visit my brother, a side-trip to Warehaven will in no way deter me from my duty.'

His statement confused her. 'Your lands are in Normandy?' How was it then that he served King David instead of Matilda, or her husband Geoffrey of Anjou?

'No. My home is a small isle off the coast of Scotland.' Gregor shook his head. 'It came as a surprise for me to have recently learned that my older brother Elrik has been granted the Norman earldom of Roul and I plan on finding out how that came about in person. So you see, you are in no way keeping me from any service to my King.'

She'd known full well before embarking on this verbal chess game she wasn't going to win. However, his dogged determination to see her to Warehaven was beginning to bring her worries to the fore once again.

'You travel all the way from King David's court to Normandy alone?' Granted, Matilda was in control of the lands south from Oxford and east of the

Thames, but there was much of Stephen's land to cross between Carlisle and Oxford. It would be risky for him to do so alone even if he had a writ of safe passage.

He opened the door to the chamber, letting the sound of men talking flow more freely into the room. 'My men are below.'

'Yet mere hours ago you were alone.'

'No. Like you I had escaped.' He shrugged, then explained, 'I have a penchant for desiring time alone when I need to think or to plan.'

His response set her heart racing. What was this Wolf up to that required such secretive planning on his part?

Before she could ask, he said, 'I am but a lowly shipbuilder by trade. None of my men would be of any use in the planning phase of my projects. In truth they would prove more of a hindrance, so on occasion I slip away to do nothing more than dwell on my own projects.' One expressive eyebrow rose and he asked, 'Can you now understand my willingness to visit Warehaven?'

Beatrice studied him. A warrior and a shipbuilder. No wonder his muscles were so well honed and his hands calloused. While he could be telling the truth about his reason for wanting to visit Warehaven—it was, after all, a very valid one for someone who built ships—a nagging worry in the pit of her stomach cautioned her to be wary.

He'd told her that her expression would give away any lie she might attempt to tell. However, *his* expression rarely changed—other than a winging of a brow, or the twitch of amusement teasing at his lips, she couldn't determine whether he spoke the truth or not. And after her experience with Charles, she had no business trying to judge any man's honesty. Since he'd done nothing thus far to cause alarm, the only thing she could do was to take his words at face value—for now.

'I grant you leave to escort me to the coast. But I think your visit to Warehaven would be better suited for a time when my father was present. He could more ably discuss ships better than anyone else there.'

He only nodded, then headed towards the door. 'I will give you a few moments to ready yourself for the day.' A frown creased his brow. 'I'm sure you are able, but I must ask to be certain, can you ride a horse?'

'Of course I can.' Even if she'd never ridden a horse before she'd not have said so. After being confined inside a mule-drawn cart for two days she would welcome the change. When they'd first set out from Montreau, she'd believed Charles when he'd explained that he'd procured the cart for her comfort. Now she realised he'd not been thinking about her comfort at all, but of her ability to more easily escape on horseback.

'Good. Then I will await you below.'

Before he left, she asked, 'Might I obtain some food before we leave?'

He pointed at the small table. 'This is at your disposal.'

'Oh.' She hadn't noticed the food-laden plate, pitcher or mug before. When she looked back in his direction to thank him for his thoughtfulness, she found nothing but an empty doorway.

Her rumbling stomach begged her to set aside her surprise at his silent, near-instantaneous departure and to focus on the food instead. A plea she readily fulfilled since she'd not eaten since early yesterday evening before she'd escaped from Charles.

One whiff of the waiting food set her mouth to watering. How on earth had she missed these aromas upon waking? The only explanation she had at hand was that she'd been distracted by arguing with Gregor. Not a bad distraction, but still a distraction none the less.

It took all of her willpower to eat like a lady and not shovel the pieces of fish, cheese and bread into her mouth.

The baked fish could have used an additional dusting of spices, but it was good. The bread was like heaven—soft inside with a crust baked to perfection. It would have been welcome at her father's table.

She washed it all down with milk from the pitcher before taking a bite of the apple. Fruit in hand, she walked over to the narrow window. The breeze coming in let her know that the day would be mild. Thankfully the sun was unobscured by clouds and would lend warmth to the ride.

A knock on the door frame caught her attention. Beatrice turned to see the barmaid from last night standing in the doorway and waved her into the room.

The woman gathered the dishes from the table. 'I am relieved to see the food did suit you after all.'

Beatrice blinked. 'Why would you think otherwise?'

'His lordship brought stew up with him last night and it came back untouched earlier this morning.'

'Oh.' As the woman's words set fully in her mind, Beatrice repeated, 'Oh! I was asleep when he returned, so I knew nothing about the stew.'

'Martha will be relieved to hear that. She takes great pride in her cooking.'

'As well she should.' Even though Beatrice agreed with the maid, her mind wasn't on the quality of the food.

Instead one thought ran round and round in her head. He had thought to bring her something to eat. The ruthless, heartless Wolf had taken the time…no, he had actually considered the needs of someone he barely knew. This supposedly cruel henchman of King David had taken *her* needs into consideration and acted upon them.

It was such a small thing, but it gave her pause. This was the type of action that defined a worthy man. Not his face, his form, his looks, or even his kindly spoken words. Because as she was well aware, even the kindest of words held little weight if they were nothing more than lies, or spoken merely for the purpose of manipulating her.

In the space of a few hours, Gregor of Roul had done more to show he was decent and kind-hearted than Charles had in three years.

Perhaps she had little need to worry about the Wolf's intent. Surely a man this thoughtful wasn't planning any nefarious deeds for Warehaven. She had probably fretted for naught and could only attribute her unfounded fears last night to Charles's underhanded actions and her subsequent escape from him.

'My lady?'

The maid's query drew Beatrice's attention away from her thoughts and back to the maid. 'Yes?'

The woman held a pair of soft boots and stockings. 'Will you have need of these?'

She glanced down at her ruined slippers on the floor near the end of the bed. Even had they not been beyond repair, they would do her little good for the journey home. She snatched a handful of smaller gemstones from the bedside table. 'Yes, I will, thank you. You are welcome to make use of whatever fabric you can salvage from my gown and these.'

The maid's mouth fell open. She glanced at the gown hanging from a hook near the door to the gems in Beatrice's outstretched hand. 'No, that is too much. Your lord already overpaid for what we've provided.'

Overpaid? Charles would have demanded whatever he'd wanted and then haggled the cost down to nearly nothing—or even taken what he wanted without payment of any kind. 'You will be doing me a favour. I have no desire to ever wear or see the gown again, but it would be a shame to have it thrown away or used for rags when there is quite a bit of fabric that could be used.'

She dropped the gems into the maid's hands and gently closed the woman's fingers over them. 'And these are nothing more than flawed stones, just brightly coloured baubles to use for decoration.'

'Thank you, my lady. I know not what to say. Is there anything else you need?'

Beatrice smiled at the woman's obvious nervousness. 'No. You've done more than enough already. Thank you.'

'It has been my pleasure.' The maid paused, then added, 'Safe travels, my lady.'

Once the maid left, Beatrice finished dressing and getting ready for the day. She used a ruined stocking to tie her pouch of remaining gemstones to her belt, plucked the heavy cloak off the bedpost and headed below.

Gregor awaited her at the bottom of the stairs.

She would know him anywhere by the glint of silver in his otherwise dark hair. He leaned against the wall, his back towards her, talking to one of his men.

When he turned to face her, Beatrice's breath caught and she slowed her descent. The sudden, rapid beating of her heart took her by surprise. How was it possible that a man clad in chainmail could be so striking?

He cut an imposing figure. From the spurs buckled to his boot heels giving proof to his status as a knight, to the solid black surcoat covering his mail, and the sword encased in a black scabbard strapped to his waist, he was every inch the warrior Wolf.

Two steps from the bottom, she stopped and placed a palm on his chest. Oddly spellbound by his steady gaze, she said, 'Sir Wolf, it seems I owe you more than I thought.'

He smiled slightly before he covered her hand with one of his own, holding it fast in place. 'How so?'

It was only with the greatest effort that she did not tremble beneath the warmth of his touch. While she couldn't deny the flash of desire that raced through her at the contact, it was quickly replaced by a sudden longing for things she'd never before considered.

Even though they'd only met yesterday, it was as if her heart knew this man could be trusted to keep her safe. He would see to her well-being without failing. Unlike Charles. Instead of keeping her safe, her would-be suitor had been the one threatening harm, leaving her to see to her own defence.

'I am in your debt. I owe you not just for keeping me safe from Charles, but also for the room, the clothes and the food.'

'I have done nothing more than any guardian would do for his charge.'

'But you are not—'

He cut her off with the slightest lift of an eyebrow. No, he was right, they were not going to have the same argument yet again. She nodded in agreement before saying, 'Still, I thank you for your kindness.'

The man standing behind him snorted and turned away to call out to four other men, also dressed in black, seated at a table. 'Mount up.'

Gregor released her hand and offered his arm. 'Ready?'

He led her outside to the waiting horses and before she realised what he was doing, he grasped her round the waist and hoisted her up on to the saddle of the smallest animal. She flung one foot over the saddle and secured the skirts of her gown and chemise beneath her legs. Thankfully there was enough fabric in the garments to do so properly.

After handing her the reins, he said, 'Should anything happen and I order you to ride, promise me you will ride like the wind without stopping.'

And again he was concerned for her safety even in advance of anything happening. Apprehensive, she asked, 'Do you expect trouble?'

'Nothing we can't deal with, but I don't want you to get caught between the crossed blades.'

'No, I'm sure I wouldn't like that either. So, yes, I promise.'

He then left to sling his shield, also black with a silvery-grey silhouette of a wolf in the centre, over his shoulder before mounting his own horse.

The men surrounded her. Gregor to her right. An older man rode at her left and the other four split up, two in front and two behind.

Intent on covering as much ground as possible, they rode with little conversation and Beatrice soon found herself being lulled into a semi-sleep state of being by the steady gait of the horse beneath her.

'Beatrice.'

She jerked awake, startled by a hard grip on her shoulder. It took her a few heartbeats to realise Gregor was shaking her.

'What?' She sat up straighter on the saddle and adjusted her grasp on the lax reins.

'I know you got little sleep last night, but I didn't want you to fall off the horse.'

'I'm fine.'

She was far from fine. The woman was clearly exhausted, but it was too early to stop for the day, so to keep her awake and discover more about this woman he would soon wed, he asked, 'Are you anxious to arrive at Warehaven?'

'I've been gone so long that, yes, I am eager to return.'

'How long have you been away?'

'Nearly three years. My sister was taken captive and held on Dunstan Isle. Since nobody knew why at first, my parents sent me north to stay with my brother and his wife as a precaution.'

'She's been held all this time?'

'No. Since she ended up married to the man, I can only assume she hasn't always been a prisoner.'

Surprised by her scathing tone, Gregor turned to look at her, asking, 'You don't approve?'

'I have never met him, nor have I heard directly from Isabella, so I fear she may not have become his wife willingly.'

Willingly? Was an agreeable marriage so important to her that she balked at what might have been an unwilling one for her sister? He stared at the spot between his horse's ears, seeking a moment to put his question into words that wouldn't alert her to the plans already in motion for her future. Plans which would unquestionably force her into an unwanted marriage.

Finally, he asked, 'Such an arrangement is common, is it not?'

'Being kidnapped and then forced to wed the knave?'

'Perhaps not the kidnapping part, but have you

not known others who were defeated in some manner and forced into a marriage for convenience, to establish peace between the families involved, or even at the order of their lord?'

She laughed softly as if he'd told an amusing story before answering, 'My parents fit that description.'

'How so?'

'King Henry sent my father to take control of Warehaven and to wed the oldest available daughter, which was my mother at the time.'

'Did that not work out for them in the end?'

'According to my father, he was smitten the moment he sallied his horse through the bonfire and landed at her feet.'

'And your mother?'

Beatrice's burst of laughter startled the other men, who turned to her until Gregor's glare forced their attention elsewhere. 'My mother claims that she is still unwilling and is only biding her time until he finally gets bored enough to leave.'

Certain this was nothing more than teasing between the older couple, Gregor commented, 'This must be a jest between your parents.'

'Of course it is. My mother knows that she is fooling no one. She would be heartbroken were my father to leave her.'

'Then their forced marriage did work out for them.'

'Perhaps. But regardless of how they spin the

tales of their meeting, the beginning wasn't as idyllic as they'd like us to believe.'

'What makes you say that?'

'Instead of arranging our marriages, they gave each of us the gift of choice, because they didn't want us to go through what they did before finding someone to love. And I worry that choice was stolen from Isabella.'

Gregor blinked. He could understand Warehaven giving his adult children a say in the arrangements made for their future—to a point. As their lord and father it was his responsibility to ensure their continued health, wealth, safety and security.

Love—or any shared emotion—was something that could develop and grow over time. But said emotion was not something that needed to be considered beforehand. Love, attraction or even lust would prove a sorry substitute for food, shelter or safety.

'Perhaps your sister is better off.'

She jerked straighter on the saddle, then shot him a look of disbelief. His comment had obviously angered her. 'Why would you say such a thing?'

'If this man was cunning and bold enough to capture her without being caught in the first place, he will most likely be strong enough to keep her fed and protected.'

'Fed and protected?' Her tone rose with each

word. She paused to swallow before continuing in a milder manner. 'That is all that should matter to her?'

'Considering she would die without either food or safety it should matter greatly.'

In answer, Beatrice turned away from him and directed her frowning stare at the top of her horse's head.

Gregor knew he was right, but knowing so didn't help dispel the sudden heaviness in the pit of his stomach at her silent response. He felt compelled to explain. 'My lady, I freely admit to not understanding this fascination you seem to have with putting love before all else.'

'Oh, yes, you are King David's Wolf. His heartless warrior without the capacity of feeling, or caring.'

He *cared* about many things—his family, men, ships and the future. But love and tenderness was something that should be allowed to grow slowly, naturally between two people who'd learned to know each other well. It was not something to be taken lightly or rushed into blindly like a starry-eyed lackwit.

Instead of learning what he could about his first bride-to-be, he'd focused on hopes for their future. He'd dreamed of falling in love. In doing so he'd been unprepared for her weakness of spirit and had ultimately failed her. His wife's safety had been his responsibility alone and he'd let hopes and dreams distract him from what had truly mattered.

He felt deep sorrow for Beatrice. She would be denied her gift of choice. She would not wed for love, nor would she ever have the chance to discover love with the man she would have as her husband.

Would he fail her, too? In the end would she choose to take her life rather than endure a loveless marriage to a man with so many stains upon his soul that he would spend his eternity in hell?

A shiver of dread made him shift on his saddle. No. He could not—would not permit the past to repeat itself.

Gregor felt her expectant gaze and replied to her comment about his heartlessness in the only way he could. 'Yes. What you say is true.'

'Please, my lord, I have been in your company an entire day and I have yet to see this cold, uncaring warrior that all have spoken about. I think the tales carried are a bit overblown.'

While that also was true, she would soon learn first-hand that some of those tales were based on nothing less than solid truth. It would be a lesson she wouldn't enjoy learning any more than he would take pleasure in the giving of it.

'You think that you know me with only a day in my company?'

'I know enough.'

Before he could debate this subject further, one of the men behind him shouted, 'My lord!'

Gregor turned to look in the direction his man pointed and saw four riders coming up quickly from behind them, with their weapons drawn. He swatted the rump of Beatrice's horse, ordering, 'Ride. I will catch up to you.'

Chapter Five

Beatrice tightened her legs along the sides of the beast and gripped the reins securely as the horse bolted ahead.

She didn't fear falling from the animal, but she did worry about something happening to Gregor. Even though she'd only just met him, she didn't want him to get injured, or killed. He was kind, brave, and strong—in short, he was everything her parents would consider worthy. And maybe, with time, someone she could easily come to care for.

Selfishly she thought that it would be a great shame for anything to happen to him before she had a chance to find out if that were true. More selfishly she knew her own safety would be in grave danger should anything happen to him.

Soon the sound of hard, rapid pounding of hooves behind her sent her heart racing. What if it was the attackers who followed at such a brisk pace? Worse—what if it was Charles? Oh, please, let it not be the scoundrel she had once hoped to wed.

Beatrice's mind conjured terrifying images of what that man would do to her once he had her again in his grasp. He would make her pay dearly for not only escaping, but for the beating he and his friends took at Gregor's hands.

She gripped the reins so tightly that her fingernails pressed into her palms as she hung on for dear life.

'Beatrice!' Gregor's familiar voice rang in her ear as his gloved hand clamped down over hers.

Relief flooded her body, leaving her shaking uncontrollably as he pulled on the reins, slowing the horse to a stop. After a quick glance down at her, Gregor dismounted and stood at her side. He wrapped a hand around the calf of her leg. 'All is well.'

'Those men?'

'Those men were thieves who will never seek to harm another, at least not in this realm.'

Without a second's thought she threw herself from the saddle and into his arms. Arms that instantly closed around her, giving her a renewed sense of safety and chasing away the shivers of combined fear and relief that had beset her.

Over her head, he ordered his waiting men, 'Find some place to camp for the night.'

Beatrice leaned away from the warmth of his chest and looked up at him. His eyes seemed to glimmer behind his half-closed lids. The frown that normally creased his brow had softened. It was a pleasing expression, one that she would like to see more often. And one that hinted at restrained passion, setting tremors of nervous anticipation to skitter along her spine. 'I am fine, there is no need to stop for the day.' She glanced at the sky, then back to him, adding, 'There remains a few hours of daylight.'

Gregor brushed a hand along the side of her head before cupping her cheek for the briefest moment. 'No. We break for the day.'

'Truly, I am fine and well able to travel further.'

When she started to turn away, intent on remounting, he grasped her shoulders. 'You are still trembling.'

Before she could admit it was his nearness that had set her nerves aflutter, she swallowed hard, then said, 'It is nothing more than the lingering exhilaration of the ride. I am fine, truly.'

He laughed softly. 'You are such a bad liar, Beatrice of Warehaven.'

Overcome with a sudden embarrassment at his assessment, she looked down at the ground between them. Somehow he knew that his touch, his nearness, caused the tremors teasing at her. Why did she have to be so easy to see through? And why did he have to be so observant?

With a shake of her head she claimed. 'No, you are mistaken. Never have I ridden so fast with such a dire need to get away.'

Without responding to her outright lie, he retrieved the dangling reins to both horses and handed her the ones to her mount. 'Since it's doubtful my men went far, we'll walk. It'll give you a chance to calm the over-excitement from your hard ride.'

Beatrice ignored his teasing tone. She knew he still didn't believe her explanation and was grateful he wasn't intent on pursuing the truth—especially since she would never be able to explain how, or why, his nearness and his touch set her heart racing.

In truth, she was also grateful for the opportunity to regain her composure before joining his men. Doing so right this moment would only alert them to something odd having happened between the two of them. The last thing she needed, or wanted, was one or more of them noticing the flush still warming her cheeks.

If his men were anything like those at Warehaven, they would leap on any opportunity to start tales and poke their noses into things that were best left undisturbed.

She walked alongside of him. Neither of them seemed willing to speak—she had no idea what to say and he appeared to be lost in his own thoughts. Unable to bear the uncomfortable tension or the deafening silence, she said, 'I am sorry.'

'For what?'

'It seems I have upset you in some manner and I am—'

He cut her off by briefly raising an arm. 'Don't.'

'Don't what?'

'Apologise for something that is not your fault.'

'But—'

'How is my reaction your responsibility?'

'But—'

Again the raising and lowering of one arm stopped her words.

'There are no buts, Beatrice. I am solely responsible for the way I do or don't react to something. It's not up to you to walk on eggshells, making certain your words, or actions, upset me not. My moods are not your responsibility. They are mine alone and I'd thank you to leave them to my care.'

If that wasn't the strangest thing she'd ever heard, she didn't know what was. 'You are an odd man, Gregor of Roul.'

'How so?'

'My mother would never say anything she knew would anger my father. She'd find a way to sweeten her words, or say nothing at all.'

'So, you have learned to think that speaking your mind is a bad thing?'

'If it only serves to upset someone else, then, yes.'

'It must be hard living your entire life afraid to speak the truth.'

'In my case I wouldn't say it was fear exactly. Respect, perhaps. Besides, I think there's a difference between truth and kindness.'

'Having never had the luxury of choosing kindness, I am not in the position to say if you are right or wrong.'

His statement gave her pause. She doubted that his life in King David's service had been anything close to kind. If even a small portion of the rumours about David's Wolf were true, there had been no kindness to greet him anywhere. But he hadn't always been that man. At one point he'd been a boy without cares. Surely there'd been some measure of kindness then.

'Are your parents alive?'

'My mother died birthing my youngest brother. I have very little recollection of her.'

'And your father?'

'Had four boys to raise on his own, along with the responsibilities of his holdings.'

Meaning his father had little time for any of them. Beatrice's heart tugged with sympathy for the child he'd once been.

He glanced down at her. 'Oh, no, you don't.'

'What? I am doing nothing.'

'You are feeling sorry for me and what you think was my hard life. Don't waste your time.'

'It had to have been hard without a mother and a father who was only there a little of the time.'

'I suppose it was a harder life than some had and a better one than many experienced. We were boys. We played, got dirty, fought, acted like boys do. When we became men, we acted like men.'

She nodded slowly. 'Sure. Sure.'

'What does that mean?'

Beatrice sighed. 'Gregor, when was the last time someone hugged you just to make you smile?'

'Now who is the odd one?'

She did feel sorry for him. These last couple of years at her brother's keep had been made harder due to the simple fact that there'd been no welcome touch from a loved one. She'd been so used to sharing a chamber, a life, with Isabella that she hadn't realised how much she had depended on a hug, or touch, or a kind word from her sister on a daily basis.

It was nearly impossible for her to envision an entire life spent in that manner.

Thankfully she didn't have to. Soon, she would be back at Warehaven and if they weren't already there, her parents would shortly arrive. Both her mother and father were demonstrative people and she would quickly find herself the beneficiary of more embraces than she could ever hope for in a lifetime.

Gregor nudged her arm with an elbow, tearing her from her thoughts. She answered his last query with a small, unfelt laugh. 'I do not think myself odd. Simply loved.'

Before he could respond in what she assumed would be a negative, or derisive, manner, his man waved to them from the side of the road just ahead.

Without another word, they led their horses into the small encampment and tied them near the other animals.

Beatrice reached to unbuckle the saddle only to have Gregor gently grasp her shoulders and steer her towards the fire. 'Sit. The men will see to the horses. I need to speak to Simon.' He glanced at his men before adding a little louder, 'You are safe here.'

He eased her down on to a log before the flickering flames and handed her a leather flask. 'It's just water.'

'Thank you.' Grateful, she took it from him. 'Water is more than welcome.' Beatrice waved her hand at him. 'Go. I am fine.'

She watched him walk away and wondered at the sudden longing washing over her. She understood lust and desire, as both were fleeting and readily dismissed. But this...this was something more—something deeper than just a physical reaction.

It was more a yearning of her heart. A need—a desire she didn't quite understand—as if her heart knew something she'd yet to recognise. Which was ridiculous considering she'd only known the man a very short time. Unfortunately, no matter what her head said, what logic dictated, neither seemed to be in control of her heart.

Beatrice took a long drink of the water, nearly spilling it on herself when a loud thud hit the ground behind her. All four of Gregor's men dropped their saddle bags at once and sat on the other logs ringing the fire facing her.

The older two had the cold-edged appearance of men well used to the duties they performed as the Wolf's men. Hard, unyielding were words that could describe them. They were men she wouldn't want to run into if she was alone.

The younger two were less imposing. One was quite a bit larger—taller, longer of limb—than the other, but neither had yet lost the obvious eagerness of youth. They talked softly with each other, taking turns to look around as if curious about everything within sight—including her.

She found their attention amusing, just as she would if they were all gathered in her father's hall. If that were the case, these would be the two with whom she would converse to pass the time. They appeared safe, unimposing and, to be completely honest, easier to manage than the other two.

The youngest one waved towards the supplies, saying, 'If you are hungry we've plenty of food.'

To her surprise, she wasn't hungry in the least. Her glance flitted towards Gregor. Food was the last thing on her mind. 'No, thank you, not right this moment.' She glanced behind her at the bulging bags, before turning back to add, 'Besides, I wish not to deplete stores you need for the remainder of your journey.'

The glare from one of the older men intensified. She wondered what she'd said to displease him. Finally, her error dawned on her. It was likely that, in his opinion, she, a mere woman—worse, an outsider—had just taken the men to task about the correct use of their supplies.

Not wanting to start off on his bad side, she turned her full attention to him. 'I know the offer would not have been made were there not enough to share. However, there are times I could eat more than the four of you combined and that would not serve you well.'

It took a moment, but to her relief the corner of his mouth twitched before curving up to a half-smile. 'My lady, I seriously doubt if you could even eat more than just Harold here, let alone the four of us.' He jerked a thumb towards the tall, gangly guard. 'We have decided that he is hollow clear to his toes.'

'Besides,' the man sitting next to him added, 'it is obvious you don't overfill yourself on a regular basis.'

'And I'll take that as a compliment. Thank you.' Beatrice laughed softly, more with relief at having avoided angering the Wolf's guard than anything else.

The youngest one jumped up. 'I need to check the nets before it gets dark.'

After he left, she asked the remaining three men, 'Have you all been in your lordship's service long?'

The oldest nodded, the one in the middle stared at the ground, while the one called Harold shook his head. They really didn't need to be so closemouthed, it wasn't as if she was trying to ferret out secrets, just simply thought to pass the time in conversation.

To her relief the one in the middle finally replied, 'The four of us were all born on Roul Isle where upon reaching adulthood the options are either to leave the isle, learn shipbuilding, dock work or join the family's guard.' He hitched a thumb towards the oldest, saying, 'James here was so adept with tools that he lost a finger the first day at the shipyard.'

James held up his left hand to give proof of the missing digit. 'Seemed to me I'd be safer with a sharp weapon in my hand.'

Harold offered, 'Like Daniel...' he nodded in the direction the youngest had just gone '... I followed in the footsteps of my father and brothers by taking up arms for the Rouls.'

The choices were the same for the men on Warehaven. 'All worthwhile reasons for your choices.' She looked at the man in the middle, wondering about his reason for joining Roul's guard.

He shrugged a shoulder before saying, 'I just wanted the opportunity to kill.'

Beatrice's stomach clenched, then felt as if it would plummet to the ground.

The oldest man punched the other one. 'Colin! You will frighten the girl to death.'

Colin rubbed his arm and hung his head before giving her a sheepish half-smile. 'I apologise. In truth, the old lord forced me into his service to keep me from causing any further mischief at the docks.'

Beatrice laughed. 'Now that I understand since there have been a few hellions on Warehaven coaxed out of their wayward ways with a little training.'

Harold stared as if in shock at Colin. He opened and closed his mouth a few times before finally finding his voice. 'You were a troublemaker? *You?*'

Colin glared at Beatrice. 'Now see what you did?' He lifted his chin and turned his face away as if grievously wounded. 'You've ruined my *golden* reputation.'

James rolled his eyes. Harold shook his head.

'Pray forgive me, Sir Colin, I meant not to sully your good name.'

The man looked back at her, laughing as he lifted a foot. 'Do you see any spurs on these boots? I am nobody's *sir*.'

'Did you ever aspire to be?'

In unison all three of the men said, 'Hell, no!'

Her lips twitched at the emphatic reply.

'Do you see Sir Simon over there?' Colin asked.

She turned to look at where Simon and Gregor were deep in conversation, then looked back at the men seated around the fire with her. 'Yes, why?'

'He was knighted on the battlefield along with

the old lord. That *sir* before his name came with responsibilities most of us desire not.'

James added, 'It is much easier to follow orders than it is to give orders that may or may not prove to be the right ones.'

'It's more than just coming up with the right orders without any advance notice.' Colin shot a quick glance back towards Gregor and Simon, before continuing. 'It also involves ensuring the lord doesn't place himself in too much danger.'

'Does Lord Gregor take too many risks?'

Harold snorted as he rose, saying, 'I'll go and see what's keeping Daniel.'

Once the young guard had left, James asked in a near-whisper, 'Have you heard the rumours about Lord Gregor?'

'Just that he's King David's Wolf and from what I can gather, someone to be avoided.' She kept her voice just as low as James had, realising he didn't want Gregor to overhear.

'He was married once.'

'Really?' That was something she hadn't heard, or if she had, she hadn't paid any attention since Gregor of Roul wasn't someone she would ever come in contact with under normal circumstances. 'I didn't know that.'

Colin cleared his throat and quickly jerked his head towards Gregor and Simon. 'Perhaps it would be best if that tale came from him.'

'I wasn't going to tell her about his marriage,'

James insisted, 'but you and I both know that was when he started taking more risks than was necessary.'

At Colin's glare, James closed his mouth. Both men fell silent and by the stiffening of their bodies, Beatrice knew the conversation was over. Which was fine, since they'd already given her enough to think about.

So, Gregor had been—or was—married. Interesting, considering he never mentioned a wife, nor did he act as if he currently had one. She wondered what had happened. Who had he married? When? What was she like? So many questions she wanted to ask, but it was apparent the men weren't going to supply the answers.

Would Gregor answer them? She glanced towards him and noticed his rigid stance and the scowl on Simon's face. They were arguing.

About what? she wondered. When Simon nodded in her direction, she had the sinking feeling it was about her.

Chapter Six

After settling Beatrice on the log before the fire, Gregor joined Simon out on the road. Before he could say anything, Simon asked, 'May I speak freely, Lord Roul?'

If the cold tone and use of his title wasn't enough, the added fact that Simon asked for permission instead of jumping right in let Gregor know that his captain had once again assumed the role of nursemaid.

He groaned and waved the man to continue. It would be pointless to deny him. The man would have his say whether it was wanted or not.

'What are you thinking?'

Gregor looked up at the tops of the trees where the birds had gathered to sing. They were probably laughing at him in a tongue only they understood. Their chiding was understandable—after all, how many men permitted their underlings the freedom to voice their opinions knowing full well the offering was going to be unwanted? He drew his attention back to Simon. 'That you are about to take me to task for something.'

Simon's eyes widened, before narrowing to mere slits. 'I saw you. You were holding her in your arms and from the look on your face you'd wanted to do more.'

Why did he suddenly feel as if he'd just been caught in the stables with the cook's daughter? They'd been thirteen when her mother had tossed a bucket of ice-cold water on the two of them. At least the woman hadn't spoken a single word—there'd been no need for a lecture since her action had made her displeasure quite clear. The cold, greasy gravy that night had only reinforced her opinion.

He knew that he wasn't going to get away as lightly this time. Simon looked like he had words a-plenty that he was about to spill.

'She was afraid and threw herself into my arms. What would you suggest I should have done? Toss her aside?'

'Have you lost your good senses?'

'Not at all.' Although he was fairly certain his man had.

'Mere days from now you will take her home from her and kill her father. Have you forgotten that?'

'No. I've forgotten nothing.' He couldn't forget it. The knowledge consumed him.

'Do you think your actions now will make anything about to happen less hard for her?'

'Nothing will make it less hard for her. But in time the pain will lessen.'

'That girl will hate you, Gregor. With every drop of blood in her body, she will hate you.'

'At least it will be hate and not fear. Besides, she will be my wife. I have no choice but to shoulder her hatred.' He was familiar with hatred, withstanding it would be nothing he'd not done before.

'Shoulder her hatred? Is that what you intend to do for the rest of your life?'

'What other choice do I have? No matter what, she is going to despise me. I see nothing wrong with the two of us getting along now, while we can.'

'There is another choice. Take that damn island for King David. Hand the shipyard over to the Empress and let the girl die with her father. It would be more merciful to you both.'

Gregor's body tensed. His breath caught in his throat as if Simon had just punched him in the gut. No. Regardless of the tales told, he'd never killed a woman and he wasn't about to start now.

Simon grasped his arm and stared up at him. 'Dear Lord, you are smitten with her.' He released his hold, stepping back as if burned, and shook his head. 'You will get us all killed, Gregor.'

The older man was testing his patience. 'None of us is going to die.'

'We're headed into a battle against someone who will believe you betrayed her in the worst way possible. Someone is going to die.'

'Enough. Simon, none of us is going to die. I am not smitten.'

His man snorted. Nodding towards Beatrice, he asked, 'Are you lying to yourself or trying to convince me?'

'I am lying to no one. I admit I find her desirable. But that's not a bad thing considering she will be my wife. I have not forgotten my duty to my King, nor have I forgotten how to fulfil his orders.'

'A desirable wife who will want you not.'

'Wanting me is something that's not determined by her head or heart.' She would hate him. He knew that. But he also knew that in their marriage bed, her body wouldn't care what her heart said. More than before, she was full of nervous tension when he touched her, a nervousness that had nothing to do with fear and much to do with desire. It was evident in the shimmer of her lingering gaze and the easiness in which she rested in his embrace. She would likely despise herself for it, but she would eventually come to him willingly.

'I'll not argue with you, Simon, she deserves better, but I am all she will be given.'

'Bah. Deserves better. What manner of talk is that? What about you, Gregor? Don't you deserve something better?'

'No.' He shook his head. 'No, I do not. To be given a wife who hates me, yet doesn't fear me, is more than I could ever hope for in this life.'

'What is wrong with you? You cannot go

through life worrying that every woman is like Sarah. She was weak of spirit, broken before you ever came into her life.'

'That is something we will never know, will we?'

'Gregor, when is this unwarranted guilt going to stop?'

He was not going to have this conversation. Not with Simon. Not with anyone of this world. In due time he would answer to a power greater than either of them—whether it be God or Satan was yet to be determined. Although he was fairly certain it would not be God. Gregor turned away, ready to return to the fire and leave his man here to fret over things that could not be changed by himself.

'Boy, answer me.'

Boy? This man playing nursemaid dared to call him *boy*? Clenching his fingers into a fist, Gregor swung back around, prepared to do something he'd never before dared imagine.

What could have been a punishing blow met nothing but empty air. Simon easily dodged his fist with a laugh. 'Surely you don't think you are the first Roul to try that?'

'One of these days you will go too far, Simon, and end up dead. This conversation is finished.'

'I have known you all of your life, Gregor.' Obviously the man was going to ignore him. 'Had you been able to stop her, you would have. Lad, it was not your fault.'

'She is still dead.'

'But not by your hand.'

'You saying so does not relieve me of the burden.'

'The burden of what? Sin? Gregor, you are not a man of the cloth, nor do I see you becoming one. Accept what happened and pay your penance in gold if you must.'

'You can't buy your way into heaven.'

'Heaven is for the dead. You are not yet dead.'

'One day I will be.' Sometimes he felt that he already was.

'So will we all.' Simon heaved a heavy sigh. 'Lad, until that day comes grasp what joys you can.'

Beatrice's laugh broke into their conversation. Gregor closed his eyes at the tendrils of warmth brushing across the back of his neck.

Simon groaned, but said nothing.

Lingering in the warm caress, Gregor said, 'A little bit of joy is all I seek right now. If the possibility of shared desire is all we will have between us, what harm is there in stirring the embers now before anger and hatred have a chance to taint the passion?'

'You risk spinning a fanciful web that in the end could entrap you just as surely as it will her.'

'No web is being spun around either of us. I go into this knowing full well that it will not last. Once the keep is taken and the marriage validated,

I will take my leave just as I had planned, no worse for the experience.'

'And in the meantime you grow more attached to the girl and she to you. How will that leave either of you no worse for the experience?'

'Yes, she will despise me and I will take that hatred with me when I go. But we will both have these few days of easy pleasure to remember.'

'You have lost your wits. A cherished memory or two will not make up for the fact that neither of you will be free to find a life worth living, nor anyone to share it with.'

They could talk in circles all night long, but it would get them nowhere. 'It is what it is, Simon.'

'Yes, well, just remember you are not the only one taking a risk at the moment.'

Gregor glared down at Simon. 'Have I ever put your lives at an unnecessary risk? Have I ever led you into battle with an uncertain outcome?'

Simon shook his head.

'I am not going to do so now.'

The older man sighed again. 'I will badger you no further. Just be careful, Gregor, that you don't spin this web so tightly around yourself that you can't break free, or see through the webbing.'

Without another word, Simon left him standing on the side of the road. Gregor flexed his shoulders and then rolled them, trying to release the tension this useless conversation had created. He wasn't witless, he knew what he was doing. Had any of his other men even thought to query him in such a manner, they'd find themselves not only on the ground, but without a position.

What was wrong with Simon? Was he too old to be out on a mission? The only one who needed to watch what they were doing was Simon. Much more of this type of interference and the man would find himself sitting alone in Roul Hall on any future missions.

Somewhat free of the tension, Gregor headed back to the fire.

Beatrice sensed Gregor's imminent return, the tingling feeling in her belly wasn't from hunger. She looked in his direction, meeting his gaze, and forced herself not to sigh at the way her heart fluttered at his approach.

He joined her on the log, sitting so close that he gained questioning glances from a couple of his men and smirks from the other two. His second-in-command, Simon, ignored him completely by staying away from the fire altogether, leaving Beatrice to wonder if she'd been the reason they'd argued.

Conversation, which had once again become boisterous and easy-going before his arrival, now became stilted. The men began shooting glances from Simon to Gregor and back, making it obvious that they, too, felt the disquiet between the two men.

She stared at the three birds the young guard Daniel had caught in his net as they cooked over the fire. They weren't done yet, but she couldn't simply sit here, doing or saying nothing. The air seemed to thicken with the building tension, especially since she was fairly certain she was the cause.

Beatrice jumped to her feet. When Gregor rose, she looked up at him. 'I'll be right back. I just need to…go for a walk. And I don't need your help.'

'Ah.' He sat back down.

Colin offered, 'There's a stream maybe twenty paces off the road to the left, just past the upcoming curve.'

'Good. Thank you.'

She walked quickly away from the gathering before Gregor decided he *had* to follow her whether she wished him to or not. Unfortunately, once she reached the road she discovered the curve ahead was a little further away than she liked. Although she was certain that if she didn't return quickly her self-appointed guardian would come looking for her.

The stream was also more than twenty paces off the road. Obviously the length of Colin's stride was greater than her own—nearly double, because she counted off thirty-five paces before she heard the trickle of running water.

A few moments later, as she bent down to swish her hands in the cold water of the stream, a branch snapped behind her. Without rising, or turning to look, she said, 'I haven't been gone that long.'

'Longer than I like.'

Beatrice froze. Her heart seemed to pause before painfully slamming against her chest, taking her breath away. Dear Lord, that familiar voice did not belong to Gregor. She jumped to her feet and spun around. 'You followed me?'

Charles leaned against a tree. 'Of course I did. You could not have expected me to do otherwise.'

'I would have thought you had learned your lesson and would stay away.' Beatrice knew she wouldn't be able to outrun him, so she started edging along the stream in the hopes she could buy herself enough time to either think of a way out of this, or delay until Gregor came looking for her.

Charles stepped away from the tree and moved towards her. 'Why would I stay away from my wife-to-be?' His expression changed from bland unconcern to one of narrow-eyed, tight-lipped anger. 'Even though she seemed to greatly enjoy being embraced by another man.'

Oh, heaven help her, he had seen Gregor holding her. If Charles got his hands on her, he would likely seek her death. The only thing she could do was stall. Eventually help would come. She hoped that help came sooner rather than later.

'Then you know nothing else happened. Even though I am not your wife-to-be, what difference does it make, Charles? He held me, it wasn't as if I could fight him off. I wouldn't win a fight with the man any more than you did.'

His lips curved into a sneer at her reminder of his beating at Gregor's hands. 'Any fool can trounce an inebriated man.'

That was his excuse? He'd been weakened from over-drinking? She knew that for the lie it was, since she'd witnessed him being beaten more than once in the past and those men hadn't been experienced warriors—in fact, onc had been a stable lad at Warehaven. The sound of shuffling leaves and snapping twigs warned her that they were not alone. A glance to her right made her stomach clench again. His two friends approached.

She quickened her steps. But Charles did so, too. He cut off her escape by grasping her arms. 'You aren't getting away from me this time, Beatrice.'

One of his companions rushed in and swept a foot against her ankles, knocking her to the ground in the worst possible position—on her back with Charles on top of her.

Beatrice did the only thing she could, the thing she should have done the very moment she'd seen him—she screamed for all she was worth.

Charles slapped her face hard enough to silence her cry, but she knew Gregor and his men had to have heard her. 'Shut your mouth.'

Through stinging tears, she warned, 'You will pay for that.'

He rose and then dragged her to her feet. 'The only person here who is going to pay is you.' He jerked her against his chest. 'And trust me, my love, you will pray for death before I am done.'

His friends' evil laughter sent a shiver down her spine.

She shoved against him. 'Let me go!'

Charles raised his arm. 'I said shut up.'

She flinched, turning away from the coming slap. She saw both of Charles's companions hit the ground at the same time with a heavy thud. James and Colin, the older two of Gregor's guards, stood over the fallen men with their arms crossed before them, casually looking up into the trees as if they'd no idea what had befallen what she hoped were the now-unconscious men on the ground.

Beatrice heard Charles grunt and looked back at him. She wasn't surprised to see Gregor resting the flat side his dagger against Charles's throat. However, the absence of any emotion whatsoever—not anger, rage, irritation, simply nothing—on Gregor's face did surprise her.

In that very heartbeat, she knew that this was King David's Wolf and also knew exactly how his enemies felt as they stared into the face of certain death. Even though she wasn't at any risk of dying, a deathly, icy chill streaked down her spine to settle in her belly before its tendrils wrapped around her heart. This was why the man she'd come to know as kind was also called a heartless killer—he had the ability to completely shut down his emotions, an ability more frightening than his sword.

'Release her.' Gregor lifted his blade slightly, causing Charles to raise his head to avoid being cut. Thankfully, he followed the order and let her go.

Beatrice moved away from the two men. Then, at the barely perceptible sound of a hushed hiss, she went towards Simon's outstretched arm. She grasped the older man's hand and stood at his side.

'You were told to stay away.' Gregor's tone hadn't changed. It was even, measured, and she had to strain to hear the softly spoken words.

Charles's face turned red as he nearly shouted, 'She is my betrothed.'

Unwilling to let that lie rest unchallenged, Beatrice said, 'I am not—' Simon tugged on her hand, stopping her interruption, and shook his head.

Gregor didn't even look her way. Still positioned behind Charles, his attention remained fully on the man. 'She is under my protection. And you think to mock me by laying a hand on her?' He turned his weapon so the sharp edge was now against Charles's neck.

'I thought only to rescue Beatrice from a man unknown to her and her family.'

'By attacking her?'

While his tone hadn't changed, the volume

had risen just enough so Beatrice no longer had to strain to hear him.

'She fought me.'

'She's a woman. How much harm did you think she would cause you?'

One of the two men on the forest floor groaned and started to move. James planted a booted foot on the man's back, keeping him pinned to the ground.

'I know she's a woman. But that doesn't make her any less dangerous.' Charles fisted his hands at his side. Perhaps the memory of being bested by a woman still stung.

'Your misplaced arrogance is the only thing that makes a weaker person dangerous.'

Beatrice knew that was true. It had been Charles's absolute certainty of being in control that had let his attention wander, gaining her the opportunity to slam the pitcher against his head.

'You don't know what she's capable of the way I do.'

'Had you treated her with a little respect, you'd have had no reason to discover whether she'd prove dangerous or not.'

'Respect? Is that what you claim to be doing? It seems to me she is at your mercy.'

Beatrice wondered if Charles had always been this witless.

'My mercy? She is not my captive and is in no danger of being harmed.'

'Perhaps not harmed, but you have taken advantage. I saw you.'

Beatrice sucked in a breath at Charles's stupidity. Was he intentionally trying to get himself killed? Did he have any idea who he was baiting?

'Do you know who I am?' Obviously Gregor wondered the same thing.

'The man who stole my woman.'

His woman? Beatrice took a step forward, but Simon tightened his hold on her hand and pulled her back to his side. He leaned his head closer to whisper, 'Stay out of this.'

She just glared at him. This was about her. Didn't she have the right to correct the lie being told about her? She turned her attention back to the two men and shook her head at herself. There was no need since Gregor didn't appear to believe Charles.

'Beatrice of Warehaven is currently under the protection of Roul.'

It took a second or two, but the name apparently sunk into Charles's mind. He stiffened and paled.

The man currently pinned beneath Colin's boot cursed softly. Beatrice couldn't make out the words, but the meaning was clear—he was cursing their bad fortune. Hopefully, if these men were permitted to walk away, they would find it wiser to keep Charles away from now on rather than let him follow her again.

'What are you going to do with me?' Fear had settled into Charles's voice, leaving it weak and trembling.

'Since you appear to be completely unable to follow orders, I see no choice but to slit your throat.'

No. She couldn't let that happen. Beatrice pulled free of Simon's hold and rushed to the men. She placed a hand on Gregor's forearm. 'Please. Do not.'

Without looking at her, he asked, 'You beg for this man's life?'

'Only to save my own soul.'

For a few heartbeats he said nothing, moved not a muscle, and she wondered what thoughts were circling in his mind.

Finally, he said, 'His death would not be your fault.'

She couldn't decide if his ability to know, or deduce, her thoughts was a good, or bad, thing. Not having to explain her reasoning was a relief, since there were times she wasn't at all certain how to explain. But the idea of someone knowing her thoughts was disconcerting. It could possibly make it impossible to hide something if the need arose.

Gregor's unblinking attention reminded her that he awaited some type of response.

'You may be right, but in my mind it would always be my fault.'

He did nothing more than nod before ordering, 'Leave us.'

Leave them? She lowered her arm and stepped back. 'Why? So that I will not be certain of your final decision?'

He said nothing. But the look he turned on her felt like a wintry blast. What had been an emotionless visage before had turned impossibly frigid.

Beatrice gasped softly at the animalistic glare piercing her as surely as any arrow. Moments ago she'd thought she had seen King David's Wolf—she'd been oh, so wrong.

Gregor twisted the dagger against Charles's neck, barely nicking him.

Beatrice shook, uncertain what frightened her more—the thin sliver of blood running down Charles's neck, the man's ear-splitting scream or Gregor's focused glare.

Without taking the time to sort through the reasons, she turned away and then ran back towards the camp.

The minute he no longer heard the sound of snapping twigs beneath Beatrice's racing escape, Gregor lowered his weapon and shoved Charles away from him.

The man raised a shaking hand to his neck, then pulled it away to look at the blood on his fingertips. 'You cut me!'

'Had she not stayed my hand I would have done more than barely nick you.'

'Obviously she cares for me.'

Gregor looked down at the witless fool. 'Obviously you suffer from some odd delusion if you believe she's anything more than a woman with too tender a heart.'

Charles shrugged his shoulders and smirked before saying, 'We shall see.'

Unwilling to listen to any more of this braggart's chatter, Gregor waved his dagger. 'No. *We* will see nothing. This is the last time you will leave my presence breathing.' Then, before Charles knew what was happening, he punched him on the chin, knocking him out.

Gregor motioned to his men. 'Let them up.'

Once the men rose, Gregor pointed at Charles. 'Now, get him out of here and keep him away. If I see any of you again, you all will die. Understand?'

The two men nodded, approached Charles cautiously, as if expecting Gregor to tear their beating hearts from their bodies, and then grabbed their companion's arms before making haste to leave, dragging the man between them.

When they'd disappeared from sight, Gregor called his men over. 'Follow them, make certain they leave the area.' As they turned to follow his order, he added, 'Alive.'

Colin grunted. James nodded.

In truth, Gregor didn't care if they lived or not, he simply wanted them gone, just as he would a pesky gnat. He would prefer Charles met his maker, but contrary to what he'd expected, Beatrice hadn't agreed. That had surprised him. He would have thought she'd have welcomed the death of the man who'd bedevilled her so much that she'd run away from him for her own safety.

'You should have killed him.' Simon interrupted his thoughts.

'I don't disagree, but he's done nothing to me.'

'He didn't follow your previous order to stay away from the lady.'

'He poses no threat.'

'No, he's just the fool who thinks to take your future wife as his own.'

Gregor snorted in disbelief that Simon would say such a thing. 'You mean the woman you recently suggested I let die along with her father? That woman?'

'You should be the one to decide her fate, not some craven coward.'

He would if it came to that, but he'd prefer she decide her own fate. Thankfully, that decision was yet a few days away. 'Yes, well, before I can decide anything for her, I need to ensure she's not now cowering in the shadows.'

'Letting her cower for a bit might prove more beneficial.'

Gregor doubted very much if letting her dwell

on her fear would prove a good thing. He headed back towards the camp. 'Simon, you deal with your women any way you wish and I'll handle mine in my own manner.'

The older man followed him. 'But I don't have—'

Before the man could finish saying he didn't have any women, Gregor said, 'Exactly my point.'

Chapter Seven

Arriving back at the camp, Gregor was relieved to see that Beatrice was not hiding somewhere. She sat on the ground before the fire with her back resting against the log.

When he stopped in front of her, she looked away. He frowned, debating his next move. He could be kind and gentle. However, she'd thought to argue an order he'd given, worse, she'd done so before his men in what could have been a dangerous situation. That was unacceptable and, to be honest, he would have thought she knew better.

Besides, he caught the sound of Simon's whispers and knew he was filling the other two guards in on the events at the stream. The three of them would be waiting to see how he dealt with Beatrice.

They'd be sadly disappointed.

Gregor extended his arm, offering her his hand. 'Come with me.'

Without looking at him, or saying a word, she batted his hand away.

He caught his smile before it reached his lips. Apparently whatever fear she'd experienced had been replaced by anger. For that he was grateful. But it didn't change anything.

He crouched down next to her, to softly say, 'You can either come with me willingly, or I can toss you over my shoulder. The choice is completely yours.'

Now she looked at him, her eyes wide and mouth open in shocked surprise. Finally, she blinked, then shook her head. 'You wouldn't dare.'

'I'd prefer not to do so, but, yes, I would.' He stroked a finger down the length of her arm, noting the slight tremor at his touch. Even when angry, her body instinctively reacted to him. 'Does that idea interest you so much that you are tempting me?'

'No!' She scrambled away and rose to her feet.

Gregor stood up and took her hand. On the way to the back of the clearing, he grabbed a blanket from the pile of supplies.

He led her behind the stacked boulders at the rear of the camp and spread the blanket on the ground before stretching out on top of it. 'Join me.'

She sat down on the far edge of the blanket, just out of his reach.

Gregor was willing to ignore that for now. He was certain he'd be able to coax her closer soon enough.

'You are angry with me.' Her voice was so soft that, had he not been paying attention, he would have missed her words.

'I was, yes.'

'Why?'

'For the same reason your father or brother would be if you presumed to question a direct order in front of their men.'

'I never...' She frowned at him over her shoulder, then turned her attention to the leaves on the ground, saying, 'Oh, yes, I did.'

'It won't happen again, Beatrice.'

'Since we'll only be in each other's company another day or two, I suppose it won't.'

He didn't correct her mistaken assumption. Instead, he told her, 'He is alive.'

She kept her face averted as she picked at another leaf. 'Who?'

'Your betrothed.'

'He is *not* my betrothed.'

'So I've heard you say. Yet he follows you about like a puppy.'

'That is not my doing.'

'Of course it is.'

'How so?'

'How many years have you led him about by the nose, telling him that you'd eventually get your parents to agree to a marriage?' When she didn't answer, he added, 'I don't care either way, Beatrice. I'm just telling you that I know for a fact that your Charles is not a leader. He'd be hard pressed to lead a barn cat around by a string let alone men, or you. So, the only person who kept the hope alive for a marriage was you. He simply followed your lead, hoping to take whatever advantage he could.'

'Advantage? Until now he'd never done anything so foolish.'

He didn't believe that for a second, but it did make him wonder why she still thought to defend him.

'So, you've no idea if the touch of his lips against your neck makes you incapable of thought? Nor are you certain if a stroke of his hand chases fire or ice along your flesh?'

She said nothing, but he saw her twist and toy with the edge of the blanket between her trembling fingers. Gregor knew it was his own arrogance that made him think her reaction had nothing to do with Charles, but with him.

'What about the warmth of his arms around you? Do you know if that makes you feel safe? Or perhaps the hardness of his chest— Is it sturdy enough for you to rest against and feel secure?'

Yet again she remained silent.

'Perhaps, if he had taken advantage, you would know if the warm slide of his tongue across yours in a kiss makes you long for something more.

'Gregor, stop.'

He sighed at her breathless request with gratitude because he was running out of questions with which to torment her further.

'Yes, you are right, he did take advantage— but only as far as I would permit.' She released the edge of the blanket and turned towards him to add, 'But never did his touch or kiss make me feel any of those things.'

She moved closer, her eyes lowered and softly whispered, 'Only one man makes me wonder at those things.'

Gregor's heart hammered inside his chest. An unfamiliar, yet welcome, tremor rippled down his spine. Simon's warning rang loudly in his mind. He realised the man might have been correct in this matter—he was in great danger of being caught in a web of his own making.

She knew it, too. Otherwise she'd not have turned his tormenting back on him so neatly.

At this moment, he didn't care.

Beatrice moved alongside him and rested her cheek against his shoulder. 'Gregor, I thank you for not taking his worthless life.'

He placed an arm around her, holding her close. 'I did it for your sake, not his.' Now seemed a good time for him to say, 'You know that you had no need to be afraid, don't you?'

'I wasn't afraid.'

He rested his cheek against the top of her head. 'I could smell your fear, Beatrice. You were most definitely afraid.'

'Isn't that what you wanted? Why else would you have looked at me in such a terrifying manner?'

'Terrifying?'

'Yes. Like a wolf about to tear apart its prey.'

He laughed at her description. 'That's a bit fanciful.'

'No, it's not. You take on an inhuman appearance, devoid of any emotion. It was as if I stared death in the face.'

'I had my knife at a man's throat. Emotion has no place in such an act. If I allowed myself to feel regret or concern for every enemy I faced in battle or even one on one, I would go mad with guilt and grief.'

'But how do you do that? I watched you change. I saw the man fade away as the animal took his place.'

'It is the way it has to be. I can't afford to let any emotion, not even anger, cloud my judgement or my movements when pitted against another—not if I want to live.'

'No wonder they call you the Wolf.'

The Wolf. King David's Wolf. Gregor gritted his teeth. He was so tired of that title and more than willing to do whatever was necessary to end this forced service to his King.

He relaxed his jaw and turned his head to whisper in her ear, 'Can I tell you a secret?'

She nodded.

'Wolves run in packs.'

Beatrice looked at him. 'That is your great secret? Everyone knows that. Even now you are travelling with your pack.'

'My guards?' He wanted to laugh at the mere idea. 'They are not my pack.'

'Then who are?'

'My brothers.'

She leaned far enough away to stare at him. 'Are you telling me that King David's Wolf is more than one man?'

Gregor nodded. 'Yes. It is four.'

She frowned, then nodded. 'Well, that makes more sense than believing you are invested with some magical powers that permit you to travel from country to country seemingly overnight. How did your family end up in this position? Was it by choice?'

He rolled his eyes. 'Oh, yes, every shipbuilder I know longs to be taken away from his work at a moment's notice.'

'My father would be frothing at the mouth.' She settled back against his side.

'I completely understand. The late Lord of Roul committed treason against the King. To save his life, my brothers and I had to place our lives in David's hands.'

'Why would he use you so harshly?'

Apparently her parents didn't involve her in family, or political, matters of the day. 'The King needs someone to do his...' He paused, looking for a way to explain without delving into any gruesome details. 'His less-than-kingly tasks. And it provides him the opportunity to blame others if something goes wrong.'

'So, essentially, it permits him to be underhanded with less chance of being caught.'

Perhaps she wasn't as shielded from politics as he'd thought. 'Yes.'

'And what happens if something does go wrong?'

'My older brother Elrik has a title, lands and property. I have the ships and warehouses. The younger two, Edan and Rory, have their lives. All of which David would take without batting an eye. So, we don't permit anything to go wrong. If, on the odd occasion something appears as if it might not run the desired course, we ensure it is taken care of before word reaches the King's ears.'

Beatrice shook her head. 'I thought King Henry's brother had been raised so piously that he'd not consider risking his soul for such earthly matters.'

'He was and he doesn't risk *his* soul. That burden is ours alone.'

'How can you or your brothers be blamed for something you've been forced into doing?'

'We could have said no.'

'And watched your father die?'

He shrugged. There were still times when he resented the position in which his father had placed him and his brothers. 'He was the one who'd foolishly decided to go against the King.'

'Gregor, don't talk like that.'

'Like what?'

'As if you'd not have cared if your father had been put to death for his crime.'

Gregor knew it was far past time to pull in the reins on this conversation. It was now going in a direction that would not bode well for either of them. 'I never said I wouldn't have cared. Why else would I have accepted the burden of his treason?'

She idly stroked his arm. 'It is sad that you and your brothers find yourselves tasked with such difficult burdens.'

'We survive. Save your pity for those who need it.'

She withdrew her touch, letting a cold breeze rush in to replace the warmth.

He grasped her hand and brought it back to rest on his forearm. 'I meant not to sound so short tempered.'

'Can I ask you something?'

'There is nothing you can't ask me. Just be forewarned that you may not always like the answer.'

'Even if it's…personal?'

'Yes. There is little I wouldn't share with you.'

'Are you married?'

Gregor blinked. Of all the things she might ask him, that wasn't one he'd expected. She hadn't come up with it on her own, so which of his men needed a heavy reprimand?

She looked up at him. 'Are you?'

'I was.'

'Was?'

Gregor swallowed his curse at himself. He'd been the one who'd told her she could ask him anything. 'She…died.'

'Died?'

'Are you telling me that you haven't heard the rumours of how I murdered my wife?'

The stroking of her fingers against his forearm stopped for a fraction of a breath and he thought she'd pull away. Instead, she slid her hand down to lace her fingers through his. 'There are many things I've heard about David's Wolf, but that is not one of them. I don't believe you capable of such a cowardly act.'

Gregor drew in a breath at her statement. Her trusting faith in him was going to one day be his undoing. 'Outside of my family and the King, no one has ever said that to me. I thank you.'

With a frown etching her brow, she looked up at him, asking, 'Do so few people know you are not truly a beast?'

He laughed softly, more out of amazement than humour, at her question. 'Fewer than you could imagine.'

'Well, that should be remedied.'

'I'd prefer it remain as is. It would be a little hard to instil fear in others if they thought I was nothing more than a lovable dog.'

'Even dogs bite.'

'True.'

'How did she die?'

He sighed. She wasn't going to let this go until she'd heard the whole sordid truth. 'Upon learning who she'd been wed to, she threw herself from the castle wall.'

'No! Oh, Gregor, that is horrible.'

Exactly the response he'd expected—horror at what he'd let happen. He uncurled his fingers and started to pull his arm free.

She grasped his wrist, stopping his retreat. 'I didn't mean *you* were horrible.'

He glanced away. 'I didn't stop her.'

'Do you believe that her death was somehow *your* fault?' Her frown returned. 'Gregor, as hard as you try, you cannot control everything, or everyone. As terrible as it may sound, had you stopped her, do you not think she'd have found another way?'

While that was a possibility he'd never considered, it changed nothing. A woman had taken her life rather than be wed to him.

'Had you known her long?' She paused, then said, 'No. That was a silly question since she didn't know who you were.'

'Stop.' He had no desire to discuss this any further. 'Just stop.'

She clamped her lips shut and stared down at her lap. Before she could pull away, he placed a fingertip beneath her chin to draw her focus back to him. 'We will arrive at the coast by this time tomorrow. I want to taste your kiss before our time together ends.'

Her eyes widened, but she hesitated.

'You need only say no, Beatrice. I will not force you. And you need only ask me to stop whenever you wish me to do so.'

'I do not worry about you forcing me.'

'Then what do you fear?'

She raised a hand to his cheek. 'That I might enjoy it too much and that you will make me long for things I can hardly imagine.'

Gregor sucked in a deep breath. Her explanation was so honest, her gaze so trusting, that for the first time in his adult life he wanted to weep at what he knew would soon be lost. This night, these few stolen hours were all they would ever share before his coming actions forced hate between them.

He wrapped both of his arms around her and dragged her across his lap. She reached up to curl her arms about his neck and pressed her lips to his.

Gregor smiled beneath her chaste kiss before easily parting her lips. She welcomed his kiss with a soft moan.

It would be all too easy to lose himself in this woman's touch. He could gladly drown in the warmth wrapping around him.

Beatrice lowered her hands to his shoulders, fingers curling into his tunic. She drew away just far enough to say, 'You still wear your armour.'

He understood her complaint. It had become

uncomfortable, but he wasn't about to remove the chainmail. At this moment it provided more protection for her than it did for him. The risk of losing control this night was great. The hindrance of the mail would give him the needed time to regain common sense were he to consider doing anything they might come to regret.

Threading his fingers through her hair, he eased her back into their kiss.

She gently pushed away to pluck once again at his tunic. 'This will not do, Gregor. Your mail is hard. I pose no threat to your life. Remove it.'

He grasped her shoulders and waited until she returned his gaze. 'The threat is not to me, but to you.'

'Very noble of you, I am sure, but silly none the less. The protection these links of metal may offer are not wanted, or welcome. Should I decide to have my way with you, this shirt of mail will protect neither of us.'

One corner of his lips twitched. Her tongue had grown bolder. 'Should *you* decide?'

'Did you not just say that you would stop whenever I asked you to do so? Has that changed?'

He reached up to stroke her cheek with the back of his fingers. She would tempt even the saints. 'No, that has not changed.'

She rose and tugged at his hand. 'I want to feel a man beside me, not a warrior ready to ride into battle.'

He bit back a heartfelt, but crude reply, but he couldn't help think that their coming marriage bed would require a warrior ready for battle. Gregor stood up and pulled off his tunic, then leaned over. Before he could request a hand in removing the hauberk, Beatrice was attempting to tug the chainmail over his head. Between the two of them, they managed to slide the armour far enough off his body so that it landed on the ground with a ringing thud.

He straightened up, glanced at the pile of chainmail and shook his head. 'You'd not make a good squire.'

'Thankfully that is a position I've never desired. We can call one of your men if you'd like.' She started working on the ties of his gambeson. 'Although, I would prefer you not.'

Once she had the ties free, he pushed her hands away and tore the quilted garment over his head. Dropping it on top of the bunched-up chainmail, he said, 'I think we managed quite well. Besides, they'd be shocked to see my armour in this condition.'

Gregor took one of her hands between his own and brought it to his lips. 'It is not too late to back away.'

Beatrice stepped closer. Pressed tightly against his chest, she looked up at him. 'If you are afraid, I promise to be gentle.'

He laughed. Not only would she tempt the saints,

she'd have them quaking in their shoes. Releasing her hands to wrap his arms around her, he warned, 'I promise no such thing.'

She shivered against him, whispering, 'I'm not sure what to do, or—'

'Hush.' Gregor brushed his lips against hers, cutting off her words. 'I was but teasing you. Nothing is going to happen that you haven't already done.'

No matter how much he wanted to make her his, he wasn't about to do that without the priest's blessing. As improbable as it was a stray arrow could take his life in battle, leaving her hard pressed to make a good marriage, or possibly carrying his child.

He swept her up in his arms and returned to the blanket. After carefully lowering her to the ground, he stretched out alongside.

Even though he'd told her nothing new was going to take place, her nervous anticipation was apparent. She'd folded her hands together on top of her stomach, clenching them so tightly her nails were pressing into her skin.

Gregor covered her hands and felt the tremors rippling through her body. He'd never been alone with such an innocent before, especially not one as brazen as this. He could only begin to imagine the trouble she could get herself into. Her bold talk and inexperience would likely be seen as a challenge worth accepting to most men.

'Beatrice, look at me.'

It took a few moments, but she finally pulled her stare away from the sky above to turn it on him.

He trailed a finger along the line of her jaw. 'I am not a stranger to you. I vowed to protect you and have done so.' He leaned over and dropped a kiss on the tip of her nose. 'Tell me what you fear.'

'I'm not sure. I do trust you with my life, so I thought this would be easier.' She shook her head, then continued. 'At first, Charles's kisses were… lovely. But then, I only wanted his kisses to end.'

'I am not Charles.'

'I know, but what if it had nothing to do with him, but instead was me?'

Gregor pried her hands apart and lifted one to his shoulder, then gathered her in his arms and rolled her on to her back. He lowered his head, pausing a breath above her lips to say, 'Hush. You worry about foolish things for naught.'

Beatrice jerked slightly at the force of his kiss before responding in kind. This was no gentle touch of exploration. It was an invasion of the senses. Far from leaving her ready to swoon at the rush of dizzying desire, it made her want more than just the feel of his lips on hers.

She shifted beneath him and tightened her hold, trying to get closer. Yet no matter how hard she strained it was not enough.

He broke their kiss. 'Beatrice, stop. Relax.'

'I cannot.' She knew what she wanted—she

wanted him. It was unlikely that she'd see him again and it was even more unlikely that she'd ever meet another man as trustworthy as Gregor. So, if this night was her last chance to be with him, as sinful and foolish as it was, she wanted this man, this man who she trusted, to be her first…lover.

In the short time she'd known Gregor, she'd learned more about him than she had about Charles in the last three years. And she'd learned things about herself, too. He'd taught her that fear was something that could be beaten if you looked at it and faced it head on. She'd come to realise that there was so much more to a man than the way he looked, or the honey-coated words that fell from his lips.

Things like honour, loyalty and strength counted for much more than she'd ever imagined. Those things would make a man more worthy as a husband than anything else.

But Gregor of Roul would never be her husband and if this one night was all she would have, then she wanted more than anything else to know what it would be like to be his wife. But even she wasn't bold enough to ask him to take her and satisfy this burning desire. 'I am so tense that I feel as though I am going to shatter.'

He groaned before moving off of her to rest on his side, then whispered hotly against her ear, 'Trust me.'

The moment after she nodded, he pushed her on

to her side facing away from him and then pulled her tightly against his chest. She could feel the pounding of his heart against her back.

With his head propped up on a bent arm, he leaned over and teased the corner of her mouth. Beatrice wanted the feel of his lips covering hers and turned her head towards his. She sighed at the return of his kiss.

He slid his free arm around her to rest heavy on her chest. The edge of his thumb stroked the curve of a breast. Her breath caught, wondering what he would do next. Gregor grazed her lower lip with his teeth, drawing her attention back to their kiss.

When her racing heart finally slowed, he pulled away to rest his chin on her shoulder. 'Go to sleep.'

His voice was rough, gravelly and it made her wonder if he, too, wanted more than just sleep. Not certain how to broach the subject, Beatrice said, 'But I thought...' She stopped, letting the question fade away into the night.

'I know what you thought.' Gregor sighed. 'But, no, your first time needs to be with your husband, in a marriage bed. Not out here in the woods with someone who is supposed to be protecting you.' Once again he moved his thumb, a gentle stroke that sent shivers to her toes. 'No matter how much I want you, and trust me, Beatrice, I do, this is not the time or the place.'

He lowered the arm that had been propping up

his head and curved his body around her. 'Now, sleep.'

She curled her fingers around the arm still tucked around her, holding him close, not wanting him to move away. The warmth behind her, the steady beating of his heart and the evenness of his breaths lulled her closer to sleep.

When all was quiet, and she was certain he had fallen to sleep, Beatrice whispered, 'It may not be the time, nor the place, but it is the right man.'

He tensed and she knew instantly that she'd sorely misspoken. He withdrew his arm and rolled away, letting the coolness of the night air rush between their bodies.

She said nothing. What could she say? It wasn't as if she could take back the wish she'd put into spoken words. So she remained still, waiting to see what he would do, or say.

Finally, he rose and covered her up with the side of the blanket he'd been laying on. She heard him walk away, heard the snapping of branches, the rustling of dried leaves and the strike of flint as he built a fire.

The blaze did little to warm her body. And the knowledge that he sat there before the fire instead of coming back to the blanket and her did nothing to warm her heart. Beatrice closed her eyes, silently cursing her foolishly spoken words and the useless moisture building behind her eyelids.

What good was having a choice, when the one she chose wanted her not?

The next morning Beatrice awoke to the sound of men's voices. She rolled over and opened her eyes to see Gregor, donned once again in his armour, and Simon talking near the fire.

When Gregor left, Simon stayed behind. He made quick work of dousing the fire and disassembling the small rock-rimmed pit.

Without turning away from his task, Simon said, 'From the sound of your breathing, I would say you are awake.'

'That I am.' She rose, finger-combed the tangles from her hair before plaiting it into a long braid which she tossed over her shoulder to hang down her back and then folded the blanket which had served as her bed.

Finished with his task, Simon turned to face her and approached to take the blanket from her. 'I'll have one of the men pack this while I escort you to the stream.'

'Where is Gregor?'

'Lord Gregor and James went ahead to scout out the road before we leave. Fear not, he'll be back shortly.'

On their walk back to the camp, Beatrice said, 'Sir Simon, I appreciate the offer, but you really don't need to escort me.'

He tossed the blanket to Daniel. 'After what happened yesterday evening, yes, I do. Come along.'

Once out of earshot of the camp, she asked, 'You don't like me much, do you?'

Simon stumbled a step, obviously surprised by her question. 'What makes you say such a thing, my lady?'

'You say little, but when you do it's as if you are ordering about one of your men.'

He shrugged. 'That is simply my way. I have not been in the company of many women since my dear Alice died in childbirth. So, any tender words or ways are unfamiliar to me.'

'You were married?'

'A long, long time ago. My Alice died over twenty years past.'

'And you never remarried?'

'No. I go to my grave free to join once again with Alice.'

Surprised by that admission, she asked, 'So, you loved your wife?'

'Not at first.' Simon laughed. 'It was no love match by any means. Our family's lands were adjacent, so the marriage was arranged by our fathers with no say from either of us. We fought continuously from the moment we spoke our vows at the village chapel. But sleeping under the same roof, in the same bed night after night, does tend to alter things a bit.'

She imagined that it did alter things. *What would it be like to sleep in the same bed night after night with Gregor?* A hot flush fired her cheeks at the thought.

'I saw that, Lady Beatrice. Tell me, do you care for him?'

'Who?' She saw little need to make this too easy for the man.

'Do not be cheeky with me, lass. You know full well that I meant Lord Gregor.'

'I've only known him for less than two days.'

'Yet both of you act as if you'd known each other for years.'

'True, and it amazes me as much as it would anyone. But he makes me feel safe and I am comfortable around him.'

'You need be extra-careful when you play with wolves, my lady.'

Did Simon fear that she sought to play with Gregor's heart? She wouldn't know how to be that underhanded. 'I do not seek to bring him any harm, Sir Simon. From what I've seen and heard he's had enough of that in his life.'

He waved her off the road towards the stream, frowning. 'It is not *his* heart I fear for, Lady Beatrice, it is yours.'

Before she had a chance to ask him to explain, he nodded in the direction of the water. 'Be on your way. I will wait here.'

When she rejoined him, she heard voices and

the stomping of horses on the road a short distance away, thus her chance to get some sort of reasoning for his fear was lost.

James, Harold and Daniel sat on their horses, waiting. Gregor stood in the road holding the reins to the other mounts.

Simon none too gently took the reins to his horse, asking, 'My lord, have you seen the size of those spiderwebs that were woven last night?' He then mounted his horse and left without another word.

Beatrice looked at Gregor, but his eyes were closed tightly while he rubbed his forehead. Finally, he lowered his hand and helped her on to the horse without a word.

In what seemed no time at all, Beatrice found herself staring out over the busy wharf. The long-missed scent of the sea, the sounds of workers plying their trade, the loading and unloading of ships—it all made her eager to return to Warehaven.

'All is in order,' Gregor said as he came up behind her.

His familiar touch on her shoulder, the warmth of his hand as he gently squeezed, before brushing his palm to the small of her back, made her long to stay here with him instead of returning home.

But his withdrawal at her comment last night and subsequent coldness since starting out this day made her aware that staying wasn't an option. She wanted to cry over how badly this had all ended after she'd begun to hope for so much more.

She pushed away the morose thoughts and stiffened her spine. 'You've found me safe passage?'

'Yes.' He urged her forward. 'The ship was heading to Warehaven. The captain swears you will know him and he vowed to take good care of you until you arrive safely at home.'

She heard his words, but they barely registered in her mind. The only thing she could concentrate on was the fall of each footstep that would take her to the ship and out of Gregor's life. It was all she could do not to throw herself against his chest and beg him to change his mind.

This hurt buffeting her was her own fault. She was such a fool when it came to men. Such a gullible, senseless fool. And hadn't Sir Simon just warned her of this very hurt just this morning? Bah, she was twice the fool.

'Did you hear me?' He reached up to grasp her shoulder and turn her to face him.

She shook her head and looked away, not wanting him to see the sudden building of moisture in her eyes.

Of course he was having none of that. With his fingertips beneath her chin, he turned her to face him. 'I said this is not goodbye, Beatrice. I will come to you, soon.'

She gasped, wondering if she could believe what she'd heard.

He cupped her cheeks and brushed at her tears with his thumbs. 'Stop this. I'd not have expected this childish reaction from such a brazen wanton such as you.'

She knew that he was but seeking to tease her out of her pitiful mood. 'Brazen and brash I have always been, but never a wanton until I met you.'

He nodded. 'That is good. Just keep it that way. Don't go chasing after the first pretty face you see.'

Pretty face. Beatrice laughed and fell easily against his chest. 'I make no promises.'

He hugged her tightly, then released her all too soon, to say, 'Go. Be safe. Be strong.'

Without another word, he turned and left her wondering at his cryptic farewell.

Chapter Eight

Beatrice stared up at the ceiling of her bedchamber. She'd nearly forgotten how much she loved this room with its curtained alcove and the four narrow window openings that permitted light to flood the chamber for parts of each day no matter the season.

Although it seemed oddly quiet without Isabella's presence. Now that she'd returned to Warehaven, she missed her sister more than she had at Montreau.

At least at Montreau she'd had Jared and Lea for company. Neither was very demonstrative, but they'd been family. Here there was no one but the guards and the servants.

She smiled wryly at her senseless contradictions. Isn't this what she'd wanted—to return to Warehaven? Hadn't she broken every convention, sinned enough to put her soul at risk of eternal damnation, taken more chances than she should have just to return?

Yes, she had. She sat up on the bed and now was not the time to dwell on her rashness, there was plenty of work to be done before her parents returned.

While the bailey, walls, kitchens, stable and

Great Hall were in excellent condition in her parents' absence, the upper chambers were…not in as good a state. It was likely that nobody had so much as come up the stairs since her parents left the last time, let alone seen that the rooms were cleaned. The chambers needed to be aired, swept, the linens washed, and the woodwork and floors dusted.

The last two days had been spent tearing down the cobwebs. After walking into one, in the dark, on the night of her return, she'd vowed not to entertain a repeat of that most unpleasant experience.

At least the work had kept her hands and mind occupied. She'd been too busy during the day to spend much time dwelling on how much she missed Gregor. Or wondering if or when he would come to Warehaven.

How she hoped he did come to Warehaven. She wanted her parents to meet him, to see that King David's Wolf wasn't any more evil or cruel than King Henry's Executioner, her father, had been. Surely they would approve a match since Gregor would meet every requirement they could devise. He was of the right age. While not titled, he did control a shipyard which would make her father happy. He was knighted. And he even met her new-found requirements—he could see to her safety, keep her fed, most likely give her the children she wished to have. He was honest, loyal, honourable and trustworthy.

Of course all of this was providing Gregor asked

for a match. That was not yet a given. Beatrice shook her head, trying to clear her mind of such wishful thoughts.

Right now she was thankful that she'd fallen into bed each night exhausted—far too tired to wish for long that his firm, warm chest was against her back while he held her close as she drifted off to sleep.

Beatrice swung her legs over the side of the bed, her feet hitting the cold floor just as one of the maids pounded on her door. 'Lady Beatrice, are you awake?'

She shot a questioning look at the young woman entering the chamber in a rush. For all she tried, she couldn't remember the woman's name. She'd been brought in from the village to assist with the cleaning and right now, from the way her body trembled, she was terrified of something.

'Yes, I am. What is wrong?'

'Oh, my lady, you are needed below.' The woman looked over her shoulder as if expecting someone to suddenly appear behind her. 'We are under attack.'

After the first rush of blood surged through her heart, leaving her head spinning, Beatrice took a deep breath. She doubted if anyone was actually attacking Warehaven. What was probably happening was that more than a couple of ships were entering the harbour at the same time. While that sight could be rather daunting if one was not used to witnessing the event, it had never in the history of Warehaven been an attacking force—at least not since her father's arrival on the island.

She ushered the woman back to the door. 'Tell them I'll be down after I get dressed.'

'Oh, hurry, Lady Beatrice. Sir Robert is pacing the hall.'

That made her frown. The man in charge of her father's guards was rarely agitated. His ability to keep a tight rein on his emotions was what made him the perfect man for the position.

She grabbed her gown from the wall peg and dropped it over her head. Thankfully, it was an over-sized garment she used when she knew she'd be getting filthy. There were no lacings to snug it to her body, so she needed only to wrap a belt around her waist, then throw on her stockings and boots.

On her way out of the chamber, she turned and went back in to grab her comb. A quick rake and braid of her hair as she descended to the Great Hall would have to do for now.

The sight that met her as she reached the bottom step nearly took her breath away. Guards, thankfully Warehaven's guards, filled the hall. They were all in different stages of arming themselves.

Just as the woman had said, Sir Robert paced—briskly—as he checked and rechecked each man and their weapons.

Her gaze flew to the long trestle table which held what appeared to be the contents of the armoury.

No. This could not be as it appeared. Nobody attacked Warehaven—at least not since her father had done so.

'Sir Robert!' She shouted to be heard over the din of men getting ready for battle.

He came to her immediately and led her to an alcove near the back of the hall. 'My lady, there is no easy way to tell you this, but an army has taken the harbour, docks and wharf district. They are now making their way through the village towards the keep.'

'I beg your pardon?' Surely she'd misheard him.

'We are under attack.'

'By whom?' What fool would attack them? Did they not realise what her father would do to them once he discovered this…this…atrocity?

'I am not sure. They carry no standard.'

This was not good. With her father and mother gone, she was the only Warehaven left to give the orders.

But what orders? Speechless, she stared at Sir Robert.

He briefly patted her shoulder. 'The men are well trained. I can advise you, but I need to see to them first.'

'I know. I know. Give me just a minute.'

'That is longer than we can spare.'

She drew in a deep breath, held it for a heartbeat, then let it out in a rush. 'Have the villagers made it to the bailey?'

'Yes, they started arriving with whatever weapons they own, the animals they could easily herd and the supplies they could carry a few moments ago.'

'Good.' She was going to have to make room for them inside the keep, but for the moment that planning could wait. 'As soon as the crowd thins, get the gates shut.'

'Men are already on hand to do so. The portcullis is ready to be lowered.'

'Our livestock?'

'Had not yet been turned out for the day.'

Which meant if it became necessary, they had enough food and with the well in the courtyard would not run out of water if this came to a drawn-out siege. Slaughtering the livestock would leave them short supplied this coming winter, but she couldn't worry about that now, she needed to focus on the immediate needs of Warehaven's people.

'Finish getting the men ready, get them on the walls, order someone to bring the villagers inside. Make certain the postern gate is secured and guarded, along with the tunnel entrance. Tell the servants to do their best for right now, we'll sort everything out later. I need to change and will join you on the wall at the main gate tower quickly.'

Sir Robert nodded and left to carry out her orders, while she raced back up to her bedchamber.

She flung open the chest at the foot of her bed, digging through the garments inside looking for her best gown. If she had to take her father's place, she wasn't going to do so looking as if she'd just come out of the pig sty.

Mistress Almedha, one of her mother's personal lady's maids, bustled into the chamber. 'Come, Lady Beatrice, let's get you ready.'

Beatrice breathed a sigh of relief. 'Thank you, Almedha. I could use some help.'

The woman reached around her and laid her hands on a brilliant green gown, then pulled it from the bottom of the chest. 'This one.'

Beatrice only owned a few, but she had forgotten about that particular gown. After Charles had claimed he hated it, she'd packed it away and hadn't worn it since.

Almedha shook out the garment, letting the matching slippers hit the floor. She then hung it on a peg and turned to Beatrice. 'There's little time to waste.' She drew her gaze from Beatrice's toes to the top of her head. 'And much work to be done.'

A young serving lad entered the chamber carrying a bucket of steaming water. His twin sister followed, her arms laden with towels, soap and a small bottle of oil.

Bewildered, Beatrice said, 'There's no time for a bath.'

While shooing the children from the room and closing the door behind them, Almedha agreed,

'No, there isn't. But there is time to clean what's seen.'

She set a large bowl on the table in the alcove, filled it with the water, poured in a small amount of oil, which filled the air with the scent of roses, and waved Beatrice over. 'Come on, child, let's be at it.'

Beatrice stripped off her clothes and while Almedha scrubbed, she unbraided her hair. Once dried and dressed, the maid pushed her down on to a stool and made quick work of untangling the snarls in Beatrice's hair before fashioning two braids which she then coiled about her head. 'I know you are unwed, but I don't think it would be wise to make that too easy for your enemy to guess.'

That was something Beatrice never would have considered. She'd have run a comb through her hair and left it to hang free to save time.

Almedha ordered, 'Up with you.'

Once she rose, the maid reached up and pinched her cheeks, claiming, 'A little colour cannot hurt.'

Beatrice's eyes teared at the stinging pinch. But she said nothing. Her mind was too busy trying to sort out what to say once she reached the wall. Since she wasn't yet certain what they were up against, stalling to find words was useless.

She looked towards the door. The urge to go hide behind the heavy curtains of the alcove grew strong, her stomach churned, twisting with cold dread. Before she could whip herself up into a ball of quivering fear, Beatrice placed her hands over her stomach, straightened her spine and strode out of the chamber. Perhaps a display of courage, no matter how false, would serve her well.

Instead of going down to the Great Hall, she climbed the steep spiral stairs leading up to the tower. Four armed men stood guard inside. They opened the door that led outside to the narrow drawbridge connecting the tower to the inner curtain wall.

She joined the two guards waiting there and walked quickly along the walkway of the battlement to the inner bailey's gate tower. The wind picked up, whipping the fullness of her gown about her legs, threatening to trip her.

Sir Robert met her at the wall. 'We lost three at the warehouses.'

She stared at him in confusion. 'What do you mean we lost three?'

'Men. Warehaven lost three men to these invaders.'

'And how do we know that?'

Sir Robert's lips thinned and his jaw clenched for a long moment before he said, 'They dumped the bodies outside the wall.'

Beatrice shivered beneath the icy chill settling in her belly, swallowing back a sourness that made her thankful she'd not broken her fast this morning.

'Do we know who they are yet?'

'No. But according to the dockmaster five ships entered the harbour just before the break of day.'

Five ships? *Five*? She did a quick calculation and felt the walkway sway beneath her feet. There could be anywhere from a hundred to nearly two hundred men marching on Warehaven.

Whoever thought to invade was as strong and wealthy as her father. Unfortunately, Warehaven's forces were only at half-capacity—the other half was with their lord and lady.

Since no sound of pitched battle reached her ears, this first meeting would be nothing more than a chance to discuss terms...terms of her surrender.

Since she would not hand over her father's keep, she could only hope and pray he'd arrive soon.

To be certain, she asked, 'Have they made any demands yet?'

'Only to converse with the Lord or Lady of Warehaven.'

Relieved that she'd assumed correctly, she nodded towards the main gate tower. 'Let's see who it is.'

Together they crossed the movable walkway suspended over the outer bailey to the main tower. Even if the attackers fought their way through the main gates, they would have no access to the keep and would have to battle their way through yet another fortified wall. Her father had taken his own attack of Warehaven into consideration when he'd rebuilt this keep.

Beatrice leaned her forehead against the cold stone of a merlon and took a deep breath to calm her shaking body. It was imperative that she control the fear seeking to overwhelm her. She didn't want her voice to tremble, or break. More importantly, she didn't want the force outside to sense her fear—or as Gregor would say—smell her fear.

Certain she had a tight hold on her composure, Beatrice moved to look over the embrasure.

No. She stumbled against the battlements. Her breath caught. This wasn't possible. The sight before her swam, wavering as if she was seeing it through wave-whipped seas.

Beatrice gripped the stone edge of the crenel, silently praying for strength and the power to remain upright without fainting.

'My lady?' Sir Robert's concerned voice broke through the thick fog shroud covering her, making it hard to breathe and even harder to think.

She waved him off, then leaned over the embrasure to stare down at the solitary man on horseback, before shouting, 'What do you want, Gregor?'

'Warehaven.'

His single-word answer made her want to scream. Had this been his plan the entire time? Was this the task King David had given him?

She was such a fool. Why had she not believed what her gut had tried to tell her when she'd first discovered his identity? How had she once again let a man sway her into believing her instincts were wrong?

She'd believed his lies. Had trusted that his

promise to protect her, his gentle touches and his kisses were real. She'd let herself imagine a life at his side, in his bed, birthing his children.

What was wrong with her that fate played her such cruel tricks by handing her useless dreams?

The need to bury herself in her chamber and cry was strong enough to nearly overwhelm her. She felt the hotness of tears building in her eyes and silently cursed the weakness, clenching her jaw until the hatred burning in her belly and chest dried the heated moisture.

She would see him dead before handing him this keep. Beatrice stood upright and took the readied bow from the shocked guard next to her.

'What are you doing?'

Sir Robert reached for the weapon, but she was quicker and leaned back into the opening.

She knew Gregor saw the arrow aimed at him, yet he didn't move. As still as a boulder, he silently stared up at her as if daring her to try something so brash.

Beatrice lowered the bow slightly and let the arrow fly. It soared true, piercing the ground in front of the horse.

Gregor's only reaction was to ask, 'Are you finished?'

She held back her smile of triumph at the flat, emotionless tone of his voice. He was angry and that made her glad. He deserved to be angry. He deserved to be dead.

'No, I will not be finished until you leave this island.'

'If your father has not yet returned, then you and I need to talk.'

'We have nothing to talk about.'

Gregor raised his arm and Beatrice heard the sound of horses and armoured men seconds before she saw them crest the hill leading up to the keep. At least fifty men formed a solid wall along the edge of the mound.

Sir Robert groaned. 'And I wager there are at least that many more behind them.'

'You are probably right, but we still have the advantage. We are in control of the keep. They are out in the open.' Her heart ached enough for her to add, 'Making easy targets.'

'Regardless, you must go and confer with him.'

'Confer? Do you know who he is?'

'No. But it is obvious you do.'

'That man is King David's Wolf, Gregor of Roul.' She didn't waste time explaining the details of the Roul family of wolves. At this moment any wolf at the gate was trouble.

Sir Robert cursed as he tore the bow out of her hand. 'I know this is not an ideal situation, but if you don't go to talk to him, I must.'

'He will kill you.'

The captain laughed. 'What matter if it is now or later? He is going to kill us all eventually.'

No, he wasn't. She knew with a certainty that

wasn't his mission. 'Had he been tasked to wipe out the people of this isle there would be far more than three bodies below.' She glanced down at Gregor, then turned back to Sir Robert. 'For whatever reason, King David wants this keep. I need to discover why.'

She then shouted down at Gregor, 'Meet me at the gate', before moving out of the embrasure only to lean back over the wall to add, 'Unarmed.'

Foolish about men she might be, but she wasn't quite as foolish about her own life, and certainly wasn't going to risk having an angry warrior slide a blade into her through an opening between the iron bars.

Sir Robert ordered the men to open the large iron-studded timber gate, leaving the portcullis lowered. 'You can confer through the bars.'

Beatrice knew her father wouldn't have done such a thing, but she wasn't her father. While she could handle a bow and arrow, a sword was another matter entirely.

She looked at the ladder leading down to the bailey. *No.* With the way she currently shook from rage it was likely she'd end up on her bottom and she wasn't about to let that happen. It would in no way gain her any confidence or trust from what was now *her* army.

Instead, she returned the same way she'd arrived, going back into the keep and re-exiting through the Great Hall. Not only did it save her from embarrassing herself in front of the enemy and her men, it gave her time to find a small measure of calm.

As she crossed from the inner yard to the outer one, she held Gregor's stare. His sword was not hanging from his side and he'd removed his nasal helm, holding it in the crook of his arm. It made it easier for her to see his anger, which was probably his intention. She didn't care. He didn't scare her. He hadn't frightened her before and now she was too angry and hurt to consider fear.

Although that might have been a mistake. He'd lied about everything else, so perhaps he'd lied about not harming her, too.

And again, she didn't care.

She couldn't care. Doing so would only make the searing pain of heartbreak worse.

To her horror, the first thing that wisped across her mind was how magnificent he looked. Dressed all in black—even his chainmail had a fresh wash of black—leaving only the silver in his hair and his shimmering blue-grey eyes to lend a splash of colour.

His shimmering eyes. She nearly tripped, catching herself quickly as she looked harder. He wasn't as outraged as he'd like others to believe. Not with that flash of colour in his eyes.

She stopped at the gate and waited for him to speak.

He reached through the iron bars, grasped her

wrist, dropped something into her palm and then released her. 'This is yours.'

Beatrice looked down at the ring in her hand. 'What is this?'

'Your wedding ring.'

She dropped the circle of gold to the ground. 'I have no need of a ring.'

'Yes, you do. Before this is over you will become my wife.'

'Like hell I will.'

'You have no choice.'

'Go to hell, Roul. I will die before I wed you.'

His jaw clenched. The colour in his eyes faded. She knew that now he was truly angered.

'This island is mine, Beatrice. The harbour, the wharf, the warehouses, the village are all mine. If you wish to save the lives of the people inside this keep, you will become my wife.'

Her stomach felt as if someone had punched her with a mailed fist. 'What are you saying?'

'You heard me. If you kill yourself, every person inside these walls will join you immediately.'

He thought his show of strength and power had turned her into someone like his first wife? 'You fool. I am not so weak of will that I would take my own life. I would fight you to the death before marrying you.'

'More blood will be spilled if you kill yourself, because I will then take Warehaven by force.'

She gasped in horror. 'You wouldn't do such a thing.'

'I would. And I will. Now pick up your ring.'

Without thinking she leaned down and retrieved the ring. Holding it in her fisted hand, she warned, 'My father will kill you.'

'He will try. And when he does, he will die.'

There was no inflection in his voice. He spoke the words like an oath, something that he would do whether he wanted to or not. She leaned closer, pressing her body against the bars. 'Gregor, no.'

'I have my orders. I will not forsake them.'

'So instead you will forsake me.' She despised the tremor in her voice.

'I give you your life and your home by giving you my name.'

'That is not a gift.'

'It is all I can offer.'

She didn't want to know the answer, but she had to ask, 'Did you know from the beginning that this was going to happen?'

He nodded.

Beatrice clung to the bars, sucked in a deep breath and closed her eyes tightly. 'You should have left me with Charles, it would have been kinder.'

He ignored her comment to order, 'You have until sunset tomorrow to ready yourself and your people for this marriage. You, along with all of Warehaven, will meet me out here, in the clearing where we will be wedded by your priest and mine. There will be no question of the validity of this union.'

'And then?'

'Your people will return to the keep under Simon's guard.'

'While I will…what?'

'Become my wife.'

Once again the ground beneath her feet rippled, threatening to drop her to her knees. Dear Lord, how was she to do this? How was she to marry and then let the man who had so betrayed her, broken her trust along with her heart, take her to his bed? How was she supposed to let the hands that would kill her father stroke her body?

She looked up at him, not caring that every ounce of her pain, hatred and fear most likely showed through the tears swimming in her eyes. 'Gregor, please, it doesn't have to be this way.'

The cold, feral glare of the Wolf froze the blood in her veins. 'Make your choice, Beatrice. It is this way, or the people of Warehaven cease to exist.'

Her tears fell hot down her cheeks. 'I hate you.'

'I know you do and I accept that hatred. I have earned it.' He reached through the bars to wipe the tears from her face. 'But I have not broken my vow to you, Beatrice. I have not, nor will I ever physically harm you.'

The softening of his tone when he'd touched her made her try to blink away the tears so she could see his face, but he lowered his hand, donned his helmet, then turned and walked back to his horse without another word.

Gregor rode across the clearing back to his men. Never before had he done anything that difficult. Breaking the heart of the woman he'd come to care for was harder than he'd imagined.

He'd seen the pain in her eyes, in the drooping of her lips and the rigidness of her body. Knowing that he'd caused it beset him with a guilt that nearly tore his own heart asunder.

Worse than witnessing her pain had been seeing the glimmer of honest fear. It was bad enough that she was heartbroken, hurt by what was to come, and scared for her father, but for her to be afraid of sharing a marriage bed was more than he could bear.

Was he fated to once again lose a wife from fear of him? And would he once again be unable to stop her before it was too late?

The guilt for what he'd caused Sarah to do haunted him night and day. How would he live with himself if the same thing happened to Beatrice? He would not only lose what little remained of his soul, he would also lose his mind.

She'd no reason to fear his touch. He had never caused her physical harm, nor would he ever do so.

Her hatred he understood—it was expected. But

to fear him in such a manner was not expected. It left him unsettled and oddly angry.

When he reached the line of his men, he dismounted and handed the reins to his waiting squire.

Simon approached, asking, 'Well?'

Had he not needed the man's assistance he'd have told him to mind his own business. Unfortunately, that wasn't the case. 'The marriage takes place in the clearing at sunset tomorrow.'

'She agreed?' The man's voice was filled with surprise.

'Only after I threatened to kill every last one of her people.'

He wanted to flinch at Simon's outraged glare. 'You aren't serious?'

'Very. Once she claimed that she'd rather fight me to the death than wed me, lying seemed a more-than-fair tactic.'

'What do you need me to do?'

'Make sure than anyone left in the wharf area and village are brought here for the ceremony.'

'And afterwards?'

'You need to choose two dozen men to escort all of Warehaven's people back to the keep. You and the men will remain there to take charge.'

'And you?'

'I am going to secure a cottage to use for me and my unwilling bride.'

'I will pick enough men to keep guard over you.'

'No!' That was the last thing Gregor wanted. He planned on helping her shed some of her pain and fear even if it meant fighting with her every step of the way. He had every intention of making her scream out her fear, facing it, enabling her to set it aside before it caused her to do something he would live to regret.

And he wanted her to cry away a portion of her pain. He knew that tears would not erase the hurt and betrayal she felt right now, but it might help to lessen it some.

Then he planned on making her scream and cry again—but this time for release, repeating the entire process until only her hatred of him remained. Hatred would fuel her reason to live, even if only to seek revenge for what he'd done. It was no less than what he deserved. So an audience of guards was unwanted.

'But—'

'I said, no.' Gregor cut off his man's objection. 'Once everyone is secured at the keep, the only person I need fear will take a knife to my back is Beatrice. I need no assistance with her.'

Simon shrugged. 'If that is your wish and there is nothing else, I'll be about putting the men to work searching for any stragglers.'

'It is.'

The only other thing Gregor needed was the willpower to see this through. Since he only needed to remind his wayward mind of what was at stake, he no longer needed Simon's help.

He waved the man away. 'Be off with you. I need to go find myself a cottage to commandeer.'

Chapter Nine

Beatrice wove her way through the crowd of people gathered in the Great Hall. She'd already been to the kitchens to ensure everything was running as smoothly as possible. Some of the women from the village had pitched in to assist the cook and baker, so there were enough hands available for the added work. While the food was not of the King's quality, it was plentiful, tasty and filling which was all that mattered.

She'd also already made another circle of Warehaven's walls and tower posts. While most of the men stationed there were experienced soldiers, there were also many young, as yet untried guards. She needed to see for herself how they were holding up. To her relief not a one seemed to be out of sorts, or overly excited or nervous. She and Sir Robert had spent quite a while shuffling the guards about to ensure that there was a good mix of new and experienced men at each location. She had insisted that only well-seasoned men guard the postern gate as that was their sole weak point in the outer wall. It was the same for the tunnel entrance—well-experienced, well-armed guards had been stationed there. If Gregor discovered that way into the keep, all would be lost.

Since this would be the last night she belonged to herself, as tomorrow night she would belong to one who wished to crush everything she held dear, what she wanted desperately to do was to hide in her bedchamber.

But she knew that Warehaven's people needed to see their lady. They needed to be reassured that she would do everything in her power to keep them safe. Hiding herself away out of self-pity would only serve to make them afraid and she wished that not to happen.

Instead, she'd done what she'd thought her mother would do under the same circumstance—make herself available, be seen and hold her head up as if she were certain of a favourable outcome from this siege. Her fears didn't matter, nor did her thoughts—what mattered most was how she was seen by her people.

Right now, as she moved through the gathered throng, she was looking for one of Warehaven's people in particular. Spying him in a corner with his mother, Beatrice waved and made her way there.

She joined them and sat on the floor next to little Johnathon, a five-year-old boy whose father and brother were among the missing. He was far too young to fully understand the complications of battle, but he was old enough to sense his mother's fear.

She asked, 'Did you have a good day, Master Johnathon?'

He giggled at her use of a title before his name, then nodded.

'I saw you watching some of the other boys playing and noticed they were without a scout to see that their way forward was clear.'

Six of the little ones had banded together, forming a make-believe group who appeared to be on a mission of great secrecy. They would huddle together looking this way, then that before crouching down to scurry to another location. The made-up world of children was so wondrous that it was hard to tell exactly what they were doing, but it amused them.

'Do you think that if you had a horse you could be that brave scout?'

He nodded vigorously. 'I could.'

Beatrice untied a string that was attached to her belt and freed the wooden horse from where it hung hidden in the folds of her over-sized gown. She held the toy out to the boy. 'This was a gift from my grandfather, but it's been very lonely these last many years having no one to play with. Do you think you could keep it company?'

He reached out eagerly, stopping suddenly to ask, 'For me?'

But before he could take it from her, his mother stopped him. 'My lady, we couldn't take a gift that King Henry gave you.'

Beatrice laughed. 'It is a toy and toys need children. I would be delighted if Johnathon could put it to use.'

The woman relented with a nod and Johnathon carefully took the horse. Holding it to his chest, he whispered, 'Oh, thank you', before running off to most likely show it to his friends.

She took her leave from Johnathon's mother, with a promise to learn what she could of the woman's husband and other son, then rose.

'Lady Beatrice!' Almedha approached with Sir Robert in tow. 'Could we have a word?'

They made their way to an empty alcove which provided a small amount of privacy.

Once she and Almedha were seated, Sir Robert said, 'Lady Beatrice, there has been much discussion of your marriage tomorrow night.'

'I can imagine there has been.'

'You need not go through with it. We will defend you and Warehaven with our dying breaths.'

She appreciated the offer, but it wasn't acceptable. 'And that, Sir Robert, is what I wish to avoid.'

'You speak as if you are certain we would be defeated.'

The look of disappointment on his face spoke volumes. She'd not meant to doubt the skills and abilities of Warehaven's guards. 'If it were anyone else outside our gates I would gladly and without hesitation set you and your men to the task of defending us. But it's not anyone else. It's Lord Gregor.'

'So you do know him.'

Almedha leaned closer. 'Which begs the question, how do you know him? And how did you arrive back at Warehaven without Lord Jared or Mistress Agatha?'

Neither question was unexpected. Beatrice had known that this day's events would bring them out into the open much sooner than she'd hoped.

'The explanation would be lengthy. Suffice it to say that Lord Gregor provided his protection on my journey home.'

Sir Robert cleared his throat. 'Forgive my boldness, but is there a reason you and he must wed?'

She almost laughed at his badly asked question. 'No, there is not.' Although, had she had her way that last night in the forest, there might have been a reason for them to wed. But nobody needed to know that.

Almedha's sigh of relief did force a small laugh from Beatrice. She patted the older woman's knee. 'I may not have the good sense my mother possesses, but I am not completely lacking in wits.'

'So, what is the problem with defending the keep?' Sir Robert frowned a moment before adding, 'Unless you worry about his safety.'

'I don't want him killed. Doing so would only gain us King David's wrath, not to mention my aunt's also.'

'He need not be harmed, we do know how to aim arrows at least as well as you.'

But she didn't want Simon or his guards injured either and how were Warehaven's men to tell who was who behind their protecting armour?

Her father's man knelt before her. 'My lady, if you wish us not to fight, at least let us stall. Keep the gates closed. Do not permit them entry. Your father should return within a week at the most.'

She sucked in a breath. There lay her biggest fear—her father's return to what would be his certain death. 'No. I wish him not to return.' She grasped one of Sir Robert's hands. 'Don't you see? He will die.'

The captain covered her hands with his free one. 'Lady, will that make any difference if you are or are not wed to Roul?'

'No. But you talk as though you would accept his death.'

'Forgive me for speaking bluntly, but a man's life is fatal. He is born with his eventual death being the only sure thing.'

She tore her hands free and covered her face. 'I cannot bear it. I cannot be the reason for his death.'

'Hush.' Almedha wrapped an arm about Beatrice's shoulders. 'Unless you are the one holding the sword, you will not be the reason for his death.'

She lowered her hands. 'I brought the Wolf to our door.'

Sir Robert rose. 'Seems to me he would have arrived with or without you.'

She nodded. 'But I didn't know that until this morning.'

'Lady Beatrice, do you truly believe they are going to permit Warehaven's men to live once they kill the lord?'

'Then that's what we need to avoid. He mustn't be allowed to capture my father.'

'How do you suggest we do that?'

Beatrice frowned. There had to be a way. Suddenly her mind caught on to the image of the standards flying from the lookout perch situated well above the highest tower on Warehaven. The addition to the tower had a clear view of the sea from any direction. She once again grasped Sir Robert's hands. 'The standards. Does my father notice them when he sails home?'

The man rolled his eyes. 'Of course he does. Every lord looks to the standards flying over their keep before approaching, which is why he never returns at night—he'd be unable to see his standards. What are you thinking?'

'That we lower both the Warehaven and FitzHenry standards and place something plain, something brightly coloured in their place.' She paused to add, 'Something not white.' She was not going to fly a flag of surrender.

His eyes widened. 'He would then know there was trouble afoot.'

'Would he understand that he was not to enter the harbour?'

'I am certain he would.'

'Would he then order his guard ships away and wait for low tide to anchor his own ship in the bay below the caves?'

Sir Robert smiled. 'You are as wily as your mother, my lady. Yes, that's exactly what he would do.'

'And from there, could you, or one of the guards whom you trust, slip through the hidden tunnel that will get you to the bay? If we could get a message to him, he could then gather enough forces to retake Warehaven.'

'That plan would work as long as we know when his ship draws near.'

Beatrice smiled. 'I was accosted earlier by six of the older lads who are too young to be on the walls, they wanted to help, so I set them to keeping watch, in pairs, from the perch on the high tower. It makes them feel important by having something useful to do.'

Something that should have been done all along—perhaps then they would have had warning of Gregor's ships entering the harbour.

Nodding, Sir Robert pulled his hands from her grasp and said, 'Yes. I think this will work. Leave it to me to make certain all is in place.'

'What if he catches on to what you are doing?' Almedha asked.

Sir Robert assured her, 'Oh, I can devise some sort of distraction if need be.' He looked at Beatrice. 'What about you, my lady?'

Yes. What about her? She was to give herself in marriage to this man tomorrow night at sunset. 'When do you think my father might arrive?'

'It could be tomorrow, the day after that, or even the next day, but according to his last missive it will be most certainly within a few days.'

She frowned. Could she hold Gregor off that long? If she didn't show up tomorrow night ready to wed him, he was going to be angry. But perhaps her father would arrive in time to stop Gregor from taking Warehaven. It was a risk she needed to take.

Finally, she glanced from Almedha to Sir Robert and said, 'I can hold off this marriage for at least another night. But if my father has not arrived by then, I am not certain delaying any longer would be the wisest course of action.'

Almedha nodded. 'Perhaps by then your parents will return.'

'I like it not, but I also agree.' Sir Robert did not look, or sound, pleased, but thankfully he didn't try to talk her out of it.

This decision would not simply decide her fate, but the fate of everyone behind these walls. It would also define her. Would she be the type of woman who meekly did as she was bid? Or, would she take even this small amount of control for her future?

Beatrice sighed. She would not choose to go meekly—not even to Gregor.

Since his ultimatum at Warehaven's gates, a night and the next day had faded away. Now, Gregor watched the stars dot the sky overhead. His anger grew with each pinprick of light that became visible. At first he'd thought she was simply taking too long to ready herself for their marriage ceremony. By the time darkness fell, he'd realised she had no intention of appearing as ordered.

He wasn't certain if this move by Beatrice was brave or senseless. But he was well aware that he'd have done the same had someone threatened Roul.

Brave or senseless on her part, neither made a difference. He couldn't let this outright show of defiance change the outcome of his task.

She was only making this harder on herself and the people inside the walls. How could she not understand that she had no choice in this matter?

Simon rode up alongside of him. 'This isn't good.'

Gregor shrugged. 'She's showing defiance. I'd not expect her to do otherwise.' Although he wished she hadn't chosen to defy this particular order.

'What now?'

'We wait until sunrise.' He glanced at his man, relieved to see that Simon didn't seem too upset by this turn of events. That meant the rest of the men were also taking it in their stride.

'What about the people we rounded up in town?'

Gregor looked back at the keep. He could feel her stare, knew she was watching his every move. 'Tie them together like the prisoners they now are. We will march them out in the morning.'

'Do you think that'll change her mind?'

'Perhaps. But if not it will add a measure of guilt to her current show of defiance.'

'How are you going to deal with her?'

'Nothing is going to change. Warehaven is mine and she will be, too. It's simply going to take a little longer than anticipated.'

'That is not what I asked.'

Gregor laughed at his man's curiosity. 'Right now I would like nothing more than to shake her until her teeth rattled.' Which wasn't exactly true. But Simon didn't need to know that even with his anger at her brash move, she'd succeeded in making him uncomfortably hot to bed her.

That knowledge shocked and baffled him. Never before had a woman defied him like this. While he'd originally found her lack of fear desirable, this level of boldness inflamed lust. Pure and simple lust.

She would pay for her action one night soon—in ways that would leave them both shaken and drained.

'For some reason I don't believe shaking her is

all you'd like to do.' Simon paused a moment, then added, 'Well, since nothing is going to happen tonight, I'll have the men secure the prisoners and then stand down until dawn.'

Gregor nodded. He wanted to be left alone and not engaging in further conversation seemed the easiest way for that to happen. He breathed a sigh of relief when he heard the man ride away.

It allowed him the solitude he needed to control the distracting thoughts whipping through his head.

Beatrice of Warehaven was an inexperienced leader. But the men she now led weren't without experience. He couldn't afford to face them without a clear mind.

Gregor looked up at the moon, now high overhead. The night was no longer young and he'd yet to eat or sleep this day. He turned his attention back to the keep, to the faint shimmer of light coming from one narrow window.

He smiled, then nodded in approval. 'That's right, sweeting, you watch and wait. Enjoy this night, for there will not be many more for you to spend alone.'

Gregor raised his arm high for a few heartbeats before lowering it to turn his horse about and head back to camp.

Beatrice had spent the last few hours watching the lone mounted figure stationed in the centre of the clearing. Backlit by the many torches and campfires behind him, his stark silhouette was easy enough to identify as Gregor.

She drew in a long breath at his farewell. How had he known she'd been watching? She was relieved that he'd not sent his force to attack Warehaven's gates at her refusal to join him in the clearing. But she wondered what he planned.

Not for one moment had she thought that he would let her get away with this defiance unscathed. She was certain that soon he would seek to make her pay.

How angry had this made him? She only wondered because the angrier he was, the more controlled would be his retaliation. That thought sent a tremor of worry slithering down her spine.

The worry was useless simply because she wasn't going to change her mind. She'd set out on this course of action knowing full well that it wasn't going to make him happy in the least. He certainly hadn't gone out of his way to make her happy, so what did his happiness matter?

Beatrice moved away from the window and crossed the chamber to sit on the edge of her parents' bed. She could keep track of Gregor's movements from here.

Tired of worrying, and of thinking in general, Beatrice climbed into the bed. Everything would still be there in the morning, waiting for her to plan, worry and think some more.

* * *

'I need to know what she's plotting.' Gregor sat down on the log next to Simon in front of one of the few remaining fires.

'How do you plan on doing that?'

Gregor stared out across the clearing through the darkness. The faint light in Beatrice's chamber had gone out. He hoped her sleep was troubled by dreams of him. It would serve her right since this should have been their wedding night.

'Have the scouts reported in?'

Simon nodded, yawning. 'Yes. There are guards positioned on every tower and all along the walls. So you aren't going to be able to sneak inside.'

'As I feared, FitzHenry fortified this keep well.'

He patted his man's shoulder, then said, 'I'm going to rest for a few hours. Have the prisoners rounded up and ready just before the sun rises.'

'I'll see it done.'

Chapter Ten

Morning had come far too quickly. Beatrice felt as if she'd just closed her eyes when Almedha had awakened her. And now, going down the stairs to the Great Hall, she felt as though she was struggling through a thick sucking mud.

Sir Robert met her at the bottom of the stairs. 'My lady, I hate to be the bearer of bad news, but…'

When he trailed off, she said, 'If someone has to bring me the news, I'd rather it come from you.' She motioned towards the food-laden table. 'But could we break our fast at the same time?'

'Yes, food would be welcome.'

She'd not expected any other response since they hadn't eaten more than a bite or two yesterday.

The hall was too crowded to bother with sitting down to be served. Instead, they walked the length of the long table, helping themselves to whatever they wanted.

With her stomach still in knots, Beatrice settled for a tankard of water, a hunk of soft bread and a bit of cheese.

She took her choices to the rear of the hall where the lord's chair sat upon the raised dais and sat down. It felt strange to sit in her father's oversized, ornate seat, but at this time it was her right.

Beatrice shivered at the brief passing thought of Gregor occupying this seat.

Sir Robert joined her. Hooking a small stool with his foot, he dragged it closer and sat down.

Once he was settled, she asked, 'So, tell me—what is your bad news?'

'We did a head count as you'd requested and almost thirty people are missing.'

Beatrice tightened her grip on the tankard in an attempt to keep control of her dismay. She knew there were people not accounted for, but had no idea it was that many. 'Do we know who?'

'The entire crew of one ship, some warehouse workers, a barkeep, a child and one of the serving maids.'

She swallowed her curse. 'Any hope they made it to the caves?'

The shake of Sir Robert's head dashed her hopes. 'Not likely. This invasion was so unexpected that nobody had any time to escape.'

'So they are likely being held captive.'

Sir Robert nodded. 'Probably. What do you think he'll do?'

The bread she'd been chewing took on the texture and taste of sawdust in her mouth—dry, crumbling—making it impossible to swallow and difficult to breathe.

The wolf of legend—the one of story and rumour—would kill them to set an example or give a warning.

But she feared that she already knew what the Wolf she'd come to know would do. He would use them to force her hand in marriage—a marriage that would most likely take place very soon. He possessed too much leverage not to use it to his advantage.

'Have my father's ships been sighted yet?'

Sir Robert shook his head. 'No, my lady.'

Beatrice set her trencher down on a small side table—any food had suddenly lost its appeal—and said, 'Send word to the camp. I need to speak to their leader.'

'And what are you going to say?'

'I'm not sure. All I am certain of is that he will use these prisoners as bait to punish me.' She looked down at her hands. Without realising it, she'd clasped them together so tightly that her knuckles were white. Easing her grip, she sighed deeply, knowing what she had to do. 'I cannot allow them, or their families, to suffer for my decision.'

'My lady—'

'No. I'll not listen to further discussion on this matter. I want those people released to Warehaven.'

'But, Lady Beatrice—'

'I said, no.' Once again she interrupted him, then explained, 'Don't you see, Sir Robert, he knows me and, God help me, he does care in his own way. He may make my life miserable, but he will not harm me.'

'While you are his captive, he will have the power to take Warehaven.'

'And that is what I will use as barter—the safety of all within these walls.'

'So you will become a martyr for this keep?' He scratched his head. 'Forgive me for saying so, but the role doesn't suit you.'

'I am far from a martyr.' Beatrice laughed at the thought. 'I do this not only for the people of Warehaven, but so that I retain my home—intact. This is as much for me as it is for you. I would think that makes me a little greedy for martyrdom.'

'And your parents?'

'Will be better able to devise a plan if they know I am safe. I think it will be easier to sway the Wolf if I am in his lair.'

'I think this is a mistake.'

'It is not your decision to make.' She rose. 'Send Almedha to me and have hot water sent up to the master chamber.'

She would take her time getting ready, it would help to calm her jangled nerves. If she was going to hand herself over to King David's Wolf, she would do so as the Lady of Warehaven.

As ready as she could be for whatever was going to happen, Beatrice shook out the skirt of her gown and then nodded for the men to open the tower door. Once again she walked the length of the battlements to the main tower gates.

But this time she felt as if she were going to her death.

Beatrice chased away that odd thought and joined Sir Robert. He said nothing, just nodded towards the clearing.

Just as she'd expected, the men and one woman he held were tied together like prisoners. They stood in a line behind Gregor, with armed guards at their backs.

She squinted to see better and noticed that he held the child before him on his horse.

He rode forward. Just before he reached the gates one of Warehaven's guards gasped. Beatrice turned her head to stare at the red-faced guard standing mere feet away.

'That is my sister's son.' He'd kept his voice low, but his distress was obvious in the way his words shook.

She turned her attention back to Gregor, knowing he wasn't going to harm an innocent child.

She watched, as he hauled the boy up to sit on top of his shoulders and dismounted before shouting up at her, 'I do not hold children hostage. Send someone down to get him.'

He swung the laughing boy down to set him on the ground, then waited until the child ran towards the gates before spreading his arms and saying, 'You wanted to talk. I'm here.'

As she turned away from the wall, Sir Robert grasped her wrist. 'Are you sure about this?'

Beatrice glanced back at the people being held prisoner before turning away from the wall once again to answer Sir Robert. 'Very sure.'

He released her. 'Be careful, Lady Beatrice. Hopefully this will all be over with soon.'

She couldn't agree with him more. She, too, hoped this was over soon. The worrying was eating at her. He'd already broken her heart. Could she trust him to take care of her people?

What choice did she have? She had to believe he would be merciful to those who had done nothing to him.

Regardless, no matter what he did, or didn't do, giving herself to Gregor was not going to be easy.

This time, since she wasn't shaking, she climbed down the ladder. Once on the ground, she put her hands on her stomach and took a deep breath before walking over to the gate.

'No.' Gregor tapped the bars of the portcullis. 'You come out here.' He then stepped away, waiting.

Beatrice held his stare and ordered loudly, 'Raise the gate.'

The sound of the gate being winched open grated on her ears, threatening to dislodge her hard-won composure. After it was secured open, she walked out of the keep to stand before Gregor.

'I will trade my life for those of the prisoners.'

He crossed his arms against his chest. 'Why would I agree to that? You are already mine.'

She looked down at his feet. He was going to make it difficult to keep her vow not to argue with him. She reached up and removed a chain from around her neck. Holding it up, with the wedding ring dangling from the chain, she said, 'I will wear this without argument.'

He took the ring and chain from her. 'You had that chance yesterday.'

Beatrice lowered her arm. 'Gregor, there is no need to make this harder than it already is.'

He reached out, placed his fingertips beneath her chin and lifted until she met his stare. 'You could look at me while stating your demands.'

'I will trade my life for their safety.'

'Anything else?'

She could tell that he was enjoying this by the shimmer in his eyes. 'And for the safety of those already inside the walls.'

'I have conditions of my own, Beatrice.'

She closed her eyes, waiting to hear what he'd demand of her.

'Look at me.'

When she finally reopened her eyes, he continued, 'You wish to take the place of the prisoners?'

'Yes.' Her chin trembled and at this moment she couldn't determine who she detested more—him, or her own lack of strength.

'So be it. As my prisoner, you will be led in chains to your cell. For all to see.'

Beatrice swallowed hard. He was going to ensure there would be no mistaking her status.

'Yes, or, no.'

When she didn't answer right away he said, 'Be warned, if you say no, all your people will suffer.'

'Yes.' She spoke so softly that she wasn't certain the word ever left her mouth.

'Again.'

She took a breath, then repeated louder, 'Yes.'

Gregor lowered his arm and turned to wave his men forward. Once Simon, Colin and James joined them, he said, 'Bring the prisoners to the wall and release them. Put her in their chains and lead her to the cottage.'

The two guards stared at him as if he'd sprouted a horn. Simon rubbed a hand across his forehead. 'My lord—'

'You heard me.' Gregor's low tone cut off his man's argument. 'She already knows what's going to happen. This is how she will pay for her defiance.'

Beatrice touched Simon's arm. 'If I am to go in chains, I would rather it be done by the three of you than any others. I am willing, Simon, but I beg you to get this over with before I lose my nerve.'

They didn't appear happy about their task, but they nodded their acceptance to their lord. Gregor turned away to mount his horse and ride back across the clearing.

Simon motioned to the men. 'Get the prisoners.'

'Is he very angry?' Beatrice asked.

'What do you think, my lady? He waited for you long into the night.'

'He is going to take my home and my father's life. How could I marry him?'

'You said you would.'

'I am not the only one who has lied.'

Simon looked at her and shook his head. 'Oh, I think you are. I have known Gregor his entire life. I would wager he never lied to you. Might not have told you everything, but what he did tell you was the truth.'

'An omission is the same as a lie.'

'That is debatable.'

Beatrice wanted to scream. Were all of Roul's men so contrary? 'He said he was going to visit his brother.'

'We are. After we finish here.'

'How convenient for him to have left that part out.'

'Hush. I warned you to guard your heart. Apparently you ignored the warning.'

The guards led the prisoners by them. Beatrice gasped when she saw Sir Brent. He'd been a knight for King Henry until Henry's death. Then he'd come to her father and now commanded ships. She turned to Simon. 'A moment, please?'

'Make it quick.'

She grasped Sir Brent's arm. 'Are you well?'

'Lady Beatrice, it is good to see you. Yes, we are well.'

'Sir Robert is in charge of Warehaven in my absence. I ask you to second him if you will.'

'You know I will do anything Warehaven asks of me. But I must ask something of you in return.'

'What?'

'I know not where your father is, or if he will survive his return. You are all that Warehaven has left here of the family. Take care of yourself, Lady Beatrice. We count on you to still be here when all is said and done.'

Was she the only person who did not take her father's life, or death, so lightly? Simon nudged her and she knew there was no time to argue with the man, or convince him of the error in his thinking, so she simply said, 'I will. Fear not.'

Colin and James led the prisoners to the gate and released them from their bonds one by one. She shook a little more each time one of them disappeared into the keep. By the time they had all been released and the gates were once again closed, she trembled so hard that she wasn't at all certain she could remain standing.

'Stop this.' Simon grasped her arm. 'You know me. You know the men. While this might be humiliating, it will not physically hurt you. Everyone at camp knows you are under Lord Gregor's protection. They will not touch you.'

'But I don't know what he will do.'

'That, my lady, is your own fault. But worrying about it now isn't going to help anything.'

James tied her wrists together, making sure the rope was not too tight, while Colin secured a lead rope to the bindings. Both of the men grumbled an apology before leading her back to their encampment.

She never realised how wide the clearing between the keep and the edge of the hill was until now. What was in truth only a few minutes felt like hours. By the time they reached the road leading down the side of the hill her footsteps faltered and she stumbled to the ground.

Simon reached down to help her back to her feet. 'You are working yourself into a fine lather for no reason. Would you like me to have Lord Gregor come retrieve you?'

'No!'

Those gathered along the sides of the road looked at her as if she were little more than a beetle, something to be crushed underfoot. Some laughed, others shouted obscenities, and still others had lewd suggestions as to what should be done to her. But as Simon had told her, not one of them tried to lay a hand on her.

When they turned off on to a narrow footpath, Beatrice knew that Gregor had taken over the midwife's cottage. It was the smallest one closest to the keep.

Simon knocked on the door before opening it and pushing her inside. They didn't even stay to untie her. The three men left immediately.

She turned away from the door to stare into the darkness of the cottage. When her eyes grew accustomed to the dark, her breath stuck in her throat at the sight before her. Gregor, the priest from Warehaven and another priest who was unfamiliar to her stood in the centre of the cottage.

Warehaven's priest moved his lips in silent prayer, while the other one asked, 'Gregor of Roul, do you take this woman as your wife?'

Before he could answer, Beatrice dropped to her knees. 'Please, no.'

Gregor crouched down so they were at eye level. 'Last night it would have been done properly. But obviously that wasn't what you wanted. Now you say this is no good either. So, let's try this again. Are you telling me that you will willingly wed me in a proper ceremony before all of Warehaven?'

She hung her head. What choice did she have? 'Yes.'

'Beatrice.'

She raised her head and met his gaze. 'Yes.'

Gregor stood and motioned the priests from the cottage. Once they left he slammed the door closed and dropped a long, thick wooden bar into place across the door. She glanced at the new addition of iron holders on both sides of the door frame. Obviously, she wasn't getting out of here without help.

Before she could say anything, Gregor tugged on the rope, forcing her to her feet. His eyes shimmered, a small smile played at the corner of his lips—both warned her that she was in dire danger.

Beatrice panicked and opened her mouth to scream, only to have him cover her lips with his own effectively swallowing the sound.

Without breaking the contact, he spun them around and backed her across the one-room cottage to the bed, where he dropped both of them on to the mattress.

With her hands still bound, caught between them, she had no way to fight him, except to squirm beneath him and try to kick free.

Gregor's laugh against her lips made her realise her mistake. He now rested firmly between her spread legs.

Beatrice fought to tear her mouth free from his. Finally able to gasp for breath, she cried out, 'Gregor, no. Not like this.'

He stared down at her. 'Not like what, Beatrice?'

'Do not take me by force.'

'Take. You. By. Force.' He said each word slowly. Then rose, untied her bonds and gently rubbed her chafed wrists. 'Are we not both fully clothed?'

'Yes.' She tried unsuccessfully to pull her hands away from his too-gentle touch.

'Then other than a kiss what exactly was I going to *take*?'

She looked away, confused and embarrassed. 'I thought…well, you were…we…'

'Just stop.' He placed a finger over her lips. 'I have never had to force a woman to do anything she wished not to do. And I'm especially not going to force myself on a woman who is to become my wife.'

'You are forcing me to become your wife.'

'And I am being forced to become your husband.'

'But I am not going to kill your father.'

'And who is to say I will not lose in battle to yours?'

Beatrice frowned. She hadn't thought of that. It was a possibility—slight, but still a possibility.

Gregor moved away from the bed. 'You can stop smiling. I am well aware that my death will cause you no pain.'

Something fluttered in her stomach at that idea. She didn't want her father to die, but Gregor's death wasn't what she wanted either.

'You do know that you showed outright defiance yesterday?'

'Yes.'

'And you do know that you have to pay for that?'

'I thought that's what this imprisonment was.'

His laugh drifted across the cottage. 'Oh, no, that was just to get you here.'

'Then what exactly will be my punishment?'

He had his back to her as he did something at the table. 'I am going to make you cry.'

Cry? That was it? He wanted her to cry? Nervousness and relief collided. She burst out in nervous laughter. 'That is the most ill-conceived punishment I have heard.'

'You didn't let me finish.' He turned around with a bowl in one hand, and two goblets in the other and headed back towards her where he placed the items on a small table next to the bed. He picked up a pitcher that was already there and poured wine into both goblets.

Handing her one, he sat beside her on the bed. 'Before this day is done, you will cry. But it will be for release.'

Beatrice swallowed hard before intentionally misunderstanding. She glanced towards the barred door. 'I may want to be out of here, but I'm not about to cry for you to free me.'

He held a grape to her lips. 'Make jests all you wish. You know exactly what I'm talking about.'

She parted her lips to accept the offered food and just stared at him as she tried to remember how to chew and swallow. This time the fluttering in her stomach settled low in her belly and the fear was for herself. Fear that he was serious and terror that he would succeed.

He brushed a strand of hair from her face, his

lingering touch light and too warm for comfort. 'In case you are still confused, let me explain.'

Gregor wrapped a hand around the one she had on the goblet and raised it to her lips. 'Drink, Beatrice.'

The wine was not watered, it was full-bodied and fruity, a combination that would soon go to her head. But she swallowed it, grateful for the moisture it left in her suddenly dry mouth.

'I am going to seduce you. First with food.' He held a piece of bread to her lips, not moving or saying anything else until she accepted that offering. 'Food is a necessity of life. By feeding you, I tell your heart and mind that I am capable of providing the sustenance you require to live.'

He once again brought the goblet to her mouth and, after she drank, he said, 'And with wine because not only will it alleviate the dryness of your mouth, it will relax you and make every touch, every breath more sensuous.'

Returning the goblet to the table, he then raised a hand to her face to cup her cheek briefly. 'Then I will pay attention to you, to every part of you.' He traced the edge of her ear, then trailed his touch down the side of her neck. 'I will stroke and kiss the soft flesh of your neck. Paying close attention here,' He lightly stroked the soft spot below her ear. 'And here.' His touch moved to the place where her neck met her shoulder.

He inched away, reaching into the bowl, and

came up with a slice of apple. He bit off half of the slice and chewed slowly, holding her gaze without blinking, and then held the other half up to her mouth.

While she chewed, he ran his fingertips across her shoulder, down her arm and then to her breast. 'I will caress your breast until your nipple cries for my touch.' As if on command her nipple hardened and he rolled it between his thumb and forefinger.

Beatrice whispered, 'Don't.' But her body refused to back away, making her word appear nothing more than a meaningless sound as she leaned into his touch.

A touch which he immediately removed. This time he fed her a bite of cheese before resting his hand on her chest. Drawing lazy circles, he mused, 'I wonder if your skin here is as soft as that which covers your neck.'

His touch fell lower, to trace more circles on her belly, before trailing his touch even lower. Beatrice froze and he reached over to pluck another grape from the bowl. Holding it to her lips he whispered, 'Shhh, just eat.'

When his hand returned to her body, it came to rest on her hip. His caress continued the length of her leg. 'I can hardly wait to trace these luscious curves all the way to your ankles.'

Once he reached her ankles, he moved his hand to the inside of her leg, sliding it along her calf and up her thigh. 'But it will be my lips that follow these curves until I come to rest here.' He stopped, his hand cupping her, not moving, yet not moving away either.

Eyes closed, Beatrice drew in a breath, waiting, wondering what he was going to do, wishing he would stop tormenting her, yet hoping he would never stop this seduction.

He rested his forehead against hers long enough to say, 'I'll not have you fearful, Beatrice. Look at me.'

Her cheeks burned with embarrassment and desire, but she forced herself to meet his unwavering gaze.

'A few days ago you found pleasure in my kiss. When I kiss you here...' he pressed his fingers against her once '...you will weep with pleasure.'

She trembled beneath not just his touch, but his intense stare and his deep, throaty voice. She grasped his wrist. 'Stop.'

Once again he placed his forehead against hers. 'Sweeting, any other time you cry stop I will obey. But not this night.'

He lowered his lips to hers. 'Today is for us, just you and me. There is no Warehaven, no Roul, no King David or his orders. Nothing outside of this cottage exists. Until the sun rises tomorrow, you are mine and I am yours.'

Beatrice moaned. 'Please, Gregor. Torment me no more. I ache for you.'

His lips met hers and she wrapped her arms

about his shoulders, drawing him closer, more than willing to have one day and night of bliss with the man she would soon learn to hate.

Chapter Eleven

Beatrice sighed. Right here, in his arms, was where she had longed to be. Yet…something wasn't right. Was she making yet another mistake? Hadn't she already proven to herself that her ability to judge men and their intentions was flawed? Did she need yet another hard lesson?

She pulled away. 'No.' Shaking her head, she repeated, 'No, no, no, no, *no*.'

Gregor leaned back on his elbows. 'No, what?' His tone remained steady, giving her no hint at his mood. 'I've already warned you that saying no will gain you nothing.'

Beatrice moved quickly off of the bed. 'I don't trust you.'

'Why should you?'

She glanced over her shoulder at him. He didn't appear angry, or even impatient. But then she'd found that judging his moods by the expression on his face was an impossible task at times.

Crossing to the other side of the cottage, she asked, 'What makes you any different from Charles?'

'For one thing, instead of leading you on with false words, I have told you exactly what is going to happen here. And for another, I haven't laid a hand on you in anger.'

Oh, yes, he'd taken great care to explain what he intended to do to her. The ripple of anticipation started at the base of her skull and raced its way down her spine. She tried to ignore the shiver of pleasure by slicing away at the block of cheese on the table.

And, no, he hadn't physically hurt her. It was odd that such a meek man as Charles would resort to force, yet the warrior they called Wolf would most likely be the last person to ever raise his hand to her in anger.

Frustrated by her confusion, she stabbed the tip of the knife she'd been using into the top of the table.

'I would prefer that you not destroy the property of another.'

'But it is fine if you do so?'

'What property have I destroyed?'

She spun around, shouting her accusation, 'You took my keep.'

'Last I saw my men were still gathered outside the walls.'

His softly spoken reply made her feel like an imbecile. She hated the way he left her flustered and confused by her own thoughts.

'You killed three of Warehaven's men.'

'The guards who committed those acts have already been dealt with severely. Payment will be made to the families.'

'So you will simply trade gold for blood?'

'I am certain the loss of those men will be felt by their families. The gold is not to replace their loved ones, but to ensure they do not go without a roof over their heads or food in their bellies.'

The same as her father had done for the families of those lost at sea. And again she felt like a fool.

He slid off the bed and approached her slowly until they stood toe to toe. Gregor placed his hands on her shoulders. 'Beatrice, what is this?'

She shook her head. There was so much confusion, so many tumbling thoughts and emotions that she could make neither head nor tail of anything.

'Are you afraid?'

'No.' She shook her head, then paused, adding, 'Yes, but not of you.'

'Then of what?' He drew a thumb along the line of her jaw. 'Or of whom?'

'Of myself. Of what I feel, what I want. I fear caring too much when I know that tomorrow, or the day after I will suffer unbearable pain. Right now my heart, my body desires a wolf more than life itself, while my mind is well aware that eventually he will tear me asunder.'

It wasn't until he brushed at her tears that she knew she'd been crying. 'You are stronger than this.'

'Apparently, I'm not.'

'Ah, but you are, Beatrice. You have the strength of a warrior and a warrior might become confused or frustrated, but they don't cry about what may or may not happen.'

Beatrice leaned against him with a small laugh at his absurd comment. 'Thankfully, I am not a warrior.'

He rested his chin on top of her head and slid his arms around her. 'Whose idea was it to hoist a red flag from the perch above the high tower as a warning to any who approached?'

'Mine.' So he'd noticed the warning for her parents.

'And who studies the walls, guards and placement of the enemy in the morning, afternoon, evening and again late at night?'

'Me.' She knew he'd been watching her last night, but hadn't realised he kept such a close eye on her.

'Who shoulders the responsibility for all in Warehaven?'

'Me.'

'Who took charge and brashly threatened King David's Wolf with a well-aimed arrow?'

She groaned at the reminder. 'That would be me.'

'Then I would have to surmise from your answers that you are a warrior and, as such, you don't cry. Instead, you could try telling me what is wrong.'

'Even if you are what is wrong?'

His hands were warm as he cupped her cheeks to tilt her head back. Staring down at her, he said, 'But I thought I was the right man.'

She'd suspected that he had heard her whisper that last night on the road. Now she knew for certain that he had. 'I thought so. My heart swallowed your lies. I let myself believe that was true. But then you showed up at my gates prepared to take all from me.'

'Your heart was given no lies.'

'What would you call it, then?'

He arched an eyebrow. 'What would you have done? If roles were reversed, how would you have proceeded?'

'I certainly wouldn't have stayed. I would have left me at the inn.'

Gregor rolled his eyes. 'And left you alone to wait for Charles and his friends to arrive?'

'Yes.' She pulled away from his touch. 'No. I don't know.'

He sat on the corner of the table. 'It wouldn't have mattered who you were, I couldn't have left you defenceless against three men.'

'I am defenceless against *you*.' She paced the width of the cottage, hoping the movement would help drain her growing tension.

He watched her closely. 'How so?'

'You could snap me as easily as you could a twig.' She glanced at him. 'Stop that.'

He jerked back slightly. 'Stop what?'

'Stop watching me.'

He just smiled and shook his head. 'Are you ever going to tell me what's wrong?'

'I thought that's what I was doing.'

'No.' He reached out and caught her wrist as she passed by and stopped her ceaseless movement across the floor. 'All you've done is look for an argument. Tell me what frightens you and don't say nothing, because something does.'

Beatrice closed her eyes. 'I don't know.'

'Yes, you do. You simply refuse to look at it.' Gregor eased her closer, pulling her between his legs. 'Worrying and fretting will only give it teeth. You are not alone. I am right here. I am going nowhere.'

'But you are.' Beatrice's heartfelt whisper surprised her. From where had that admission come?

'No. I'm not. Even if the worst thing you could ever imagine were to happen, I will still be here.'

'Why?'

'Willingly or not, you will be my wife.'

She tried to pull away, but he wouldn't let her. He held her fast, asking, 'What?'

'I will only be your wife because it was ordered.'

'Yes.'

Why did his one-word answer cause her pain and sadness? She pushed against his chest. 'Let me go.'

'No.' Gregor grasped her upper arms, holding her in place. 'This is not some fanciful tale of love sung about by the troubadours. This is real. This is our life, the one we will share together. Can we not make the best of what we've been given?'

'I don't know.'

'What would be the harm in trying?'

When she didn't answer, he said, 'I am tired of talking.'

'That makes two of us.' Since sadness had replaced her tense frustration, she agreed, this talking was getting them nowhere.

He released her arms, only to sweep her off her feet and into his arms. Startled, she clung to his neck, and asked, 'What are you doing?'

'What do you think?'

Since he was headed back to the bed, she didn't need to think too hard. Her heart picked up its pace along with her breathing. Her stomach fluttered. When he turned his head to look at her, she felt the flush of embarrassment and uncertainty fire her cheeks.

His soft laugh didn't help. She buried her face against his shoulder.

'Warriors don't hide.'

Without moving her face away from his body, she repeated her earlier claim, 'Thankfully, I'm not a warrior.'

He sat down on the edge of the bed, holding her on his lap. 'It's going to be hard to kiss you if you keep your face hidden.'

She lifted her head to glance at him and, before she could turn her face away again, he cupped the back of her head and drew her close for a kiss.

She wondered if she would always surrender

so easily to this thought-stealing caress. It would be all too simple to crave the feel of his lips and tongue on hers.

Distracted by his kiss, her mind barely registered the touch of his hand on her leg. The calloused warmth caressed her ankle, moving to calf. Beatrice frowned. His touch was flesh to flesh. When had he discarded her shoe and stocking?

His hand swept to her other leg, which was also bare. He was either very, very sly, or had far too much experience. She quickly pulled her mind away from that thought, it would only pose questions she didn't want answered.

Gregor eased her off his lap to stand before him and tugged at the belt wrapped low about her waist, then dropped it to the floor. 'Is this your finest gown?'

Suddenly dizzy at the implication of his question, she steadied herself with a hand on his shoulder. 'Yes.'

'Then I guess a knife is out of the question. I will make a bad lady's maid.' He touched the tight sleeves by her wrist. 'Will we be able to get this off?'

'It went on, so I'm certain it'll come off.' She tugged at the sleeve, folding her hand to pull the tightly gathered fabric over it. 'You are going to have to help.'

He fought with the other sleeve, but once he had pulled it over her hand, he grasped the hem of the gown and lifted it over her head. To her relief he didn't drop it on to the floor, instead he hung it from a wall peg.

Clad in only her chemise, she felt naked and crossed her arms against her chest.

Gregor studied her from head to toe, before waving a pointed finger at her. 'That has to go, too.'

Beatrice wondered if her blush reached her toes. 'But I…this…maybe…'

He reached out, grasped the hem of the garment and lifted it as he said, 'Don't worry, your embarrassment will be short lived.'

She squeezed her eyes closed, wishing that by doing so she would somehow become invisible.

His touch beneath her breast made her jump. 'You are as beautiful as I knew you would be.'

She opened one eye to see if he was just saying that to be kind. But his rapt attention on her body made her think that perhaps he actually meant the words.

Gently he uncrossed her arms and took her hands in his own, brushing his thumbs across the tops before pulling them to his belt. 'Now me.'

Beatrice froze. She couldn't. While she was fairly certain she wouldn't die from embarrassment, she wasn't as certain that the heat building on her face and chest wouldn't burn her alive.

He leaned in to drop a quick, chaste kiss on her forehead. 'Tunic and shirt.'

She almost laughed at her sudden release of the breath she hadn't realised she'd held. Making quick work of removing his clothes, she handed each piece to him and he simply reached back to hang them on pegs next to her gown.

Once his chest was bare, he placed his hands on her shoulders to ask, 'Have you never bathed guests to Warehaven?'

Eyes closed, Beatrice shook her head. 'We were only permitted to assist my mother with the older men. The ones with barrel-shaped chests and guts just as large.'

'Ah. We have all night to take this as slow as you need. But first, you have to open your eyes.'

She blinked her eyes open, darting her gaze everywhere but towards him.

He lifted one of her hands to his lips for a kiss before placing her palm on his chest and holding it there. 'Just flesh, hair, nipples, no horns, no strange body parts are growing from my chest.'

She burst out laughing at his nonsense. Looking at him, she shook her head. 'You are impossibly silly.'

'And you are impossibly innocent.' He waved a hand before his chest. 'Anything there unexpected?'

No, there wasn't. She tipped her head and studied the muscles cording his chest and stomach. She'd seen the men loading and unloading the ships working bare chested. Her rapt attention was what had made her father forbid her from visiting the harbour without an escort.

But seeing them from a distance was far different from being close enough to touch. Lifting her hand slightly, prepared to stroke the hard planes, she asked, 'May I?'

'Oh, I wish you would.'

The hair peppering his chest was soft and dark without a trace of silver. She ran both hands across his shoulders and down the bulges of his arms. He didn't gain these muscles from holding a shield and sword. Obviously he did more than just design ships, he helped build them.

Beatrice trailed her fingertips down his arm to stroke his forearm. When he flexed his muscles, she wondered how many men had met their end with their head and neck trapped between the muscles of his bent arm.

To turn her mind away from such dark thoughts, she placed the palms of her hands flat against the ripple of muscles on his abdomen.

His skin was surprisingly soft beneath her touch, the smoothness broken by a thin jagged scar slanting from his navel nearly up to his armpit.

This had not happened during a battle. He would have worn his armour and the force it would have taken to slice through his chainmail in this manner would have cut him in two.

She traced the scar, asking, 'How did this happen?'

'I let my attention wander and found myself captive in a cell.' He stepped a little closer to her.

She could feel the warmth of his body. 'You were tortured?'

'No.' Gregor raised both of her arms, so her hands rested on his shoulders, and then pulled her against him. 'I killed a man in a fight and this is how his brother thanked me.'

She tried to focus on the conversation, but the feel of her breasts pressed against the warm hardness of his chest teased at her mind, breaking her concentration. 'It must have hurt.'

'A bit.' He lightly stroked her back, chasing the shivery tingles with his fingertips. 'But it taught me not to lower my guard at the wrong time.'

Beatrice gasped slightly when he brushed a hand across her hip, then caressed her bottom. 'I imagine it did. He could have killed you.'

'That had been his plan.' The hand on her back shifted to stroke up her side. 'But my men showed up before he could get any further along.'

He cupped a breast, teasing the nipple with his thumb. Beatrice moaned softly and leaned into his touch. 'It would…have been a…shame if they… hadn't.' She was quickly losing the ability to talk.

Her attention wandered to the glide of his calloused palms. There was no doubting that a man's hands created the subtle friction against her skin. Hands well used to employing weapons and tools. Hands capable of creating and taking.

Right now he was expertly creating a fiery anticipation that left her shaking with longing. Soon he would take, and Beatrice knew she would do nothing to try to stop him. It didn't matter, right or wrong, she wanted him, wanted to feel his strong body over her, entering her, taking her, making her his.

Gregor reached up and traced the edge of her ear, then trailed his touch down the side of her neck. He leaned his head down to tease the soft spot below her ear, then slowly moved to the crook of her neck.

He turned his head, rubbing his stubble-covered chin across her shoulder. 'Do you want to know how we escaped?'

What? 'Who?'

'Me and my men.'

What was he talking about?

His soft laugh against the side of her neck sent another shiver down her spine. She didn't know what he found amusing, nor did she care. What attention she could muster was more focused on his mind-stealing exploration of her body.

He drew a line from the base of her neck, down her spine, over the curve of her bottom, coming to rest where the back of her thighs met. The building tension rushing through her made it impossible to stay still. She squirmed against him.

Gregor gasped and caught her hips between his hands, stopping her movements. 'Easy, Beatrice.'

He pulled her tight against him, pressing the length of his erection against her belly. Beatrice tensed, then relaxed. Isn't this ultimately what she wanted?

There wasn't any part of her body or mind that feared what was going to happen. In this, she trusted him. Instinctively she knew that her warrior Wolf would do everything in his power to make her first time, their first time together, unforgettable.

She realised that he'd been correct, her embarrassment had been short-lived. She also suddenly understood that his running conversation had been an attempt to distract her, to give her time to become accustomed to his hands and body touching hers.

He'd succeeded. Except now, she wanted more.

She pushed her hand between them to rest her palm against his hard shaft. 'How did you and your men escape?'

Groaning at her touch, Gregor paused, his face tight with concentration. He asked, 'What?'

Beatrice laughed, not at his obvious lack of concentration, but at the knowledge that she was just as capable of making him lose his ability to think as he had been with her. Slightly tightening her grasp, she teased, 'From the man attempting to kill you, how did you escape?'

He growled softly before lowering her to the bed. She reached up for him, whispering, 'Gregor, please.'

After quickly stripping off the rest of his clothes, he stretched out alongside her on the bed. His hands and fingers seemed to dance along her skin, caressing her, stroking her with his fingertips, then gently dragging the tips of his nails along the same path. Each touch bolder than the last, sending her anticipation soaring.

At times he was gentle, coaxing a sigh from her lips. Other times demanding, making her moan with need. She grasped his wrist as he stroked her belly, then cupped a breast. She wanted more than his mind-robbing touch. Beatrice gazed at him through half-closed eyes. 'Tease me no more.'

Gregor wanted nothing more than to satisfy her plea. However, no matter how brazen she was, or how sweetly she begged, she was a virgin. He wanted her first time to be pleasurable and something she would be more than willing to repeat.

He knelt on the bed, leaned over to kiss her, claiming her lips, drawing her focus to the sweep of their tongues.

Her body was warm, her breast soft and pliable beneath his caress, the pebbled nipple hardening at his teasing fingers.

Beatrice's belly contracted as he slid his hand down to settle it between her legs. He sighed at discovering the heat. She didn't flinch. After an initial pause, she pressed up against his touch, moaning softly when he moved his hand back to her hip.

Her breathing quickened as he trailed the tips

of his fingers down the length of her leg, pausing to stroke the back of her knee, making her laugh and try to twist away from the tickling touch. He stopped and moved his touch to her calf. Her laughter quickly turned back to sighs of pleasure.

But when he reached her ankle, and drew his fingertips along the inside, she froze. Gregor smiled and then, even though he knew there was nothing wrong, asked softly, 'Is something wrong?'

She shook her head.

He wasn't about to give her time to become too shy to continue, so he slipped one of his legs between hers, easily parting them enough for him to slide his hand up the inside of her leg. When he reached the soft flesh of her thigh, she tensed.

Again, he asked, 'Is something wrong?'

This time she hesitated, but to his relief finally shook her head again.

He rose to kneel between her legs, ignoring the widening of her eyes and lifted one of her legs. He worked his way from her ankle to her knee, trailing kisses until her limb shook in his hold.

Gregor stroked his tongue along the back of her knee, drawing not a giggle, but a long sigh from her lips.

Halfway up her thigh, she tensed again and he stopped to look at her. 'Am I hurting you?'

He knew he wasn't, but he hoped the question would distract her even a little.

She shook her head.

'Are you afraid?' He knew that she had to be afraid. Not of him, but of the unknown. Fear was the last thing he wanted her to feel.

At first she shook her head, but then she drew in a breath and said, 'A little, maybe.'

'Trust me, Beatrice, there is nothing to fear. The only thing you are going to experience is pleasure. And I am here to fall into it with you.'

Without taking his eyes from her face, he resumed his journey up her thigh. She shook so hard and he hated it. He hated her trembling, hated knowing that he was the cause of it. She had outright defied him without a thought to the consequence, so her fear of this surprised and baffled him.

He knew that he could tell her a hundred times that nothing was going to hurt her and that there was nothing to fear, but until she saw the truth of that for herself, she wasn't going to believe him. And making light of her senseless fear would only embarrass her more. To her, this nervousness was very real, as real as her fear of the unknown.

'Take my hand.' Gregor held a hand out towards her. 'Just hold on to me.'

She entwined her fingers with his and closed her eyes. 'Please, get it over with.'

With his lips on her thigh, Gregor stopped. Earlier she'd worried that he was going to take her by force. Now she wanted him to get it over with?

This was without a doubt going to happen, but assuredly not like she obviously expected.

He lifted his mouth from her leg. 'Look at me.'

She opened one eye.

'I don't know who told you about what happens between a man and a woman, but apparently they weren't fond of the act.'

When she didn't reply, he said, 'You and I are going to be wed. God willing it will be for a long time. And this...' he stroked his tongue along the length of her thigh '...is one of the things we will share. Often.'

He lowered her leg and ran his hand up the soft skin to settle over the mound of soft curls. 'So, you need to forget what you've heard, or what you were told, and discover the truth for yourself.'

Gregor held her one-eyed stare and dipped a finger against her warmth. When she closed both eyes, he ordered, 'Look at me.'

It took a few heartbeats, but she opened her eyes. He stroked light gentle circles, holding her now wide-eyed gaze and said, 'There will be days when we hate each other, perhaps more than just days, but this won't change. The body doesn't care what the head thinks, or the heart feels, it wants what it wants.'

Before she could sense his next move, he slipped past the now-slick folds to stroke the heat inside. 'When all is said and done, you may wish me dead. But trust me, Beatrice, even while screaming your hatred for me, after this day and night you will cry for me to share your bed.'

The hand still holding his fell lax and she parted her legs further. He leaned down without breaking their eye contact. 'I am going to kiss you and if it hurts, feel free to say so. The last thing I want to do is cause you pain.'

With his tongue, he traced the path his finger had just traversed and thankfully, the sounds she made had nothing to do with nervousness, or fear and most decidedly not from any pain.

Her gasp was from surprised shock, not fear. But she quickly settled into his intimate caress, sighing with pleasure and finally, when she cried out, 'Gregor, please', he knew without a doubt that her gasping cry wasn't from frustration, but from a desperate need for release.

He moved over her, worried for half a second that he might have lied to her. His concern vanished the second he filled her and she fell into his rhythm without so much as a flinch.

They fitted together as if made for each other. Before long, Gregor curled his fingers into the coverlet beneath them, fighting for enough control to hold off long enough for her—

'Oh.' She tensed beneath him, her toes curling into his legs. 'Oh, my.'

Beatrice's eyes flew open. He recognised her look of surprise the second before her eyelids fluttered closed and she hung on to him as if for dear life.

He released the coverlet and wrapped his arms tightly around her, wanting to hold her close as they shared their first climax together.

Spent, he relaxed, dropping his full weight on top of her. Beatrice gasped for breath and pushed at him. 'I can't breathe.'

Gregor rolled over on to his side, pulling her close. He didn't care what the next few days brought to them, he wasn't letting her go.

She turned over, her back against his chest and hung on to his arm. She sighed weakly. 'So much for being a warrior.'

He laughed softly. 'I'd say you faced and conquered your fear of the unknown', then kissed the back of her head. 'Go to sleep for a...'

Before he completed his suggestion she'd relaxed in his arms. Her light and steady breaths let him know that she'd already fallen asleep.

Beatrice opened her eyes as she slowly woke up. The sunlight still streamed into the cottage, so she knew they hadn't done more than take a nap.

She stretched, savouring the warmth curved around her. Gregor's chest was against her back, one foot hooked over her ankle. The arm he'd draped over her to pull her close was still wrapped around her. Her head rested on his other arm.

She wanted to stay right here, snuggled down

into the softness of the bed and against the man keeping her warm.

He nuzzled her neck, asking, 'Are you hungry?'

Yes, she was, but she didn't want to move, nor did she want him to leave the bed. 'A little.' She wrapped her arm over his and curled her fingers around his wrist to hold him in place. 'But food can wait a while.'

He sighed, his breath brushing across her ear. 'I'll not argue.'

A pounding on the cottage door drew a groan from him. He rolled on to his back and shouted, 'Who is there?'

'Simon, my lord. I am sorry, but I must speak to you.'

Gregor rubbed a hand over his eyes. 'Now?'

'Yes, my lord, now.'

'Stay here.' He patted her hip. 'I'll make this brief.' Then swung his legs over the edge of the bed and rose.

On his way to the door, he grabbed his tunic from the clothes peg and dropped it over his head. Gregor made easy work of removing the wooden beam from across the door, setting it against the wall and then opened the door a crack.

Beatrice couldn't hear what they said, but she recognised Gregor's tight tone of voice. Whatever news Simon shared wasn't welcome.

Gregor glanced back at her a moment before he left the cottage, closing the door behind him.

Beatrice rolled over, snuggling deeper into the warmth of the spot he'd just vacated. She buried her nose in his pillow, breathing in his scent, hoping he'd return soon.

Her wish was granted faster than she'd expected. The door swung open and he strode inside. 'Get up.'

Shocked by his coldly issued order, Beatrice sat up and looked at him. This was not the same man who'd so tenderly and thoroughly made love to her. The teasing, attentive lover had been replaced by the emotionless warrior.

He tossed her gown and chemise on the bed. 'Get dressed.'

Except he wasn't quite as emotionless as he would probably like to appear. She heard the tension in his voice. 'What's wrong?'

Gregor retrieved her stockings and slippers. 'You are going back to the keep.'

'No. I exchanged myself for the captives. I will not trade back.'

'I don't want your captives. I just want you gone.'

Beatrice jerked back as if he'd slapped her. His words hurt much more than a slap ever could. Her hands shook as she dressed as quickly as possible. But she fumbled with the sleeves of her gown. Unable to get her hands through, she cursed softly.

Gregor came over to the bed and slid a knife through the wrist edge of both sleeves. Decorative beads and gemstones, free of their anchoring threads, pinged off the floor of the cottage. 'Hurry up.'

She stared in confused dismay at what had been her best, most expensive gown. What was wrong with him?

Her feet hit the floor and she marched across the cottage to where Gregor had retreated by the table with his back to her.

She grasped his arm to force him to turn around and face her, but he easily pulled free of her hold.

'Gregor, tell me what is wrong. Did I do something to displease you?'

His answering laugh was cold and cruel. 'Not everything is about you.'

Beatrice breathed deeply and stared at his back. Something wasn't right. For one thing the man who repeatedly demanded eye contact while discussing anything refused to meet her gaze. For another thing he was visibly upset. She placed a hand on his back. He stiffened at her touch, but not before she felt a tremor shake his body.

'Gregor.' She softened her tone. 'I have willingly given you all I had to give, don't cast me aside now.'

He spun around and engulfed her in a hard embrace. 'I will never give you up, or cast you aside. But I need you to return to Warehaven.'

Give her up? What was that about? What was he not saying?

She pushed away from his embrace far enough to see his face. 'Have my parents returned?'

'If only it were something that easy.' He cupped the back of her head and leaned down towards her. 'As far as I am aware, no, your parents have not yet returned.'

She raised up on her toes to meet him half-way and stroked his cheek whispering, 'Kiss me, Gregor. Kiss me like there is no Roul, no Warehaven, only you and me.'

If only there was a way to freeze this moment, to keep his lips on hers for ever, his strong arms holding her tight against his chest.

She sighed knowing how impossible that would be and rested her cheek against his chest, over the steady pulse of his heart. Right now he was her lover, her protector. But the moment she left this cottage he would set all of that aside to once again become David's warrior, the man who would follow his King's orders, letting nothing and no one, not even her, stand in his way.

'Thank you.'

'For what?' He rested his chin on top of her head. His voice was rough, distant, as if he were already setting her aside.

'These last few hours. It was more than some people are given in a life time.' What would happen next was nothing new. Armies had always attacked armies and the victors had always laid claim to the remaining valuables.

She would be a part of the remains. And like many women before her, she would be expected to accept her lot in life.

But she was luckier than many of them—while they had likely gone to their captor's bed a frightened prisoner to be used and abused, she had this day to hold close to her heart.

He released her and moved away. 'It is time for you to go.'

She stretched an arm out towards him, wanting one more minute. 'Gregor.'

'Go.' He reached beneath the bed to retrieve his weapons and tossed them on the bed. 'Just go, Beatrice.'

She stared at the scabbard ensconcing his sword and raced for the door, slapping a hand over her mouth to hold back a cry.

Chapter Twelve

Smoke billowed above the flames still shooting up from the pile that used to be a warehouse. They'd fought the blaze for hours, before Gregor had finally called a halt to what had proven an impossible to win battle.

He sat on his horse at the edge of town, exhausted and angry at those responsible for such an act. When he found them, there would be no mercy. No more than what had been given to the seven men trapped inside the burning warehouse when it had fallen.

Simon rode up alongside. He had sent the older man to check on the status of the ships and knew that his quick return would not be with good news.

'How many?'

'Three ships lost. And five men still unaccounted for.'

'The round ships?'

'Yes, and your new one.'

Gregor cursed. Two of his largest ships had been refitted for moving troops and now their burnedout shells rested at the bottom of Warehaven's harbour next to one of his finest clinkers—the one he'd recently finished building.

'How?'

Simon squinted his eyes against the smoke blowing their way with the shifting of the wind. 'The men said that after the warehouse caught fire they heard men screaming, so everyone rushed to the aid of those caught in the warehouse.'

'Leaving the ships unprotected.' Gregor finished the explanation, then asked, 'And were there men caught in the warehouse fire?'

'Not then, no.'

'Didn't think so.'

The warehouse had been a diversion. It had been done by someone who knew the layout of Warehaven's wharf.

They were well aware that the building on the end held household goods—fabrics, candles, wooden furniture—items that would add ready fuel to the fire. Which was the reason this building was set far apart from the other warehouse buildings.

Had they chosen one of the other ones for the distraction, the fire could have easily leapt to the inn, bakery and on down the line, setting the entire row of buildings on fire.

The question was—why? The ships they torched were empty. Two of them were fitted for moving troops, nothing else.

If the goal had been to keep him here, it was a waste of time and energy, because he wasn't going anywhere to begin with. If it was done simply to anger him, they'd succeeded. What they didn't realise was that that tactic would only make him more dangerous.

So far, he'd been *nice...fair-minded...chivalrous*. And he'd done so because of a woman. It wasn't her fault. It was his own.

But he was done playing.

Simon asked, 'Do you think it was one of them?'

'If not, then it was one of ours.'

Simon shook his head. 'No. I don't think any of our men would intentionally cause this much damage.'

Gregor didn't bother telling the old man that he'd been spouting sarcasm out of frustrated anger—of course it was one, or more, of Warehaven's people. Instead he said, 'I'm taking the keep tonight.'

'Why tonight? You've let her hold it thus far.'

'Because apparently everyone is uncertain as to who is in charge. Perhaps taking possession of the keep will clear their uncertainty.'

'What about Lady—?'

Gregor stopped his man's question, by saying, 'She will do as she's ordered.' He hoped for her sake she did. Otherwise there would be more than one battle taking place this night.

She'd already interfered by sending men from the keep to help with the fire. He'd sent them back, amazed that his own men had let it happen. They essentially permitted the enemy to walk right past them into the village and down to the docks.

Rage had consumed him until he'd realised that he'd been the one to permit such confusion to exist. Nobody was certain who was in charge. Some thought he and Lady Beatrice were equally in control.

By the time the sun rose, the confusion would be gone.

Beatrice leaned against the stone wall of the battlements. She'd been here since before nightfall yesterday and now the sun had just begun to rise at the dawn of another day. Torches mounted around the walls supplied additional light that wouldn't be needed for much longer.

'You might not hear anything until later.'

Sir Brent stopped beside her.

She waved him on, not willing to talk to anyone for fear she'd burst into tears of utter frustration.

She'd seen the smoke from the fire yesterday and had sent men to help douse the flames. Men Gregor had only sent right back to the keep, with orders to stay put.

Apparently he hadn't needed the extra hands. But he had to know she waited to hear what had happened. Had anyone been injured, or worse? Had any of the ships been lost? What about her father's warehouses? Or the other businesses near the wharf?

Finally, when she thought she could stand it no longer, she heard the faint jingle of armour and clang of weapons as the men in the clearing began to move.

In the faint light of dawn, she could see that they marched in two single file lines towards the keep.

She shouted, 'Hold!' at her archers on the wall. Before ordering them to loosen their arrows, she wanted to see what Gregor was up to.

The lines of men stopped at Warehaven's gate, forming the human walls of a corridor that stretched nearly to the edge of the clearing.

A lone rider approached. He wasn't halfway across the clearing when she realised that it was Gregor.

He, too, stopped before the gate and shouted up at her, 'Send out the villagers and your men. Leave only your priest and servants inside the walls.'

Without waiting for any answer, or question, he turned and rode back the way he'd come.

She stood there dumbfounded. He was ordering her to leave herself and her servants defenceless, unprotected inside the walls. She studied the columns of his men. They were armed. And he wanted those inside to walk through that corridor of men?

He'd lost his ability to reason.

A shrill whistle broke the silence of the morning.

The corridor of men moved as one, wheeling about to form a double row of men lining her wall. An opening was left in front of the gate. Before she could finish wondering why, she heard the rumble and looked towards the edge of the clearing.

As the men in front of the gate raised their shields, locking them against each other, a battering ram rolled steadily towards her keep.

Beatrice blinked twice, before turning to shout at those in the bailey. 'Drop your weapons and assemble here, now.'

Not about to see her keep destroyed because she'd failed to follow an order quickly enough, she ordered the guards in the tower to raise the portcullis and swing open the heavy gates.

She pulled Sir Brent aside. 'Get the villagers out here. Line them up behind the soldiers.'

'What about you, Lady Beatrice?'

She glanced over the wall, then back at Sir Brent. 'He told me to stay, so I'm staying. He is probably taking possession of the keep. We should be thankful he is permitting Warehaven's people and the guards to leave first.'

'Do you think…?' He let his question trail off.

She was in no mood for his half-questions. 'Do I think what?'

He nodded towards the men in front of the wall. 'That they'll let us pass unharmed?'

'I know nothing more than you do. But I doubt that he'd be that underhanded.'

Her heart skipped raggedly at the brief thought that he might possibly be. There was nothing, no one to stop him from doing whatever he wanted. She pushed her worry aside, unwilling to give it power by dwelling on something that had yet to happen.

'I can't leave you here alone.'

'I won't be alone. Almedha and the others will be here with me.'

Sir Brent looked at her and shook his head. 'Not much protection in that lot.'

'It is my responsibility to protect them, not the other way around.'

'And what is a lone woman going to do against an armed force?'

The rumble of the battering ram grew louder as it moved closer. She pushed him towards the ladder. 'Sir Brent, go! Get the men and the villagers out of here.'

As soon as Sir Brent started leading the people of Warehaven out of the gates, the battering ram stopped and was pushed off to the side making room for them to pass.

Beatrice stood at the wall, watching. Waiting. Not certain what would happen, not willing to look away.

She saw Sir Simon approach, then enter Warehaven. He climbed the ladder to the wall and stood beside her. 'The villagers will return to their homes. Your men will be permitted to make camp at the far side of the clearing for now—unarmed.'

Something had changed, but she couldn't put her finger on it. So she asked, 'And what about me?'

He fell silent, but awkwardly patted her shoulder.

Beatrice swallowed her building fear, drew in a steadying breath and asked softly, 'What is happening?'

'Lord Gregor will be here soon. I am certain he'll explain all.'

He then left her alone.

Beatrice rested her forehead on the cold stone and closed her eyes. A blind person could tell that Gregor was, or had, taken possession of Warehaven. But why now? Had something happened in the village to make him change into the cold-hearted warrior of rumour?

She heard him enter the keep. The bridle on his horse and the spurs on his heels jingled, announcing his arrival in the eerie silence that had fallen over Warehaven.

Beatrice turned to look down at him, but he paid her no attention. After dismounting, he handed the reins to a stable hand and then strode into the keep.

Apparently if she wanted to talk to him, she'd have to request an audience, inside the…his…hall.

His men entered the keep and within moments the red flag was lowered from the high-tower perch, to be replaced by the standards of Warehaven and FitzHenry. Her father would now have no warning of what was afoot.

She stayed on the wall until the thudding of her heart eased and the pounding in her temples slowed. It would do no good to argue with him, Gregor didn't argue. The last time she'd tried he'd made her look and feel like a fool. They'd been alone then, with no one to witness her shame.

Uncertain if she could retain her composure, Beatrice climbed down the ladder and walked towards the keep. The moment she set foot inside the Great Hall she felt every pair of eyes looking at her.

The men and servants were waiting to see what she would do, or what she would say.

But Gregor watched her—studied her closely… as if seeking to determine the right moment to launch an attack. His unwavering stare sent shivers down her spine.

He sat in the lord's chair, in the centre of the raised dais. Knowing she couldn't speak to him without becoming emotional, she headed for the stairs.

'Lady Beatrice!'

She came to a halt at his shout. Without turning around, she replied, 'Yes, my lord?'

'A word.'

Beatrice shook her head. 'Can this not wait, my lord?'

'No.'

She jumped at the feel of his warm breath against the back of her neck. She'd not heard his approach. A quick glance over her shoulder confirmed her fear. He was standing right behind her and did not look pleased to see her in the least.

He extended his arm past her, motioning up the stairs. 'After you.'

The twittering of the servants let her know that she'd made a mistake—she'd given them something to talk about. The hardest thing to control in a keep of any size was gossip. And gossip they would. Beatrice knew they'd take every little word, the slightest movement, and blow them completely out of proportion.

By morning she'd not be able to recognise the tale of her entry into the keep. She knew anything she did or said now would only embellish the tales further. So, as sedately as possible, given the drumming of her pulse and the whirling of her thoughts, she walked up the stairs.

Once at the top, she turned to her left along the corridor, heading to her own chamber. Gregor skirted around her, grasped her hand and led her in the opposite direction.

Since there were a few options—a tower cell, the door leading out to the wall and a couple of empty chambers, she asked, 'Where are you taking me?'

'The Lord and Lady's chamber.'

'That is my parents' chamber.'

'Nothing in Warehaven belongs to your parents.'

Two armed men unfamiliar to her stood guard outside the open chamber door. They moved aside, giving her and Gregor entrance to the room. Once inside, Gregor closed the door behind them.

Beatrice's eyes widened at the sight of what had been done to the chamber. Gone were the ceiling-to-floor curtains that had surrounded the bed—curtains she and Isabella had helped her mother embellish with stitched scrollwork along the edges. The matching coverlet had been replaced with fur covers.

Also missing were the curtains that lent privacy to the alcove, along with the comfortable pillows that had lined the stone bench inside the alcove. Gone, too, were the small fancifully carved side tables and the two cushioned chairs that used to flank the brazier.

There was nothing left in the chamber that had made it her parents' solar, the one room in the keep that had been solely reserved for family.

Unable to speak past the lump in her throat, Beatrice crossed the nearly bare room to stare out of the tall windows.

Gregor paused behind her and turned her round to face him. Silently he untied the belt around her waist and let it fall to the floor. When he reached up and started to brush her gown off her shoulder, Beatrice grasped his wrist. 'No.'

He paused for a heartbeat and then continued removing her clothing. 'I have already been played for a fool. It won't happen again.'

'Not by me.'

'No?' He stared at her, capturing her as surely

as a huntsman's trap. 'Before today, who was in charge of Warehaven?'

Beatrice closed her eyes. 'Me.'

'Look at me when you answer.' He waited until she opened her eyes to ask, 'And who was responsible for all on this island?'

'Me.' Her answer came out as a breathless whisper.

He shoved her gown down her arms, trapping her, then leaned closer, his lips against her ear and whispered just as softly. 'Then, my lady warrior, you killed twelve of my men.'

'No, Gregor. I would never—'

He effectively stopped her from talking by brushing a knuckle across the curve of her exposed breast. 'Everything in this keep, on this island, is mine.' He tipped her chin up with a forefinger. 'Including you.'

One tug of his hand sent her gown and chemise sliding down the rest of her body to pool at her feet.

Suddenly shy beneath the intensity of his stare, she tried to shield herself from his perusal. He pulled her arm away from her breasts and grasped the wrist of the arm reaching down to cover her mound.

He pinned her arms behind her, easily holding both of her wrists in one hand. 'You waste your time trying to fight me.'

He glanced down at her body. 'If I wish to look at you, I will and you will not naysay me.'

Then he stroked a fingertip across one breast, down her chest and belly until she tried to squirm away from his touch. He slid his hand between her legs, cupping her, holding her still. 'And if I wish to touch you, I will.'

She despised the burn of tears in her eyes, but couldn't stop them as she stared at him, asking, 'Why are you doing this? Of what am I accused?'

'Twelve of my men died in your fire. Three of my ships now rest at the bottom of your harbour.'

'I had nothing to do...' She paused. Had the fire been one of Sir Robert's distractions? No. He wouldn't be careless with her father's property. 'I had nothing to do with either your men, or ships.'

His raised brow warned her that he'd noticed her hesitation. 'You were responsible for all of Warehaven at that time.'

'We were both at the cottage when the fire was started. I had nothing to do with it.'

'So you claim. Yet I'm not certain I believe you.' He released her to scoop up her clothing and then headed towards the door. 'Until I find the person or persons responsible, I hold you in their stead.'

He was going to leave her in this chamber without clothing? That would prevent her from trying to find the culprit and from running the keep. 'You can't do this.'

Gregor balled her clothing up in his fist and marched back to her. Standing toe to toe he nearly growled, 'This is what happens when you seek to play a wolf false. I can do whatever I want, Beatrice, and there is nothing you or anyone else can do to stop me. It is time you learn that truth.'

She gasped at the coldness of his voice and the utter lack of any emotion in his dark stare.

Before she could say, or ask anything, he spun around and left the chamber.

She stood in the centre of the room, brushing her hands up and down her arms for warmth. This was the reason every creature comfort had been removed from the chamber. She glanced at the bed, cursing at the single piece of furniture that would become her only way to stay warm.

Gregor could hear her vile curse float through the door. He looked at his men. 'Nobody enters, except by my order.'

After both men nodded, he walked to what he knew had been her chamber and entered, tossing her clothing upon the already overladen bed. He'd stripped the master's chamber and had stacked everything in here.

He knew full well she hadn't personally started the fire. They'd been…occupied with other things…at the time it'd been started.

However, someone in her service had, he didn't yet know who, although her odd pause made him wonder if she did. Had she known ahead of time it was going to happen?

It was possible. Unlikely, but possible.

Until he found the cur who'd caused such damage and death, she was going to remain in the master's chamber unable to leave.

By keeping her confined he would know where she was at all times. By having her under constant guard, he would know who spoke to her, or who tried to visit her.

Not only would she quickly learn who now controlled this island, she would be safe.

It was impossible to know the thoughts of those responsible for what happened at the wharf. While it was obvious the attack was against him, they'd also burned one of her father's warehouses. Did that mean she might also be in danger?

It was a risk he was not willing to take with the woman he would soon call his wife.

He couldn't help but wonder if perhaps her father was guilty. If that were the case, then it was even more imperative to keep Beatrice under guard. Otherwise she might attempt to find and join her sire.

Gregor wasn't about to let that happen.

Not now.

He'd taken her to his bed. Treated her as one would a wife. She could be carrying his child.

He would die before he'd let anyone take that from him.

Chapter Thirteen

Beatrice huddled in the corner of the alcove, her teeth chattering, shivering from the cold. She would freeze to death before climbing beneath *his* covers. For hours she'd sat here, watching the darkness chase away the light of day.

The chamber door opened and she glanced towards the entry way to see Gregor walk in carrying a trencher of food.

His attention went first to the bed, making her snort in amusement, but also drawing his attention to her.

She pressed tighter against the corner of the walls, hoping to disappear into the darkness.

He said nothing, only shook his head, placed the trencher on the bed and walked towards her.

'Leave me alone.' Beatrice pointed a shaking finger towards the door. 'Just go back to where you came from.'

He pushed her arm away and wrapped his arms around her, lifting her against his chest. 'If I had wanted you dead, I'd have taken care of it in a much less hurtful manner.'

To her horror, she found herself drawn to the warmth of his body, realising too late that she had instantly curled against his chest without so much as a thought.

He climbed on to the bed, his back pressed up against the wall, his knees bent, with his booted feet on the bed, holding on to her tightly, keeping her in place, and pulled a cover over her body.

'What were you thinking, Beatrice?'

'That I would rather die than be your prisoner.'

'There are other ways to accomplish that than sitting in a cold room.'

'I thought about jumping out of the window, but I didn't think I'd fit through the opening.'

He glanced at the window, then back at her. 'I'm certain you would have.'

'How do you know? Did you measure just in case the idea seemed feasible?'

'No. But the opening appears to be about the same size as the one my first wife threw herself from.'

She whipped her head up to look at him. His expression hadn't changed from the emotionless visage she'd seen before. His tone was flat.

'Forgive me.' Beatrice sighed before resting her cheek against his shoulder. 'I was simply being…'

'Disagreeable.' He finished the sentence for her. 'I am well aware of that. Since it was unlikely that you'd perish from the chill in this chamber, you sat in that corner simply to make me feel bad for so mistreating you.'

'Do you?'

'Not in the least.' He chastely kissed her forehead. 'So not only did you waste your time, you only succeeded in making yourself uncomfortable.'

'I hate you.'

'Of course you do.'

She pushed away from his chest. 'I meant, I really hate you.'

'Be still my heart.' He leaned his head back against the wall with a forced sigh. 'I am not at all certain I can bear your tender words.'

'You could leave.'

'This is my bedchamber. I have a bed, warm covers and a soft woman at my disposal. Why would I go elsewhere?'

'I am not at your disposal.'

'No?'

'No.'

He dropped his legs to the bed, tore the fur cover from her and motioned towards the alcove. 'You are free to go sleep on the stone if that is your truest wish.'

Beatrice stared at the darkness of the alcove and shivered. She leaned back against the warmth of his chest. 'Now I really, really hate you.'

He pulled the cover back over her and held it fast by tightening his arms around it, before bending his knees once again, securing her in a warm cocoon. 'That is too bad.'

'Why?'

'I had other ideas for warming you.'

She groaned softly. His simple words created images in her mind that left her heart racing.

To dispel those thoughts, she said, 'I thought you were angry with me.'

'I am. But that does not mean that I don't still desire you.' He reached up to stroke the side of her neck. 'I am quite capable of doing both things at the same time.'

'Then we are lucky that I am too angry with you to do anything else.'

His laugh rumbled in his chest before escaping.

'What do you find so amusing?'

'The woman sitting naked on my lap issuing such a tempting challenge.'

'I offered no challenge.'

He lifted his head away from the wall and looked at her. The second he raised one eyebrow, Beatrice pushed against his chest, thinking only of the need to escape.

Before she could fully formulate a plan to free herself from his embrace, he removed the cover, dropped her to the bed on her back and leaned over her, resting on his elbows while his body half covered hers. 'Are you angry with me, Beatrice?'

'Very.' She cringed, knowing she should have kept her mouth shut.

He smiled before lowering his lips to hers. 'Show me just how angry you are.'

She narrowed her eyes. No. She was not going to play this game with him. Instead, she remained still, refusing to return his kiss.

Gregor lifted his head, warning, 'I will win at this game, too.'

She closed her eyes as if ignoring him. But it was soon impossible to ignore the feel of his hands caressing her breasts, teasing the tips with his fingers before covering them with his mouth. And she knew he'd won the moment he pushed his hand between her tightly clenched legs and stroked the warmth she'd tried to keep hidden.

She reached for him. 'Gregor.'

'Hmmm?' His voice warmed her ear. 'Something you want, Beatrice?'

'You.' Had this been another time, another place, she'd have laughed at the breathless tone of her voice.

Thankfully, he didn't laugh. Nor did he laugh when she moaned in pleasure as he entered her, or even when she cried out with her release.

He saved his soft, deep chuckle for afterwards when they lay beneath the covers, wrapped in each other's arms.

'That was not quite the welcome I'd expected.' He lifted his head to glance down at the floor. 'And I hope you aren't hungry.'

Beatrice pulled his head back down to the pillow. 'Not in the least.' Adding, 'At least not for food.'

'Brash and wanton.' He settled her more securely against his chest. 'I couldn't be a luckier man if I tried.'

Beatrice had woken up once during the night and listened to the sound of his deep breathing. It wasn't loud or obnoxious like her brother's, but more of a gentle rumbling that lulled her back to sleep.

When she woke up again the sun had risen, filling the chamber with light and blessed warmth. Gregor was gone and from the coolness of the sheets he had been absent for a while.

She sat up stretching and saw that one of the small tables had been returned. It held a bowl of still-steaming water, soap, a wash cloth and a towel. A chamberpot sat alongside it on the floor.

All welcome items to be sure, but she wished he'd have remembered a comb and maybe something to wear. She flung back the covers and frowned at the sound of something hitting the floor by the bed.

Beatrice leaned over to look and saw a comb lying next to one of his shirts and the belt from her gown sticking out from beneath the shirt. She rose and retrieved the items, holding the shirt up in front of her. The sleeves would be a bit long, and the body a bit short, but it would be better than nothing.

She quickly finished with her morning necessities, pulled the shirt over her head, capturing the pleated width with the belt, and sat down on the edge of the bed to comb the tangles from her hair.

The opening of the door surprised her and she jumped to her feet to see Almedha enter holding a trencher of food and a pitcher of something to drink.

'Thank goodness.' Beatrice rushed towards the woman, stopping when Almedha shook her head and glanced over her shoulder at the guards standing in the open doorway.

Apparently, speaking to anyone other than Gregor wasn't permitted. An assumption that was confirmed when one of the guards warned Almedha, 'No speaking to the prisoner.'

She sat back down on the edge of the bed and waited for Almedha to hand her the trencher. The woman leaned low to give it to her, whispering, 'Are you well?'

Beatrice just rolled her eyes.

'His lordship is working hard to find those responsible for the fires.'

His lordship? He'd also been working hard to establish himself as lord and master of Warehaven. Beatrice sighed. What was wrong with her this morning? Perhaps this forced confinement was working on her nerves more than she'd realised.

While she didn't want the woman to get in trouble with the guards, she also had no desire to be rude to one who was only seeking to help her.

She touched the older woman's hand. 'I know he is. Thank you.'

After Almedha left and the guards closed the door, she picked at the food. She wasn't hungry, nothing piqued her appetite. In truth, she was… tired. Which made no sense since she'd had plenty of sleep last night.

She placed the trencher and pitcher with the other items on the small table and went to stare out of the window. Not even the activity outside the keep held her interest.

A scuffle outside the chamber door caught her attention. Curious, she slowly crossed the room, heading towards the door. A hard thud against the wood brought her to a halt in the centre of the chamber.

The door swung open and she jumped back at the intrusion. To her dismay, Charles stepped over the prone body of a young guard from Warehaven to enter the room.

She stared at the guard before raising her gaze to him, asking, 'What did you do?'

'I've come to your rescue.'

Not even with some miracle from God could Charles have defeated the guards. Beatrice prayed her disbelief didn't show on her face. She backed away. 'Do I look like I need to be rescued?'

He ran his gaze around the chamber before focusing on her and answering, 'Yes.'

Perhaps her question should have been phrased

differently. He'd been at Warehaven countless times and knew this chamber was normally furnished in a more lavish manner.

For a reason she couldn't determine, she felt it important to make up some explanation for the condition of the room. 'With my parents still away, I thought it the perfect time to gut and clean their chamber before their return.'

He cleared his throat and she focused on his open expression of lust. He hadn't given the chamber's furnishings a single thought. His mind was elsewhere as evidenced by the look on his face. Eyes half-closed as if he'd either just risen from bed, or was going there directly. His mouth was half-opened, as though he was ready to devour something sinfully luscious.

When his sleepy-eyed gaze fell to her legs she realised she was standing there in nothing but Gregor's shirt. It came down only to her knees, with a neck opening that was slit to the V of her breasts. To make matters worse, she'd tightened the waist with her belt.

From the lewd, hungry look settling on his face and the warmth at her back, she also realised that the sunlight streaming through the window emphasised the thinness of the shirt, leaving little, if anything, to his imagination.

Beatrice moved slowly toward the alcove—away from the sunlight and away from the all-too-available bed.

Surely someone had seen Charles enter the keep and by now had alerted Gregor to their uninvited visitor's presence.

She wanted to shout at him. To loudly question his reason for tempting his own death. But again, something held her back. It might have been the odd glint in his eyes, the strange jerkiness of his movements, but something warned her that all was not well with Charles's state of mind. And she wasn't about to discover that something alone with him in a bedchamber.

Instead, she tried to act as if nothing untoward had happened between them—as if he hadn't tried to attack her not once, but twice—as if he hadn't threatened her, or thought to force her into a marriage.

'When did you arrive on Warehaven?'

He moved along with her, his steps just as slow, never once taking his lewd stare off her breasts. 'A few days ago. The same day as you.'

So the fool had followed her again. It was apparent he wasn't going to leave her alone. Ever.

That was something she would deal with in all due time. Right now she wanted to know how he had been here without her knowledge. Why had nobody told her of his arrival? As far as anyone on Warehaven knew, Charles was a potential betrothed. They didn't know anything about what he'd done, or had tried to do.

'You should have made your presence known to me.' She moved into the alcove.

'I wanted to surprise you.'

'And so you did.' Oh, yes, he'd most definitely succeeded in doing that.

She sat down on the cold stone bench, motioning him to take a seat opposite her. Which he did, but then he leaned forward to clasp one of her hands between his.

The moment he touched her, she wanted to scream. To pull away. But she forced herself to remain calm.

'Are you happy to see me?'

'Well, of course I am. How could I not be?'

He smiled as if to himself and nodded. 'I told Robert you would welcome me and my help. It was too bad he had to die in the fire.'

Robert? Sir Robert was dead? Her heart sank to her stomach. Keeping her tone light, she asked, 'And how do you plan on helping me?'

'Now that your lover's time is consumed clearing the rubble from the warehouse it will be an easy enough task to spirit you away just like Lady Isabella was.' He leaned a little closer to ask, 'Won't it be romantic?'

She now knew who was responsible for the destruction at the wharf—Charles. She felt safe in guessing that the scuffle she'd heard before Charles entered the chamber was the young Warehaven guard fighting with Gregor's guards. She didn't need to ask how Charles had entered the keep—he'd coerced the guard into letting him in through the tunnels that Gregor had most likely left unguarded since he knew nothing about them. And Charles had then killed the young man to keep his mouth shut.

His hand tightened on hers. 'Has he been a good lover for you?'

Beatrice snapped her thoughts back to Charles. 'I have no lover. I've been waiting for you.'

He tightened his grip a little more. 'You can't lie to me. I smell him on you. Besides, you wear his clothing like a whore.'

Charles pulled her to the edge of her seat and reached out to grasp the front of Gregor's shirt, tearing the thin fabric down the front.

The whoosh of a blade as it whipped through the air to rest against Charles's neck had never sounded so welcome.

'Give me your hand,' Gregor ordered as he reached towards her with his free arm.

Beatrice hesitated.

Gregor repeated, slowly, 'Give me your hand.'

She placed her hand in his and when he pulled her away from Charles, she looked up at him, whispering, 'He has lost his wits.'

Gregor stared down at her and clenched his jaw. 'Cover yourself.'

She pulled the shirt closed. The sound of heavy footsteps in the corridor alerted her to the arrival of Gregor's guards and she rushed to grab a cover off the bed to wrap around her body.

Sir Simon entered the chamber at a run, coming to a rocking halt as he looked from Gregor and Charles to her. He used the side of his already drawn sword to clear a path through the guards gathering in the chamber. 'My lady, come with me.'

She looked at Gregor, not certain she should leave Charles to his care.

Without turning around, Gregor ordered, 'Go.'

She followed Sir Simon out into the corridor and down to her chamber, where he suggested, 'Wait here a moment,' while he went inside.

Finally, he came back to the door and beckoned her inside, asking, 'Does this door lock?'

Beatrice shrugged. 'It has a lock, yes. But the key was lost long ago.'

He glanced up towards the top of the door. The old iron holders were still in place. He turned around, his gaze settling on a tall floor sconce, which he lifted into the holders. 'The fit is crooked because of the legs, but if you can reach it, it will work.'

Beatrice retrieved a stool from the corner of the alcove. 'I can stand on this.'

He removed the sconce and handed it to her. 'Secure the door behind me. Open it for no one except Lord Gregor. Do you understand me?'

She nodded. As he turned to leave, Beatrice said, 'I know who set the fires.'

'So do we. It was your Sir Charles.'

She bristled at the unspoken insinuation. 'He is *not* my Sir Charles and his deeds were *not* done at my bidding.'

Sir Simon made some type of indiscernible sound before leaving the chamber.

Beatrice slammed the door closed behind him and then climbed up on the stool to wiggle the sconce down into the iron holders.

She stepped off the stool, dropped the cover she'd wrapped around herself, then turned to place her fisted hands on her hips as she stared at the disaster that had once been her nice, neat chamber.

At least she now knew where all the comforts which had once been in her parents' chamber had been stored.

She retrieved her patched and re-patched house-cleaning clothes from a wall peg and some old stockings from her clothes chest. Once dressed, she went to work trying to uncover her bed and make some order out of her parents' things.

Hopefully the items would soon be returned to their rightful place and she would once again have use of her chamber. But in the meantime just dumping them in a pile was unacceptable.

She was folding the last sheet when a pounding on her door made her jump.

'Open up.'

She knew it was Gregor, but had to ask, 'Who is it?'

'Open this door, now.'

His surly tone of voice brought back her own disagreeable mood. She was tired of being ordered about, especially in her own home.

So she ignored him.

He pounded harder on the door. 'Beatrice, open this door.'

She stared at the door and shouted, 'Try asking.'

This time the pounding came from the bottom of the door. It moved on its hinges. 'Open this damn door or I will kick it in.'

For half a second…half a heartbeat, she wondered if he could. But when the door bowed once again under the force of his kick, she yelled, 'Stop. I'll open the damn door.'

Once she removed the sconce and stepped away, he shoved the door open so hard that it sent the stool flying across the room, bounced against the wall and then swung back to slam closed on its own. He barrelled through the instant it opened, not stopping as he marched up against her, pushing her backwards across the room until the wall on the far side stopped their progress.

She stared up at him. 'What is wrong with you?'

'Did you order Charles to set those fires?'

She shoved against his chest. 'Have you lost your wits, too?'

'Answer me.'

Speechless, she said nothing.

Gregor grabbed her upper arms. 'I said answer me.'

He was beyond angry, had gone far past irate. His face was expressionless, his eyes as dark and lifeless as midnight. The only emotion she could read was in his voice and that contained only rage.

Beatrice instinctively knew that this moment was going to set the tone for the rest of her life with this man. No matter how much she wanted to cower and beg him to believe her, this was not the time. A show of weakness at this moment would only make matters worse now and for the future.

Whether he realised it yet or not, he needed her right now. He needed someone safe to rail at, someone who could face his rage without flinching, or running a sword through him. He could take nothing from her that she hadn't already freely given him. And as hard as it was to convince her whirling mind and trembling heart, he was not going to abuse her physically.

He was seeking to frighten her and was determined to show her who was now in charge. He'd succeeded at both tasks, but he didn't need to know that. He was angry at the senseless loss of life and property. And she didn't blame him. She shared that anger.

She took a deep breath, stiffened her spine, ignored the shaking of her body and met his hard, unfeeling stare. 'Do whatever it is you must to spend this rage, Gregor. You cannot break me.'

'You think you know me?' He spun her away from the wall and forced her towards the bed. 'You think you know what I will or will not do?'

He pushed her down on to the mattress and leaned over her, a hand on either side of her head. 'Break you? I could kill you with one hand.'

Beatrice knew she was about to tempt fate, but she couldn't help herself. She reached up and placed a hand against his cheek. 'I die a little with every touch and each kiss.'

His eyes widened. And finally—finally she saw a flicker, a shimmer of life in the dark orbs. Thankfully, she'd been right.

He pushed off the bed and stared down at her. 'Woman, you will get yourself killed one day.'

'Perhaps.' She grasped the hand he extended to help her from the bed. Once on her feet, she placed her palms against his chest and gazed up at him. 'But not by you.'

With a heavy sigh, Gregor turned away. 'You never answered my question.'

She couldn't believe he had to ask her such a thing. *Had she ordered Charles to torch the warehouse and ships?* As much as she wanted to rail against his mistrust, she knew better than to bedevil him further. Repeatedly poking the Wolf with a stick might not kill her, but it could possibly gain her the feel of his fangs.

'It matters not who is lord here.' She kept her voice as steady as possible, fighting the urge to scream.

He turned back to look at her, so she continued, 'This is still my home. These are still my people. I would never do anything to bring harm to either. I am insulted that you could for one heartbeat assume otherwise.'

She stood silently, holding his stare until he nodded. Relief flooded her with a force that made her knees weak. She wanted nothing more than to sit down on something sturdy before she fell.

Gregor walked over to the door and tested it to be certain it was not broken. Seemingly satisfied, he said, 'I need to see to my prisoners.'

Prisoners? He hadn't killed the man already? 'Charles is still alive?'

'And another.'

'Who?'

'Randall FitzHenry.'

Chapter Fourteen

Beatrice stared at the now-closed door. Unable to catch her breath, she held a hand to her chest, praying her heart didn't burst through flesh and bone with its wild beating.

He had her father.

'No. No. No. No. *No!*' What had started as a whispered plea ended as a scream.

She jerked opened the door, only to find her way blocked by two guards. 'Let me pass.'

When they remained frozen in place, their shields and bodies preventing her from exiting, she screamed, 'Let me pass!'

'Let her pass.' Gregor's voice echoed up the stairs.

Her way cleared, she nearly flew along the corridor, trying to reach Gregor before he could get to his prisoners. She stumbled down the stairs, catching herself from falling twice before her feet hit the floor of the Great Hall.

He hadn't stopped and was halfway across the hall. She raced as fast as she could to catch up. Not knowing what she would say, or what she would do, and not caring who watched, or what they thought, she sped around him and threw herself on the floor at his feet.

'Gregor, I beg you, don't do this.'

When he tried to step around her, she wrapped her arms around his ankles. 'Please, please, don't.'

'Get up.'

She ignored his order to cry, 'Take my life instead.'

He stared down at her in shock. He'd expected a display of emotion from her. But never this. 'Get on your feet.'

Again she ignored him. Through the sound of his heart thudding in his ears he heard her ragged cries and realised she was sobbing too hard to hear anything.

He wanted to gather her close and tell her that all would be well, but that would be a lie and he couldn't do that to her. He couldn't give her hope when he didn't know if any existed. His men had captured her father and he'd not yet had a chance to speak to the man.

A commotion at the rear of the hall caught his attention. An older man had shoved his way past Gregor's guards and was now striding determinedly in his direction.

Gregor's hand instantly flew to the grip of his sword, wavering when he saw the man was unarmed and from the way he scowled at Beatrice knew that it had to be FitzHenry—her father. Gregor raised his arm, silently ordering his men to hold their weapons.

Stopping to stand over her, the man shouted, 'Beatrice, get on your feet.'

To Gregor's surprise, she freed his ankles and rose to throw herself against her father's chest, still sobbing and now babbling incoherently.

FitzHenry grasped her arms to pull her away from his chest, ordering, 'Cease.'

When her cries didn't lessen, he raised his hand as if to slap her.

Rage rushed to the fore, firing his blood, clouding his vision with pure red. Gregor pulled his sword free of the scabbard and held it to FitzHenry's neck. 'Touch her and I will kill you.'

The man raised an eyebrow and stared from Beatrice to Gregor and back before he released her.

Not only had she finally stopped crying, she was now standing silent, her hands folded together in front of her as she looked down at the floor.

In that instant, Gregor knew two things—she could be broken and he never wanted to see her this submissive again.

Her father brushed aside Gregor's blade, then reached out to cup her cheek and shook his head. He then kissed her forehead. 'Oh, how I've missed you, child.'

'Father, Sir Robert is…he died in the fire.'

'I heard, he will be greatly missed. Beatrice, go up to your chamber and stay there.'

She nodded and walked towards the stairs without a backward glance.

An invisible hand closed around Gregor's heart at the sight of his little warrior looking so defeated and forlorn. He replaced the point of his weapon against the older man's chest. 'I could kill you for that.'

'You could try.'

The two men stared at each other, neither willing to stand down. Gregor knew he faced an opponent who would not go down easily. But neither would he.

'If you so much as think to raise a hand to her again I will gut you. Slowly and with great pleasure.'

FitzHenry looked towards the stairs, then back to him.

He said nothing, but Gregor could feel his assessing stare. Taking a step closer, so there was no doubt in the older man's mind, he said, 'She is mine.'

The man relaxed, his shoulders visibly lowering. Responding to Gregor's comment, he said, 'It is about damn time.'

Gregor lowered his weapon and stepped back to motion for Simon.

When Simon arrived at his side, he handed Gregor a missive. 'This came a few minutes ago.'

Gregor barely glanced at the Empress's wax seal before breaking it to unroll the small scroll. He read the note quickly and then cursed. Knowing his man was awaiting his orders, he said, 'Secure him in the cell next to our other guests until I can make proper arrangements.'

Without waiting to see that his orders were carried out, he took the missive to the small chamber off the rear of the hall, stowed it in a chest and then turned to head back up the stairs, taking them two at a time. He paused outside Beatrice's chamber door, seeking to calm this unfamiliar concern running through him.

Once certain he was again in control of himself, he opened the door and entered the chamber. He scanned the room and, not seeing her, went into the alcove. The only things there were the items from her parents' room.

He frowned—where was she? Where would she have gone?

A guard waylaid him as he left the chamber. 'If you seek Lady Beatrice, she's out on the wall, my lord.'

Gregor followed the corridor to the open door leading out to the wall walk. He breathed a sigh of relief to see that she hadn't gone far, she stood just beyond the door, leaning into a cut-out portion of the crenellated wall.

'Beatrice.'

She straightened and leaned away from the wall to look at him. His anger grew anew at the sight of her reddened eyes, but it was hard to determine who he was angrier with—her father, or himself.

'Is he alive?' she asked softly.

Gregor walked to her side and stared out over the far edge of the clearing. 'For now, yes.'

'Thank you.'

He wanted to scream his ire aloud at the soft, flat tone of her voice. Instead, he gripped the edge of the wall. How was he to coax her out of this melancholy? And why did it matter so much to him? Shouldn't he be pleased to know she could be so easily controlled?

That question made his stomach churn until he had to swallow hard to steady the sickening twisting.

She traced the veins on the top of his hand. 'What is wrong, Gregor?'

He shook his head.

Beatrice leaned against his arm. 'I can count on one hand the number of times my father has raised a hand to the three of us. He is not cruel. I am fine.'

He frowned down at her. How did she know what bothered him?

She smiled. 'I heard you. On my way up the stairs, you threatened to kill him if he raised a hand to me again. I think the threat was to gut him, slowly and with great pleasure.'

'You were far from fine.'

She stroked his hand. 'He is my father, Gregor.

I am not going to argue with him the way I will with you.'

'Do you fear him?'

'Heavens no. I fear hurting him, or causing him distress, that is all.'

'Would you say that you love him?'

'Well, of course I do.'

'If that is love I'll have none of it.'

Even though the air was warm, she shivered and he wrapped an arm around her, pulling her close.

'Gregor, that is the love of a child for a parent. There are invisible boundaries that my siblings and I would never cross out of respect. You are angry that he thought to slap me and that I turned around and followed his order without question. What did you expect me to do?'

'I know what would have happened had I been the one to raise a hand and then issue an order.'

'But as of this moment, you are nothing to me other than the lord of the keep where I reside.' When he stiffened at her comment, she rushed on, asking, 'Am I not still an unmarried woman?'

'By your own choice.'

'Regardless, I am unwed. He is my father and he gave me an order.'

'So if we were wed and I were to slap your hysteria away and then order you to your chamber, you would react the same?'

She laughed. 'You are not my father and I am

not your child. Were you to do anything so foolish I would make your life a living hell.'

'And why is that? Because you love and respect your father, but not me?'

Beatrice fell silent. Was he looking for some sort of declaration from her? Did she love him? Sometimes she thought so. Other times she wasn't certain if it was love or lust that made her dizzy with an emotion so strong she wanted to weep.

She turned into him, resting against his chest. 'Gregor, I don't know if what I feel for you is love or lust. But I do know that I do respect you. I respect you as a strong man who does not resort to violence against those smaller and weaker. I respect you as an honourable man who keeps his word.'

'I do not want your love.'

'And why is that?'

'Because some day you may have greater reason to hate me. Love would only make it worse for you.'

She had no reply for that, so she simply wrapped her arms around his waist and listened to the steady beating of his heart.

Gregor sighed and kissed the top of her head. 'Have I told you lately that you are an odd woman?'

'Not for a couple of days you haven't.'

'Well, my little warrior, you are an odd woman.' He tightened his embrace around her. 'But I don't think I'd have you any other way.'

Beatrice closed her eyes tightly to hold her tears at bay. Heaven help her, but she was fairly certain the emotion filling her heart and making her want to weep was not lust.

Gregor caressed her cheek, then tipped her head back and wiped a thumb over a tear she'd been unable to hold back. 'What is this?'

'Nothing.' She shook her head. 'Just silly tears for nothing.'

'Stop. I don't like it.'

She burst out laughing. There was little else she could do when he spouted such nonsense.

He stroked her cheek. 'That is better. I can't have you crying when your visitors arrive.'

'Visitors?'

'Did I forget to mention that we will be having visitors join us for the evening meal?'

She lowered her arms and stepped back. 'Yes, you did.'

'Well, I am telling you now. And since your bath should be ready, perhaps we should go inside.'

He turned to leave and she grasped his arm. 'Gregor!'

Turning back to face her, he raised an eyebrow. 'Yes?'

'Who are these visitors?'

'Your mother and aunt.'

She leaned back against the wall for support. 'Not my Aunt Matilda.'

'I didn't realise you had more than one.'

'I have four, but are you speaking about Matilda?'

'She's the only one I know.'

'If you don't answer me, I may become ill.'

Somehow, Gregor managed to appear innocent. 'Honest, as long as you aren't facing her or her troops across a battlefield, the Empress isn't that bad a person.'

Beatrice dropped her chin to her chest. 'Yes, I am going to be ill.'

Gregor laughed then took her hand. 'It will not be that bad. Come, we have things to do.'

'Things to do? We have three days' worth of things to do.' Beatrice realised her voice had risen to a near-scream. She swallowed, then added in a softer tone, 'And you have left me mere hours. I swear, Gregor, if you ever do something like this again—'

He cut off her words in a manner that never failed to work. He pulled her into his arms and covered her lips with his own.

Once she relaxed in his embrace, he lifted his head to ask, 'You'll do what?'

She rested her cheek against his chest. 'I don't know, but I promise it will be something quite horrible.'

A few hours later, they stood together in the centre of the Great Hall as the doors opened. Beatrice took another look around the hall, ensuring everything and everyone was in place.

Her heart raced as her mother and the Empress entered the hall. She longed to throw herself in her mother's arms, but restrained herself and instead knelt. 'Aunt Matilda, welcome to Warehaven.'

Matilda took her hands to bring her to her feet before kissing her cheek. 'Yes, thank you, child, it is good to see you are well after your recent ordeal.'

The Empress turned her attention to Gregor. 'Roul.'

When Gregor rose, the Empress pierced him with a glare that should have had him quivering in his boots, but he seemed to take it in his stride.

She then sighed, loudly, and said, 'Since the last time you were at court, you showed so much concern for Lady Emelina, I brought her along.'

She motioned the lady forward. 'Lady Emelina, I'm sure you remember your champion, Sir Gregor of Roul?'

Before the lady could respond, Matilda said, 'He will be glad to see to your needs while we are here.'

Beatrice felt her eyes widen. She knew she'd clenched her jaw because her teeth were grinding against each other. She pinned Gregor with a stare that he ignored as he took Lady Emelina's hand and led her away from the welcoming party.

Matilda called out across the hall, 'Randall, no greeting for your sister?'

Beatrice half-watched her father's approach—her attention was more focused on Gregor and his Lady Emelina. If that tiny red-haired wench thought for one second…

'Beatrice.' Her mother drew her focus away from Gregor. 'She is already betrothed to another.'

'What do I care? He is free to do as he pleases.' She hated the tremor in her voice. Hated more the way she felt at seeing him with another woman. She trusted him. He wasn't going to do anything unseemly, so what was wrong with her?

She heard her father snort before he leaned in to give his wife a kiss. 'Brigit, my love, the girl has made her choice, I don't think you are going to be able to reason with her at the moment.'

He then turned to his sister, saying, 'I see now why you saw fit to delay our return by three days. Since Roul's men took me from the ship, leaving you behind, this was obviously your doing.'

'Not entirely.'

'Ah, you had Uncle David's assistance.'

Matilda moved away from the entrance to take his arm. 'Perhaps, dear brother, we should talk.'

As they walked away, Beatrice heard her father reply, 'That would be something different for us.'

'Child, do we have need to talk?'

Beatrice turned to her mother and nearly cried. 'Mother, I have missed you so very much.'

Her mother gathered her close. 'I have missed

you, too. What is this about you having made a choice?'

'It is a long story.'

'And we have all night. Longer if needed.' Her mother linked an arm through hers and led her towards the high table. 'Tell me everything, Beatrice. Start at the beginning.'

Beatrice sighed. 'If I start there, you will only be disappointed.'

Taking a seat on one of the end chairs, her mother admitted, 'Perhaps. But I must ask, are you happy with this choice?'

Beatrice looked at Gregor, who was standing near a wooden support beam listening intently to whatever his Lady Emelina was telling him while she placed a hand on his chest.

As if feeling her stare, he turned to look at her and smiled before he rolled his eyes towards his talkative companion.

Beatrice returned his smile, then told her mother as she sat down next to her, 'Yes, I am happy with my choice. But it presents grave problems for all of us.'

'I know about David's orders to his Wolf, orders that I'm sure Matilda had a hand in since she explained them to me while we rode here from the docks. I am well aware that Randall is no longer the Lord of Warehaven. He was nothing more than King Henry's bastard warrior when I married him. His title didn't matter then and it doesn't matter now.' She placed a hand on Beatrice's. 'This is not the first time Warehaven has been taken, my love. It is simply the first time someone might die because of the taking.'

'Mother, don't speak so.'

'Have the two of them even talked about this yet?'

'I don't know.'

'Well, then, we have no way of knowing what is going to happen. Beatrice, I have had a good life with my husband, a long life. I worship the ground on which he walks. But I am not foolish enough to believe he is immortal. Some day he will die.' She paused to swallow, before continuing, 'Tomorrow or ten years from now will make no difference, it will hurt the same, my grief will be no different. But I am not alone. I have our children, our grandchildren and my memories to sustain me until I, too, die.'

Even though her mother's voice remained steady, Beatrice gasped at the raw pain etched on her face. She worried greatly for her husband. 'Mother, stop it.'

'No. You stop worrying about me or your father. You need to start taking care of your future.' She grasped Beatrice's chin, holding it tightly between her thumb and forefinger to ask, 'Do you know how much we love you, how greatly we have missed you and how much we have longed for you to find someone worthy of being your choice?'

Her mother released her, then asked, 'Is he worthy? Is he brave? Do you respect him? Do you trust him? Is he strong enough to hold you should you swoon from his kisses?'

Beatrice gasped in shock.

Her mother laughed. 'You thought I couldn't hear you and Isabella talking about the boys at night? Your father was outraged by your conversations, but I found much amusement in them. You were so naïve. So young and full of dreams. Have you found those dreams, Beatrice?'

She once again glanced at Gregor, only to find him watching her closely. His steady attention made her warmer than was welcome while sitting next to her mother. 'Yes, Mother. I think I have.'

'Have you discussed your futures?'

Beatrice turned her gaze back to her mother, admitting, 'Somewhat. I have already missed one wedding and begged off another one.'

Her mother tried unsuccessfully to hold back a laugh, but she managed to say, 'From the way the two of you look at each other, I am fairly certain you did not miss the wedding night.'

Beatrice felt her embarrassment race hot up her face. 'No. We didn't.'

'Then I would say your father has more to discuss than just the surrender of Warehaven.'

Beatrice grimaced and shrugged. 'I would hope he does.'

'Now tell me, how did you manage to escape from Jared? Don't tell me you waited until Lea went into labour.'

Again she felt the flush warm her cheeks.

'Oh, Beatrice. What were you thinking?'

Chapter Fifteen

Gregor stood in the shadows of the corridor, waiting for Beatrice to walk by. The sleeping arrangements for the night were not to his liking, but he'd had little say in the matter.

Empress Matilda was in Beatrice's bedchamber with four of her ladies. Beatrice's parents had resumed possession of the master's chamber, taking the bed while Beatrice and Almedha shared a pallet in the alcove. Lady Emelina and the other four ladies who'd accompanied Matilda were in the extra bedchamber.

The men who had come with the party had pallets on the floor of the Great Hall with the guards. Those who had drunk until they passed out slept where they'd fallen.

He had his small chamber at the rear of the Great Hall. It was more of a study, a place to do accounts and such, than a bedchamber. But it did have a pallet, along with a door that locked.

He ducked further into the shadows as her parents walked by, followed by two of Gregor's guards who were FitzHenry's constant companions. The one good thing about FitzHenry being of royal lineage was that the man didn't have to suffer the bite of shackles. As long as he did nothing foolish, he could be treated as an honoured guest of sorts. Which would be easier on Beatrice. The constant guards were more for Gregor's own sake—he didn't trust the man not to stab him in the back if given the opportunity.

What seemed hours later, Beatrice walked past him. He reached out and clasped her hand to pull her into the shadows, whispering, 'Spend the night with me.'

She fell into his arms. 'I thought you'd be too busy with Lady Emelina.'

He knew she wasn't complaining, but just teasing him. 'I tried, but she seemed unwilling to share my bed.'

'Oh, so I am your second choice?'

'My third, actually. There was this pert little serving maid—'

He gasped when she bent her leg and lifted her knee against his groin, asking, 'You were saying?'

He threaded his fingers through her hair and pulled her closer. 'I was saying I want you in my bed this night.'

'And I would like that, too.' Beatrice sighed. 'However, the keep is a little too crowded for sneaking about.'

'Oh, I know. If we were caught, what would people say? They might force us to marry, making certain you actually showed up for the ceremony.'

'Are you going to hold that over my head for the rest of our lives?'

'Only until you are my wife.'

He felt her lips curl into a smile as she pressed them to his. 'Those arrangements need to be made with my father now that he is here.'

She was wrong. FitzHenry might be free to walk about, but he was in control of nothing. 'As Lord of Warehaven the decision is solely mine.'

'Gregor.'

'Do not start, Beatrice. Nothing has changed except that nearly all of the parties involved are in attendance.'

She tried to pull away, but he held her in place. 'Are we going to argue about this each hour of every day? Can you not concentrate on this moment? Must you worry about tomorrow before it is here?'

'Is that what you would have me do? Not concern myself with the future? My future? Or what could possibly be our future?'

'Could possibly be? You seem confused, as if you have a choice in this matter.'

'There is always a choice.'

'Is there?' He released her. 'What would your choices be?'

She had no response and he wondered why she was intentionally trying to anger him. He moved away from the shadows. 'Join me or don't. Those are your choices right now. But hear me well, Beatrice. You will marry me. That choice has already been determined.'

He left her standing there as he went back down the stairs and wove his way through the sleeping bodies strewn about the floor of the Great Hall and into his private chamber.

A soft tap on his door moments later surprised him. He opened the door and waved her into the chamber, closing and locking the door behind them. He tossed the key on to the desk before asking, 'Changed your mind? Again?'

'Gregor, I am tired. This day has been far too long. I am sorry for arguing for the simple sake of arguing.'

She wasn't getting out of it that easily. 'I don't want your apology. I want an explanation. What choices do you think you have?'

'I could always run away.'

'Oh, yes, because you've already proven how good you are at that.'

'I could give myself to the church.'

'I don't know about that. I don't see you becoming celibate. I doubt it would suit your temperament. You need a man, Beatrice.'

'I could find another one.'

'Sure you could and you also know that I would simply get rid of him.'

'I could kill myself.'

He stared at her, certain he'd lost his ability to understand words because she couldn't have just said that she'd kill herself rather than marry him.

He retrieved the key from the desk, unlocked the door and pulled it open. 'Go.'

Beatrice's eyes widened. She rushed to stand before him. 'Oh, Gregor, I didn't mean to say that. I am so sorry. Please.'

He refused to look at her. 'Leave.'

'Gregor.'

'Get away from me.'

He slammed the door behind her, locked it and then threw himself on the pallet to stare up at the ceiling. This was not proceeding to plan. Somewhere along the line he'd lost sight of the fact that once he took her father's life she would bear nothing but hatred for him. He'd known that all along and had been determined not to permit himself to become too close, too attached to her.

Somehow he needed to remedy this situation— and quickly, before it was too late to pull away.

'Beatrice, wake up. You need to get ready.'

She opened her burning eyes slowly and stared up at her mother. 'The sun hasn't risen yet.'

'I know, but your wedding takes place at dawn.'

She sat up, shielding her eyes from the light of the wall torch. 'My what?'

'Nobody told you?'

'Please, Mother, I had a bad night. Told me what?' She knew that she had nobody to blame for her bad night except herself. Her mouth had once again caused her more distress than the person she'd used it against.

'Gregor spoke with your father and Matilda yesterday. He requested the marriage take place today.'

She'd seen the three of them huddled in the alcove after the meal last night, but had assumed it had something to do with Warehaven, not her. No wonder he'd been so angry over her comment about having choices. She groaned and fell back down on her pallet. 'I am a lack-witted fool.'

Her mother sighed. 'What happened?'

'We argued.'

'About?'

'About whether he had to speak to Father about marrying me or not. I didn't know he already had. And then I said something about having choices.'

'What choices were you speaking about?'

'That's what he asked.' Her mother's groan made her cover her eyes.

'And your answer?'

'One of them was that I could kill myself rather than marry him.'

'Were you aware that is what his first wife did?'

She admitted, 'Yes.'

'Someone needs to take a switch to your backside, Beatrice. You are no longer a child and should know better. Speaking your mind is unacceptable when you intentionally hurt someone else with your words.'

'I know that.'

'Obviously you don't.'

'It probably won't matter, since it is unlikely a wedding is going to take place.'

'Oh, I'm certain there will be. I'm also certain it will not be pleasant. But trust me when I tell you that your wedding night is most likely going to be hell. This is not a good way for this marriage to start.'

'I could claim sickness.' She did feel rather ill.

'Oh, no, you don't. Get up. You created this mess, you are going to face it.'

Reluctantly she rose and let her mother and Almedha do whatever they needed to do to get her ready. She sat when told to sit and stood when told to stand. The entire time her mother's scowl of disapproval never faltered. Which served to make Beatrice more nervous with each passing moment.

A maid entered carrying her green gown. The sleeves had been repaired and the gown cleaned. Lacings had been added to the back and the neckline widened, so that it would easily slide off her shoulders and down her arms. The sleeves would still need a good tug to get the gown off, but at least a knife wouldn't be needed.

While the matching slippers had also been cleaned, Beatrice knew the belt had been a lost cause.

Her mother reached under the bed and pulled

out a paper-wrapped package. She removed the string holding the package closed and lifted out the finest chemise Beatrice had ever seen. It was so white and so thin that it appeared almost transparent when held up to the light. And was as soft as fur against her skin.

Once dressed, her mother walked around her, picking at the fabric of her gown here and there, tugging the neckline into place. 'It needs a belt.'

She retrieved a small chest from the corner of the room and pulled a gold-woven girdle from the contents. 'Here, try this.'

Almedha wrapped it about her waist and fastened the clasp at the back. 'That seems fine.'

Once again her mother performed an inspection. This time she included Beatrice's hair, which had been drawn back into her usual single plait. She undid the braid and finger combed the waves to spread them about her shoulders.

Beatrice picked at the strands which had fallen on to her gown. 'Mother, I hate wearing my hair down. It gets into everything.'

'One day won't kill you.' She went back to her jewel chest and found a thin braided-gold circlet which she placed over Beatrice's head. 'This will help hold your hair in place.'

When her mother once again went back to the chest, Beatrice cried, 'No more. I feel overdressed as it is. Please, Mother, no more.'

To her relief her mother put a gold torque back

into the chest. The last thing Beatrice wanted was something heavy around her neck. It would only make her feel as if she were being choked. Which, considering how she'd behaved last night, was a possibility.

Her father knocked once on the door before entering. 'Is she ready?'

'As ready as she's going to be, yes.'

'Good.' He came over and took Beatrice's hands in his. 'I must warn you. The groom is in a surly mood.'

Her mother chortled. 'I can't imagine why.'

Honestly confused, her father said, 'Neither can I considering this was his order.'

Beatrice explained, 'He is surly because I said things I shouldn't have last night.'

'And can I safely assume your mother has sufficiently berated you?'

'Yes.'

'No,' her mother answered at the same time.

'Beatrice.' Her father looked down at her. 'Do you enjoy making things hard for yourself?'

The question didn't need an answer, so she remained quiet.

'Well, what's done is done.' He nodded at her mother and Almedha. 'We will be down in a moment.'

Her mother came over and gave her a quick peck on the cheek. 'It will work out. Have faith.'

Once the women had left the chamber, her father asked, 'Are you certain he is who you want, Beatrice.'

She laughed softly. 'It's a little late to change my mind now.'

'No. It isn't. I can have you away from Warehaven and safely on your way to Dunstan, Montreau, or to one of your aunts in Wales before anyone knows you are gone.'

'No, Father. I am not going to run. I angered him that is all.'

'That man's anger can get you hurt, child. Once you are wed there is nothing I can do to stay his hand short of killing him.'

She looked up at him. 'I'd prefer you didn't. Besides, how many times did you strike my mother, or even any of us, in anger?'

'Never. How can you think to ask such a question?'

'Gregor will not harm me either. He will be surly. He may ignore me until I want to scream just to get his attention. He may even shout or rage. But, Father, he will never harm me.'

'Are you trying to convince me that David's Wolf is kind?'

'Was King Henry's Executioner kind to those he cared for?'

Her father smiled and kissed her forehead. 'Fair enough.'

He took her hand and placed a gold band in her palm. 'For your husband's hand.'

She closed her fingers over the ring. 'Thank you.'

'I wouldn't tell him from where it came. At least not any time soon.'

Beatrice laughed. 'He's going to know it came from somewhere. But I doubt if he'll ask.'

Her father shook his head and sighed sadly. 'My baby.'

'Don't you start.' She shook her finger at him. 'If you cry I am lost.'

He sniffed and then extended his bent arm. 'Ready?'

She placed her hand in the crook of his elbow. 'Yes.'

Her father led her down the stairs and across the Great Hall to the small family chapel. Gregor waited for her at the entrance.

Their exchange of vows was brief and to the point. He took her as his wife. She accepted him as her husband. The only time he touched her was to place the ring on her finger. It was the same for her, she touched him only when she placed the ring on his finger.

They entered the chapel together, side by side, but not touching, and knelt before the altar for a blessing from both Warehaven's and Roul's priests.

When he kissed her it was a quick peck of his lips to her cheek.

Beatrice fought to harden her heart against his obvious anger. This was not the wedding she'd dreamt of as a child. Today, a kind word or touch would have been welcome. She gritted her teeth, refusing to cry. And she refused to beg his forgiveness. Yes, she'd said terrible things, but she'd apologised. The only thing she could do now was wait out his anger, without saying anything further to send his anger soaring.

They left the chapel to share a morning meal in the Great Hall. He led her to the dais and pulled out a chair in the centre of the high table, leaning over her shoulder to whisper, 'If you start to cry, I will leave.'

She couldn't remember a more miserable meal and felt nothing but relief when it was over and she could leave her seat next to him to move about the hall. What she wanted to do was to escape to the wall for a few moments, but she knew that would be deemed inconsiderate and rude.

So she accepted congratulations and best wishes from people she didn't know, faces she didn't recognise through her fog of self-pity. She spent a few minutes talking with her aunt about things she forgot about the minute Matilda moved on to speak to others.

She found a seat on a bench that had been placed against the wall out of the throng of people who visited and laughed and drank as if this were some festive occasion.

The whole time she kept telling herself that this was her fault. She had no right to be angry at Gregor, but she was. And each time he laughed with, or smiled at, Lady Emelina, her anger grew until she had to clasp her hands together to keep them from shaking.

'Still feeling sorry for yourself?' her mother asked as she sat down next to her. 'Stop it.'

'Stop what?' Beatrice was surprised by the venom in her own tone.

'That, for one thing.'

Beatrice swallowed and tried again. 'Stop what?'

'That's better. Now smile.'

'I don't think I can.'

'It is easy. Loosen your jaw and curve the corners of your lips up towards the ceiling instead of the floor.'

She turned to face her mother and grinned like a sodden fool.

'Well, that's rather ugly. Try again.'

She laughed. 'Mother, you have lost your wits.'

'See. That wasn't so bad, was it?'

'No.'

'Good. Now for the hard part.'

Beatrice dreaded asking, but knew her mother wasn't going to cease. 'What?'

'Take that softer tone, smile and that easy laugh and go join your husband.'

'He doesn't want me to.'

'I didn't ask you what he wanted. I told you to go join him.' She leaned her shoulder against Beatrice's. 'He isn't going to openly attack you on your wedding day with everyone watching. He is going to pretend that everything is wonderful. Trust me, the man knows his way around David and Matilda's courts well enough to know when to put on a happy mask.'

Beatrice doubted if that was going to happen, but sitting here sulking was doing nothing more than adding heat to her anger. She rose, shook out her skirt, looked down at her mother and smiled. At her mother's nod of approval, she turned and walked towards her husband and Lady Emelina.

Gregor saw her and frowned.

Beatrice hung on to her smile as if it had been carved in stone. She might be lacking in court experience, but she was determined to see this through as well as he and greeted people here and there as she crossed the hall. He wasn't going to scare her off with a frown.

When she was close enough he extended his hand and pulled her to his side. Her mother had been correct, he was going to use his finest court manners.

She knew he wasn't happy to see her in the least by the darkness of his eyes and the coldness of his touch.

This had been a mistake. His show only served to make her angrier. The simple fact that it was false and lacked any welcome or feeling whatsoever made her want to run from the keep. But he kept a tight hold on her hand where it rested on his arm. He knew she was far from happy with him and was determined to make her suffer more for her cruelty last night.

After a few minutes Matilda joined them. She, Gregor and Lady Emelina chatted about something that had happen at court, but before she left, she leaned over to whisper in Beatrice's ear, 'Stand strong, girl.'

Gregor looked down at her and she noticed that the hardness of his glare had lessened slightly. She smiled up at him and lightly squeezed his arm.

But when she looked back at Lady Emelina she met a calculating stare and realised that everyone had been wrong about this woman. While she might be betrothed to another, she wanted Gregor.

Beatrice squared her shoulders. The woman could *want* all she wished, it was never going to happen.

Gregor must have felt a change in her stance, because he looked down at her again, this time with that all-too-familiar winged eyebrow.

She reached up with her free hand and caressed his cheek, coaxing him to lean down for a kiss. Just before breaking the contact of their lips she moaned softly as if with regret.

By the winging of both his eyebrows she knew she'd taken this pretence a step too far. He now knew she was up to something and briefly narrowed his eyes before looking back at Lady Emelina.

When she returned her attention to Lady Emelina, the woman excused herself and walked away.

Gregor tightened his hand that covered hers. 'What was that about?'

She looked up at him from beneath her lashes. 'What?'

'She is simply an acquaintance from Matilda's court.'

'Really?'

'Yes. Her former betrothed thought to teach her a lesson by using force. When I happened upon them in the garden she was sobbing, begging him to stop.'

Beatrice knew the answer, but she still asked, 'And you went to her rescue?'

'Of course I did.'

He made a habit of defending the weak. It was a fine and noble trait, but it was also one that could gain him a knife in the back one day. For a man who was supposed to be a dangerous, frightening warrior, he certainly did seem to come to the aid of ladies in need quickly enough.

'Who do you think she is?'

'A woman who wants to be in your bed.'

He released her. 'You have lost your wits. She is betrothed to another.'

'I don't care if she's married to someone else. She wants in your bed and I promise you, that isn't going to happen as long as I draw breath.' Beatrice kept a tight rein on her temper and suggested, 'If you think I am wrong, go after her. See what she does.'

'Perhaps I will.'

She waved him away. 'Go.'

'You must be very sure of yourself to send me to another woman's arms.'

'Gregor, you are far too honourable to take another woman to your bed now. But that doesn't mean they don't want you to.'

He strode away without another word.

From behind her, her mother said, 'That may not have been wise.'

'If I know nothing else about Gregor, I know for a fact that had he possessed any desire to bed that woman he'd have said so.'

'You can't know that for certain.'

'He's made it clear that I'm not to ask him a question I don't want an honest answer to.'

'That should provide some interesting conversations.'

'It has.'

After her mother left, Beatrice wandered around the hall for a while before Gregor finally returned, the darkness of his eyes bleak even for him.

He tucked her hand in the crook of his elbow.

From the coolness of his touch she knew he did so for appearances's sake and not for any desire for physical contact. 'Well?'

'You have taken your distrust of me and unfairly placed it on others. She was and always is the perfect lady. I don't understand this sudden cruelty from you. It is not acceptable, Beatrice.'

She knew she hadn't mistaken Lady Emelina's intent. He was either lying, or wouldn't recognise a woman's advances unless they hit him with a shield, knocked him out and dragged him off to bed.

She was amazed that a man with such dark good looks wasn't well experienced at fending off female advances. Did he really believe that his reputation repulsed women? He might frighten *girls*. And while *women* might not wish marriage with David's Wolf, they would be sorely tempted to taste the danger he presented. And to think he'd called *her* innocent.

She peered around him towards the lady in question and met the woman's ice-filled, smirking glare. Beatrice's first impression still held firm. However, it now appeared that Lady Emelina intended to make her look like the shrew.

Beatrice drew her focus back to Gregor. 'I apologise if I was wrong.'

He leaned closer, keeping his voice low so those passing by wouldn't hear, and said, 'You need to practise your court face, my lady. You aren't sorry for your accusation in the least. I know not what you're thinking or planning, but this needs to stop now.'

She nodded in reply. He was right. This did need to stop. Now. And since he wasn't going to put an end to it, she would.

'Beatrice.'

His warning tone might have been more threatening had his breath against her ear not been so warm.

'Of all the things you could worry about, I would think women chasing after me would be the last on your list. After all, they would rather kill themselves.'

He couldn't have slapped her any harder had he physically used his hand. 'Gregor…' She'd found her voice too late. He had already walked away.

Beatrice chewed on her lower lip. She had to fix this. Somehow, she had to make him understand she'd not meant that awful thing about choosing death rather than marriage to him. She had spoken such cruel words only because she'd wanted to argue and had let it get too far out of control. It had been mean, childish and she'd never before in her entire life felt so guilty and ashamed of herself.

She was a married woman now, and needed to start acting like one, instead of like a child.

A chill raced up her spine, making the fine hairs on her neck rise and dragging her out of her thoughts. Beatrice looked up to see Lady Emelina's calculating stare and satisfied smile as she clung to Gregor's arm.

Chapter Sixteen

Gregor leaned against the side of the stable, breathing in the air and soaking in the blessed quiet. He was thankful the Empress had drawn Lady Emelina's attention away, permitting him to escape.

He knew Beatrice was truly sorry for what she'd said last night. Why she found it necessary to argue simply for the sake of arguing was beyond his understanding, but it was time to put an end to this festering anger that he had wanted to embrace. In their short time together, the two of them had perfected the ability to set off each other's rage with nothing more than unmeasured words.

Before meeting her he'd been in control of himself, his mood or emotions his responsibility alone. He'd been capable of not permitting the words and actions of another person to affect him.

Now? He closed his eyes, sighing. Now he found himself constantly chasing his suddenly elusive control. Unfortunately, it was quicker than he, always managing to stay just beyond the reach of his fingertips. One minute he wanted nothing more than to hear her cry his name in the throes of lust and the next he longed to shout at her in frustration.

Less than a day into the marriage and already

it wasn't going well. Of course, part of the reason for that was because he'd acted like an ass during the exchange of vows and blessing.

Gregor cringed at his childish behaviour. He stepped away from the stable. It was doubtful they would find any measure of peace between them this day without yet more accusations and hard words. But maybe they could argue away their misunderstandings long enough to still end up having a real wedding night in each other's arms. Since it would be one of the few nights left to them before he dealt with her father, he wanted it to be one both of them would remember fondly.

He stared towards the keep, knowing there would be no possibility of finding the privacy they needed there. The small huntsman's hut near the cove was too far away. Any of the ships was out of the question—since the fire every one of them was manned with guards.

Gregor smiled; he knew the perfect place. The midwife was in London visiting her sister, so the cottage was unoccupied and far enough away from the other villagers to provide the privacy he desired.

He headed back to the keep. Since he hadn't planned on having a wedding night, he was unprepared and needed to gather supplies—food since she'd only picked at the morning meal and he'd seen her eat nothing since. No wine, he wanted both of them fully in control of their senses, if not their tempers. No torches, but candles, just enough light so that later, after the sun set, he could still see every nuance of her expressions.

Thankfully he had men to help carry everything to the cottage. He just had to hope they would keep their mouths shut about his whereabouts at least until tomorrow. He also needed to give Simon his orders for the rest of the day and night, as he didn't want anyone thinking FitzHenry was in charge and then he could kidnap his wife willing or not.

'Lady Beatrice, a word?'

Beatrice stopped to look over her shoulder at Lady Emelina before turning around to see what the woman wanted. 'Yes?'

Emelina's cheeks pinked and she glanced around the crowded hall, asking, 'Is there somewhere private we could talk?'

In truth, Beatrice didn't want to spend any time talking to this woman, but at the sight of the lady's blush, her curiosity about the woman's need for secrecy won out. She nodded towards the corridor near the stairwell that led down to the armoury and cells.

Once there, Lady Emelina folded her hands together and said, 'It seems you and I have got off to a bad start.'

What difference would that make? It wasn't as if they were going to be residing under the same roof. 'I don't understand why that would matter to you.'

'Lord Gregor is a friend, a special friend, and I think it would make a difference to him.'

'Special friend?' Beatrice had no clue what that meant…special friend?

'He put himself at risk to rescue me from my former betrothed.'

'You needed rescuing?'

Lady Emelina leaned closer to whisper, 'Yes, just the same as you.'

The same as her? What did this woman know about what had happened to her? 'Nothing happened to me.'

'Oh, Lady Beatrice, Gregor has told me how your former betrothed thought to take advantage of you.'

Something was wrong here. For one thing she and Charles were never betrothed. For another, Gregor would never have said anything to anyone about the circumstances of their meeting. He had promised not to say a word and he was far too private with personal matters to have shared that even with someone who called him a friend.

Beatrice frowned. 'He told you about my former betrothed?'

'Oh, yes, he did. He mentioned that he nearly had to kill the man to keep him away. Your suitor must have loved you very much.'

Beatrice watched the woman while she talked. Something seemed…familiar about her. Yet they'd never met before now. Something in her all-too-forced smile, in the way she used her hands to punctuate certain words. The only other person she knew who did that was…

Beatrice gasped.

She heard a noise behind her, then almost instantly felt something hit the back of her head. Before everything went black, she whispered, 'Charles.'

Gregor made one last inspection of the cottage. Everything seemed in place. He and his men had managed to smuggle away all he'd wanted and more as the table filled with food would attest. There was enough there to feed the two of them for a month.

He could probably burn down the entire village with the supply of candles in the basket sitting alongside the bedside table. He'd almost forgotten to nab a candleholder, but had grabbed a couple from the bedchamber when he'd been there to retrieve sheets and a cover.

'Lord Gregor!' Simon came to a rocking stop inside the cottage. 'You are needed back at the keep.'

Now? 'For what?'

'Lady Beatrice is missing.'

'What do you mean *missing*?'

He followed Simon out of the door as the man explained. 'Her mother has looked for her everywhere. When she couldn't find her, she enlisted the Empress's aid. Men were sent to scour the keep and the buildings in the bailey.'

'Did anyone think to check the battlements?'

'Yes, I did once I remembered she seemed to have a fondness for walking in the breeze.'

Her fondness was for the quiet more than the breeze. Mounting his horse, Gregor asked, 'Is anyone else missing?'

At Simon's tight-lipped grimace, Gregor's stomach tightened. 'Who?'

'I am sorry, my lord, the men were caught off guard.'

He was in no mood for guessing games. 'Damn it, man, who else is missing?'

Simon spurred his horse ahead. Passing Gregor, he said, 'The prisoner and Lady Emelina.'

He nearly flew past his man, shouting, 'If Beatrice comes to any harm, all of you will pay dearly.'

'Yes, my lord.'

Gregor entered the bailey at a gallop. He nearly leapt from the saddle before the beast came to a full stop. Tossing the stable hand the reins, he ordered, 'Get the other horses saddled.'

He stormed into the keep. Spotting Beatrice's family gathered on the dais, he approached, asking, 'Any news?'

The Empress shook her head. 'None.'

'How did this happen?'

'From what we could ascertain, Lady Emelina must have distracted one of the guards enough to get him to back against the cell. The prisoner broke his neck. From that point it is anyone's guess.'

While he could understand how the lady distracted the men, he didn't understand how two of them could have been overcome by one woman.

Beatrice's mother touched his arm. 'You are going after her?'

What kind of question was that? 'Of course I am.'

'Does anyone know how long they've been gone?'

Matilda shook her head. 'No. But I wouldn't think it could be any more than two hours.'

He checked to make certain Simon was gathering the men, then turned to head into his private chamber to don his armour.

'Lord Gregor.'

Startled by FitzHenry's use of the title, he looked at the older man.

'Neither of them can captain a ship, but they could have hired one. Two hours would have given them a good head start, so check the cove first, then the caves.'

Gregor stared at him for a moment. Naturally the man appeared angry, but he was also agitated, as if ready to jump out of his own skin—a nervous energy that Gregor fully understood. His knowledge of the island could prove useful, so he said, 'You have ten minutes—get ready to ride.'

Instantly about twenty years fell off the man as he dashed for the stairs.

Matilda only shook her head and said, 'You'd best watch your back. My brother isn't inexperienced with a sword.'

Beatrice's mother took immediate offence. 'He is not dishonourable. You do him a severe injustice by hinting otherwise.'

Having no time for this argument, Gregor left the two women to argue and went into his chamber, relieved to see that his squire and a page were already laying out his mail and weapons.

He dressed quickly and went back out to the Great Hall. Simon had gathered the men. Each was fully armed and ready to leave.

Gregor took four swords off the stack next to a support beam. He perused the gathering, picking out four of the men from Warehaven that he'd already decided he could trust and handed each a weapon. 'Guard the women with your lives.'

James, Colin, Harold and Daniel stepped forward. James cleared his throat, then began, 'My lord—'

Gregor cut him off with a glare. They thought he'd leave them behind? He was not about to let a stranger find Beatrice—she would not be afraid of these men. 'You ride with me.'

He pulled aside his squire and eight of his own men. 'Guard this keep. Nobody comes or goes. Make sure every entrance or exit is guarded.'

Gregor knew by the downcast look on his squire's face that the young man was not happy with his task in the least, but to his credit he said nothing, only nodded and pulled his weapon to the ready.

FitzHenry, followed by his two guards, joined them in the hall. Gregor looked at the man's sword. 'Make sure you only use that on those who took my wife.'

Beatrice's mother joined them to pat her husband's chest. 'I'd nearly forgotten the bastard warrior I fell so hard for.' She raised up on her toes to kiss his cheek before handing him his nasal helmet. 'Bring our baby back safely, my love.'

'Wake up!' A loud clap near her ear followed the shout.

Beatrice opened her eyes. Her hands were bound behind her, but she could feel the coolness of the earth beneath her. They were still on the island, which meant that there was a good chance she would be found. Had she been placed upon a ship there would have been little hope for any quick rescue.

'There she is. Thankfully you didn't kill her.'

Beatrice squinted against the shrillness of Lady Emelina's voice. It seemed to bounce off the walls around her before piercing her throbbing head like an arrow.

She kept the smile from her mouth as she realised they'd brought her to the caves. This was where she, Isabella and Jared had spent most of their childhood playing. Someone unfamiliar with the winding passages might get lost here permanently, or worse, if they didn't know which mouth was safe to use as an exit, they could walk through expecting to step out of the darkness only to find themselves falling through the air to the sharp rocks below.

Of course this knowledge was only useful if she lived and could get free. Otherwise what she knew would make no difference.

'Tell me, Lady Emelina, are you his sister?'

'Charles's? No, his cousin.'

Ah, that explained the slight differences that prevented immediate recognition. It still didn't explain one thing. 'How is it that I've never met you, or heard about you?'

'Since our parents aren't as royally connected as yours, they had no choice in taking sides between Stephen and Matilda. To keep at least some of us safe, the family split up—mine chose Normandy, where Charles's came to England. There has been little opportunity for us to communicate since then and it was deemed safer that way.'

The explanation made perfect sense, especially considering that many families had done the same thing, hoping that one day this conflict would end and they could all be together again.

'Why am I here?' She needed to keep them talking, keeping their attention less directed to what she was doing behind her back. The floor of these caves was littered with broken bits of pottery and pieces of sharp rock. She rooted around behind her in the dirt, trying to get her fingers on one she could use as a knife to cut the ropes binding her wrists.

Charles and another man walked into the light from the torch. 'So you can watch your husband die.'

Beatrice wasn't surprised to see him. Since someone had to have hit her on the back of the head, she'd assumed it had been Charles right away.

She looked at Emelina. 'But I thought Gregor was your friend.' If she remembered correctly, he was her *special* friend. Her fingers closed around a sharp-edged rock. She turned it around so she could slowly saw it against the ropes.

The woman laughed. 'That mangy beast?' She shivered. 'No. He was merely a useful tool.'

Mangy beast? Her husband was far from mangy and most definitely no beast. Beatrice took a breath against the swimming of her head. Her makeshift knife slipped, cutting into her palm. *Focus*. She needed to keep her wits about her and not let little things distract her.

'A tool for what?'

'Ships. Men,' Charles added.

'What do you need with ships and men?'

Charles squatted down in front of her. 'Why should your family be the only ones to benefit from something my father helped start?'

As far as she knew, his father Lord Wardham had done nothing more than lend her father enough coin to buy the materials for the first ship. After that, he'd wanted nothing to do with any of the work or planning. However, it wasn't something she was in any position to argue at the moment.

'So you did all of this for ships and men? After you burned three ships that you could have taken?'

'The fire hadn't been set for loss of property. I'd received word that Lord Gregor was aboard one of the two larger vessels. He was supposed to have died in the fire. Little did we know he was safely locked inside a cottage, rutting with his whore.'

Focus. Focus, she silently repeated to herself. She couldn't afford to let them distract her from her task at hand, nor could she give them the slightest hint that she was up to something.

Charles stroked a finger down her cheek. 'Which is why he must die. He has interfered in our relationship enough. So when he comes to rescue you, which we both know he will, he will be caught by surprise and put down like the dog he is while you watch. But fear not, Beatrice, you will join him.'

She was relieved to see that Charles seemed to have regained some of his wits, so she didn't fear he'd do anything to her before Gregor arrived. However, he was wrong. If anyone needed to be put down like a mad dog, it was he, not Gregor.

Her husband had given Charles every chance to

make himself scarce, but he insisted on showing up over and over, inviting trouble. How could she ever have wanted to marry this man? She still couldn't understand how she could have been so fooled.

'It is simple,' Lady Emaline explained further. 'We both seek revenge. Roul's death will ensure he never gets the chance to interfere in anyone's life again.'

'Interfered? I thought he'd rescued you.'

'I required no rescuing.' The woman made a dismissive sound, then added, 'The fool misinterpreted love-play as abuse. After his interference, nothing I said could convince Comte Souhomme back to my bed and now I am betrothed to a man with no title and little wealth. Roul destroyed my future and it's only fair I return the favour.'

The last thread of the bindings broke away and Beatrice quickly clasped her hands together to keep her arms from falling free. She wasn't strong enough to overpower three people. But she could wait. And she could warn her husband of the trap.

She hoped he didn't take too long, because the warm blood running between her hands meant she'd done more than simply nick her palm, she'd cut it deep enough that it was now beginning to throb.

Bleeding to death as Charles's prisoner was not how she was going to die. It wasn't an option. Especially not now. Not after she'd found someone

she was willing to wed even if it had been prear-
ranged.

A sliver of sunlight still glimmered through the
mouth of the cave when she heard a noise. Unfortunately, the other three had heard it too.

Charles handed Lady Emelina a knife and
waved her over to guard Beatrice while he and
the other man took up a position on either side of
the entryway.

Beatrice raised her brows when Emelina stood
over her with the knife pointed in the opposite
direction. She wanted to tell the woman that her
stance was wrong if she really needed to do any
harm. It was a mistake that Beatrice welcomed
because it would make it much easier to surprise
the woman and get the knife away from her when
the time came.

The jingle of spurs, the clanking of chainmail
and the heavy steps of booted feet heralded the arrival of armed men. She kept her stare on Charles.
He would be the first to flinch, the first to make
a move.

In the flickering torchlight she saw his shoulders bunch as he leaned low, getting ready to lunge.

She threw herself at Emelina, screaming, 'One
left, one right!'

Emelina fought like a wild animal, swinging the
knife blindly, the fingers of her free hand curled
trying to gouge anything she could reach. She
backed Beatrice down the side tunnel.

Beatrice swiftly sent up a prayer for forgiveness for what she was about to do. The second her foot hit a dip on the darkening path, she started counting footsteps while fending off Emelina. When she reached thirty steps, she quickened her pace, turned and ran towards the sound of the wind. She counted twenty more paces before she threw herself against the wall of the cave.

Not expecting the move, Emelina's momentum kept her moving forward—a step too far.

The woman's fading scream echoed through the tunnel.

'Beatrice!'

Still hugging the wall, she called out, 'I am here, hold on. Let me come to you.' The last thing she wanted was Gregor following Emelina over the edge by accident. If the strength of wind whipping just inside the mouth didn't pull you out, the overhang of the opening was deceptive. By the time anyone could realise the floor didn't extend as far as the walls and overhang, it was too late to do anything to save themselves.

'I am right here.'

She followed the sound of his voice in the dark with her hands outstretched. The instant her fingers made contact, he grabbed her and pulled her against his chest.

'Are you unharmed?'

Now that it was over, she was trembling like a leaf in the wind. 'No. I cut my hand with a rock.'

'We need to get you out of here.'

At his hesitation, she offered, 'Put the breeze at your back.'

He turned them around on the path and headed back to the main cave.

The bodies of Charles and his man lay on the floor. The sword wounds to their chests had been fatal. Her father and Sir Simon stood near the bodies, their weapons still in their hands.

The hard-packed dirt floor beneath her started buckling like storm-swept waves upon the sea. Beatrice stumbled, unable to remain upright on the moving ground. 'Gregor, I… Gregor…'

She vaguely heard his shout at the same time his one arm came behind her unsteady legs to lift her from her feet and the other cradled her back to hold her against his chest.

The next thing she knew, she was resting on a bed. 'Lady Roul, can you hear me?'

She frowned. Who was the stranger talking to?

Gregor asked, 'Beatrice, can you hear me?'

Opening her eyes to complete blackness, she said, 'Yes, I can hear you.' Her heart raced as she gasped for breath. 'I can't see you.'

Frantic, she tried to raise her arm, but it was being held down and someone was stabbing her palm. She struggled to sit up only to have strong hands push her shoulders back down on to the bed. 'Stop. You are safe.'

The bed dipped as someone sat next to her. 'It is fine,' Gregor assured her. 'Here, let me move the cloth.'

A damp weight was lifted from her face, forcing her to squint against the bright torchlight. She recognised the midwife's cottage, but not the man sitting next to the bed with his wrapped-up foot on the edge of the mattress while he stitched a nasty gouge closed on her palm.

Gregor nodded towards the man. 'This is Sir Matthew. He is Matilda's surgeon. I thought he would do a better job sewing your hand back together than your father or I could.'

She glanced at the man's foot. The surgeon laughed, then explained, 'I fell off the deck of the forecastle and broke my foot.' He leaned closer to add in a near whisper, 'I had to set the bone myself. And I have to admit, it hurt.'

Beatrice laughed, then winced as a sharp pain laced through her head.

Matthew said, 'I wouldn't advise much laughing for a day or two. They whacked you on the head hard enough to break it.'

A rumbling laugh she recognised as coming from her father rushed across the cottage. 'We always knew she had a hard head. Now we have proof.'

'Randall, don't torment the girl.'

'Mother?'

'Yes, dear.' Her mother came and sat on the

other side of the bed. She leaned over to brush Beatrice's hair from her face. 'And by the way, sweeting, *you* are Lady Roul.'

'Oh. That's right.'

Gregor snorted.

The surgeon finished the last stitch and snipped the thread. While he wrapped a cloth around her hand, he said, 'This is going to hurt for a while. If it's your sword hand, I would suggest not testing your weapon too soon. Allow it time to heal first.'

'Not something I need worry about, since I'm not very adept at fighting.'

'Oh, I don't know, my lady, hear tell you handled yourself admirably and hardly needed rescue. And I am positive this wound didn't come from any sewing session. Did you truly use a rock?'

'I had nothing else.'

'Mmm-hmm. Well, you rest.' He turned to her father. 'If you could get my assistants to help me, I'll return to the ship and check in on her tomorrow.'

Her mother reached across to tap Gregor's shoulder. 'Go back to the keep and change. See to your men. I'll sit with her until you return.'

He leaned over to kiss Beatrice's forehead. 'I will be back as soon as possible. Is there anything I can bring you?'

Beatrice plucked at her gown. 'Something other than this.' Her hand flew to her head. 'Oh, no, the circlet.'

'Is not lost.' He stroked her cheek. 'It was lying on the steps leading down to the cells.'

Once the men left, Beatrice sighed and tried to get comfortable, but she was stiff and sore and nothing seemed to ease her discomfort.

Her mother distracted her by saying, 'I think we may have a problem.'

'Don't say that.'

'The two of them are up to something and I like it not.'

Baffled, she asked, 'What could they be up to?'

'I don't know. That's what I don't like. They whisper together like a couple of young boys plotting mischief.'

Beatrice groaned. The idea of King Henry's Executioner and King David's Wolf plotting something together could be a recipe for trouble.

Chapter Seventeen

Beatrice's scream jerked Gregor upright on the bed. She fought an imaginary foe in her sleep—again. He had hoped that leaving an oil lamp burning in the bedchamber might have lessened her dreams. Unfortunately, that hadn't seemed to help.

'Beatrice.' He gently shook her, trying to drag her from another night terror. 'Wake up.'

She threw herself against his chest, sobbing. 'I killed her.'

It was the same complaint as last night. He didn't know how to make her understand there hadn't been a choice in Lady Emelina's death. 'Stop this. Beatrice, it was you or her and you certainly couldn't fight the woman with your hand torn open and bleeding. What else were you going to do?'

She'd barely slept the last two nights. That first night in the cottage had been terrible. So her parents had easily agreed to take the cottage, thinking that perhaps being back in her familiar bedchamber might lessen her distress. But it hadn't done so in the least.

The dark circles beneath her eyes and the fear that never left her darting gaze tore at his heart. He didn't know what to do for her. He hated the way she shook—terrified of the memory that wouldn't leave her alone even in her sleep.

'I led her to her death. Intentionally.'

'And she was chasing you with a knife. Do you think she would have hesitated to use it on you?'

'I should have stayed in the cave and not led her down the tunnel.'

'You followed your gut, it is what probably saved your life.' He stroked her hair and rocked her. 'What's done is done, Beatrice.'

'It was a grievous sin.' Her voice was hardly a whisper.

'Have you talked to your priest?'

'Yes.'

'And what did he say?' He'd already talked with Father Peter. So he knew the man had tried to explain to her that what she'd done was in self-defence, therefore not considered murder. In desperation the priest had given her a penance and absolution.

'That it was not murder.'

'Still you didn't believe him. Not even after he absolved you of your imaginary sin?'

She shook her head.

'Oh, Beatrice, what are we to do with you? Tell me how I can help you.' He was serious. At this moment he would do anything to give her peace from the fear eating at her.

When she remained silent, he mused, 'It is too bad you are not one of my men, I could deal with you as I did the guard who let this happen and be done with it.'

She pulled away from his chest and looked at him. 'This wasn't the guard's fault.'

'I beg to disagree. Had the two of them not let Lady Emelina distract them, they would both still be alive and you wouldn't have been injured.'

'Both still be alive? Did you put the other one to death?'

'What are you thinking?' He looked at her in shock. 'No. But at the present my squire has more responsibilities than he does.'

'That is not fair.'

'Fair? What does fair have to do with it? He is a guard. I am his liege. I gave him an order. He failed to follow the order, resulting in death and injury to others. He doesn't get to apologise and pretend nothing is amiss. Right now he should be grateful that he isn't without a position at all.'

Beatrice sniffed back tears and laid back down on the bed. Gregor looked at her. She was sad. She was upset. She was afraid. And he was at the end of his patience.

'I need something to drink. Can I bring you anything?'

She shook her head.

Gregor sighed. Never before had he been at such a loss as to what to do. He patted her shoulder. 'I will be back.'

He left the bedchamber knowing she wouldn't

fall back to sleep while she was alone. Thankfully he saw Almedha in the Great Hall and asked her to keep Beatrice company. He needed some time alone, to think, to clear his head and to soothe the anger poking at him. He was angry with the whole situation. And, yes, to his dismay, a little irritated with Beatrice.

How was he going to make her understand, to see reason?

Gregor saw Simon shaking his head as he approached. The man extended a flagon of wine, asking, 'Is she still having bad dreams?'

'Yes.'

'And of course you've explained that she is not to blame for the woman's death.'

Again Gregor answered, 'Yes.'

'So the Lady of Roul is reacting in the same manner as the Lord of Roul does.'

'What?' Gregor rubbed his pounding forehead.

'She is no more to blame for Lady Emclina's death than you are for Sarah's.'

Not willing to talk about his first wife, or himself, any further in the crowded hall, even if most of the men there were asleep, he motioned towards his private chamber.

Once behind the closed door, Simon changed the subject and asked, 'Have you told her about tomorrow?'

'No. I think it would be safer not to.'

'And when she discovers what is happening?'

Gregor smiled. 'I believe it is your task to keep the women from the field of battle.'

'You sound certain it will come to that.'

'Would you give all of this up without a fight?'

His man shook his head. 'No.'

'Neither would I.' He took a swallow of the wine, then handed the container back to Simon. 'Go find your bed. I think I'll spend the night here.'

Once Simon left, Gregor kicked his feet up on the desk. After he and FitzHenry faced each other tomorrow, he would soon discover just how much his wife wanted to be married to David's Wolf.

He should be spending this last night with Beatrice since it might be a very long time before he'd get the chance to do so again. However, with her current state of mind, he didn't see tonight being any different from the last two. Her focus would not be on his touch and later her sleep would be fitful. Besides, he needed some sleep before the sun rose. The last thing he wanted to do was to face her father without having all his wits about him.

With a soft curse, Gregor lowered his feet and shoved away from the desk. No. He wasn't spending this night alone.

When he walked back into their bedchamber, Almedha held her finger to her lips before she left. Beatrice was sleeping.

He undressed and then stood by the bed, looking down at her. Her frown creased her forehead and she mumbled in her sleep. Gregor wanted to soothe away the frown lines, but didn't want to wake her up.

But then she looked up at him. 'What are you doing?'

'Watching you sleep.'

Beatrice pulled down the covers. 'Come to bed.'

He slid under the covers and she instantly rolled on to her side and pressed her back against his chest.

She came to him so willingly. It was too bad she couldn't trust his words as easily as she did his body.

He curled an arm around her, holding her close. She entwined one hand with his, bringing it to her lips. 'Thank you.'

'For what?' Gregor moved his head closer, whispering against her ear. 'I've done nothing.'

'Your patience.'

Little did she know how much he wanted to rage from the uselessness he felt.

'How did you bear it?' she asked.

'Bear what?' She was so warm and soft against him. It was difficult to keep his attention on her words and not give in to the demands of his body.

'Killing your first man?'

'Beatrice.' This was something he shouldn't have to discuss with his wife. He was supposed to have protected her, not left her in a danger so great that she'd had to defend herself to the death.

The part that sickened him was that she'd been right—to a point. He'd known that Emelina had been up to something. But like his wife he'd thought the woman had wanted him in her bed. There hadn't been the slightest clue that her real intent had been to kill him or anyone else who got in her way.

He moved enough to roll her on to her back next to him. 'Beatrice, I am so sorry. This never should have happened.'

'It wasn't your fault.'

'Yes, it was. I knew your suspicions had been right. But like you I thought she'd wanted something else entirely.'

She looked up at him, a small smile playing about her lips. 'And here I thought you were so naïve that you didn't know when a woman was trying to seduce you.'

He laughed. 'Yes. That's me, innocent and naïve.'

She drew a finger along his collarbone. 'You still haven't answered my question.'

'It was during a battle and came down to me or him.'

'That simple?' Her finger trailed down the centre of his chest.

'Yes, it is just that simple. You either choose life, or you choose death. I much prefer living.'

'So do I, but I would make a terrible warrior.'

'Actually, you wouldn't. While accepting the outcome is simple, the taking of a life is not simple, nor easy. It was not meant to be easy, Beatrice. That is the whole idea. If you stop feeling bad or guilty for ending a life, then something is wrong with you. I would not have a soldier under my command who felt no guilt, no remorse.'

She frowned as if considering his words. And when her frown cleared it was all he could do not to sigh in relief.

'Gregor?'

'Yes?'

'Can I still ask you anything?'

'That's not changed.'

'If I am not to carry Emelina's death in my heart, why do you carry Sarah's?'

That was a hard question. One that even Simon had hinted at. While he'd been rather angry at Simon's hinting, he wasn't put off by Beatrice's question. In fact, for the first time the question didn't make his chest tighten.

'I don't know, Beatrice. I was young and I'd had such high hopes for the two of us, for our future together, that I'd never expected, or dreamed, she would do something so rash, so horrific to herself because of who I am.'

'Do you think she was perhaps weak and too fearful to be rational?'

'It's possible.' More than possible, it was most likely true.

'I think Charles was that way, too. He certainly

went out of his way to invite death of late. It was as if he wanted you to kill him.'

'I agree. Charles did seem to lack the ability to be rational.'

'Do you think Lady Emelina would have killed me?'

He was thankful that she'd turned their conversation away from Sarah. Somehow Beatrice's simple logic had begun to ease the festering pain he'd carried for so long. He needed some time to accept the idea that maybe Sarah's weakness hadn't been his fault.

'Emelina knew all was lost, so, yes, I am sure she would have.' Although right now, with Beatrice caressing his abdomen with the palm of her hand, he was more certain that she was going to be the death of him.

'Gregor?'

'Yes?'

She rolled on to her side and stroked her palm along the hard length of his erection, asking, 'Do you think we could—?'

He didn't wait for her to finish her question before nudging her on to her back and settling between her legs. When she hooked her legs around his and pulled him to her, he knew without a doubt that he hadn't mistaken her request.

What he had mistaken was her urgency. She had no wish to tarry. From the way she curled the fingers of her uninjured hand into his upper arm, the nails pressing into his skin, she had no desire to savour their time together.

Gregor scooped her into his arms and rolled on to his back. She sat up on him, straddling his hips, the wide-eyed look of surprise on her face nearly making him laugh. But her surprise soon faded as she set about mastering this new position. Awkward at first, she quickly found a rhythm that suited her need.

Unwilling to give up an opportunity to tease her further, Gregor stroked his hands along her legs, trailing imaginary paths on the top of her thighs with his fingertips, caressing her soft skin from knee to hip. All the while he watched the play of expressions flit across her face.

From surprise to determination, then to devilry once she'd found her rhythm and thought to torment him. His teasing touch at the juncture of her thighs gained him her heavy-eyed gaze of desire and lust.

When lust turned to frustrated need, he grasped her hips, holding her still, as he took them both swirling over the edge to fulfilment. Beatrice fell gasping on to his chest, her ragged breaths no steadier than his own.

Their bodies lax, they drowsed, savouring the fading ripples of desire. Gregor pulled the cover over them, Beatrice still resting warm and sleepy on his chest. Just as he was about to drift off to sleep, she moved her head, her lips near his ear, her breath warm against his neck, and whispered, 'I love you, Gregor.'

He caressed the back of her head, holding her close, wishing for all the world he could give her the words she longed to hear.

But he couldn't. He would risk much with the rising of the sun, he was not yet ready to fully risk his heart, too.

She moved off his chest, but to his relief did not move away. Instead, she rolled on to her side, the soft round fullness of her hips pressed against his groin, her back against his chest with her head tucked beneath his chin.

Just as they slept on the nights they'd spent together, she slipped a foot between his ankles and used his one arm as a pillow. The other arm he wrapped tightly around her abdomen, which she in turn hugged with both of her arms.

It was warm. It was comfortable. It felt…right. His sleep would be deep and restful. Whereas on the nights they didn't share a bed, he awoke still tired, feeling as if something were missing.

He didn't know if this was love, or a part of love. All he knew for certain was that this wife of his was brash, she was bold and, for right now, she was his.

Beatrice groaned. Something threatened to jar her awake. Refusing to give in to the urge to open her eyes, she lay there enjoying the fact that she finally felt rested and alive again. She'd slept through the night in Gregor's arms, free of night terrors, free of bad dreams.

She reached out across the bed, searching for him with her fingertips. Finding nothing but cold, empty sheets, she opened her eyes, dismayed to see that the sun had barely risen. Why had he left so early?

The distinct sound of swords clanging against each other drew her up from the mattress with a frown.

Again, weapon met weapon and she turned to look towards the direction the sounds had come from. This time the noise of the weapons was joined by cheers and jeers of men shouting.

'Beatrice!'

Her mother ran through the chamber door. 'Do you hear that?'

Beatrice swung her legs over the edge of the bed and, with a sinking feeling in the pit of her stomach, walked to look out of the narrow window.

The sight that met her tentative gaze threatened to knock her to her knees.

Her ears hadn't deceived her, there were indeed men fighting.

In the clearing, just beyond the main gate, two groups of bystanders had formed—one group from Warehaven, the other from Roul. Matilda and her guards stood at the entrance of a tent which had been erected a little further out.

In the centre of the bystanders, were two mail-

clad, armed combatants. Beatrice didn't need anyone to tell her that one was her father, the other
her husband.

She grasped her mother's arm. 'What is happening?'

'What we knew would eventually come to
pass.'

'But, I thought…' She let her unnecessary words
trail off. Obviously she'd thought incorrectly. Just
because the two men had seemed to have been getting along didn't mean anything had been settled.

'Must they settle it in this manner? Is there
nothing we can do?'

Her mother looked at her and Beatrice then noticed the red-rimmed eyes. The time for doing anything was past. Apparently her mother had tried
unsuccessfully to talk her father out of this fight
for Warehaven.

And Gregor had so expertly taken away her opportunity to try the same with him.

She closed her eyes and groaned. He'd so expertly distracted her that she'd told him of her feel-
ings for him. How could she have been so foolish?

It had been one thing to realise that, yes, she
did love her husband, but that was private, a secret
she'd shared with nobody. Something she could
think about, something she could test in her mind,
on her heart. Something not quite real. However,
sharing it had only given it strength and made it
real. And that strength would only serve to make

her pain very, very real should anything happen to him.

Another clang of swords caused her mother to jump and hide her face in her hands.

Beatrice swore softly. She wasn't going to stand here doing nothing.

She grabbed her clothing and pulled it on. Not caring whether the gown was straight, she wrapped her belt about the waist and sat to tug on her stockings and soft boots.

'What are you doing?'

'What does it look like? I cannot just sit here worrying, Mother. It will only rob me of my senses.'

'Your father forbade me to attend.'

Beatrice shrugged. 'Nobody said a word to me.'

She stormed across the chamber and pulled open the door, surprised that the entry wasn't blocked by guards.

Turning back to look at her mother, she stated, 'You can stay here if you wish. But I can't. I simply cannot.'

Chapter Eighteen

Not wanting to take the time to go down the stairs, to the Great Hall and then out to the wall, Beatrice went up the tower steps, her mother following right behind. She pulled open the door leading out to the wall walk—her way was blocked.

Sir Simon looked at her, asking, 'Is there something you require, Lady Beatrice?'

'Yes. I need you to get out of my way.'

'I'm sorry, but I can't do that.'

Beatrice took a deep breath, stood up as straight and tall as possible, threw back her shoulders and ordered, 'Stand aside.'

Sir Simon studied her for a moment, then pressed his back against the wall to let her by. 'You don't leave this wall, do you understand me, my lady? I have my orders.'

She nodded. 'I hear you.'

'That isn't what I asked. Do you understand me?'

Gregor's man was getting to know her far too well.

She brushed past him, answering, 'Yes.'

She and her mother came to a stop near the main gate tower. Sir Simon was right behind them. They leaned over a cut-out in the wall to watch.

Beatrice held her breath and swallowed hard

to keep down the threatening churn of her stomach, as they watched two well-experienced warriors battle.

Both men were about the same size, her father's chest a little bigger, a little rounder. But where her father had more experience with a sword, Gregor was younger and quicker on his feet.

Neither wasted any movement. There was no wild swinging of their weapon. No unnecessary jabbing. They circled each other, but neither one of them wasted time posturing or posing.

Gregor lunged. Beatrice and her mother gasped. Her father raised his shield, held his attacker off and pushed him away with a blow to the side of the head.

Beatrice narrowed her eyes. Something wasn't right.

Then her father lunged and the movements were repeated—Gregor raised his shield, fending off the attack, pushed her father away and while her father's guard was down, Gregor slammed his fist against her father's head.

Now her mother narrowed her eyes and looked at Beatrice.

While the two men fought back and forth in the same manner, she watched them, closely. And again thought the same thing. Something wasn't right.

Whenever each of them had the opportunity to end this fight, they didn't. While it looked legitimate, appearing viciously and earnestly fought, something was off just enough to catch her attention.

For one thing, how many times had her father told them that the nasal piece of a helmet was the weakest part? He'd said that if you wanted to kill your opponent, or incapacitate him, you must hold tight to the grip of your sword and slam that mail-covered fist straight into the nasal piece.

The narrower length of metal would break and if the blow didn't shove the broken bit into your enemy's face, killing them, it would so injure them that you could then end the fight with either a death blow, or move in to quickly disarm them and take them prisoner.

Each of them had just had more than a couple of chances to do just that. But neither one had.

Her mother nudged her shoulder, mouthing, 'Look.'

They had dropped their shields and were now fighting in close contact with each. To her amazement, from this distance, it appeared as if they were actually speaking to each other whenever they came close enough to communicate.

She could be wrong, but Simon's softly issued curse behind her led her to believe she was correct.

Beatrice looked over her shoulder at the man and from the hard scowl etched on his face, he was not at all happy with his liege lord at the moment.

Her attention flew to the Empress. If she and

her mother could see that something wasn't right, surely Matilda could, too. However, her aunt was half-turned away from the fight, talking to someone inside the tent. So only part of her attention could have been on the battle.

Beatrice wondered what the men all thought. The groups gathered seemed to be enjoying the spectacle, just as they would have had this been a true fight. So, there was nothing odd there.

The two men pushed away from each other. To her horror, Gregor raised his weapon, the blade turned flat at shoulder height pointed straight at her father's throat. Before she could think to scream, he rammed the weapon home.

What had seemed to her nothing more than a ruse had turned lethal. Her father hit the ground, blood pooling beneath him. The gathering surrounding them fell silent immediately.

Gregor approached Matilda and threw his bloodied weapon at her feet.

Beatrice's scream finally escaped and she raced down the ladder, out the gate and across the field to beat her fists against Gregor's chest. With each blow, she could feel the shattering of her heart. It ached inside her chest.

'You lied!' she shouted, ignoring the stares of those gathered. 'How many times did you tell me to trust you?'

Stoic, he remained silent beneath her verbal onslaught.

'You are a liar, Roul.' Her voice rose, the shouts tore at her throat. 'You vowed to protect me, but I am not safe, I am not unharmed. I will never trust you.'

When he still said nothing, she lowered her voice. 'I was wrong. I do not love you. I could never love you.' Beatrice gasped at the pain lacing through her. 'I never want to see you again.' She shoved her hands against his chest. 'Go back to your precious King and leave me alone. I've no need for your protection and do not desire any more of your lies or the pain you so readily inflict.'

His silence infuriated her. She glared at him, tearing her wedding band from her finger. She threw it at him, screaming, 'I hate you, Roul! I wish to God I had never met you. I would have suffered less had you left me to be tortured by Charles and his friends.'

Beatrice ignored the hushed gasps from the gathered crowd. She lowered her head, unable to look any longer at the man she'd married. Her mother came to her side and took her arm. 'Come with me. I have need of you.'

Sir Simon, James, Colin and Harold got her father on to his shield and then carried him to the keep.

She looked back into the now-dispersing crowd. Where had Gregor gone? Why did she care? She'd told him to leave and he had. She should be grateful. Yet gratitude wasn't the emotion churning in her stomach.

Beatrice followed her mother into the keep and up to the chamber she'd just last night shared with Gregor—the chamber where she'd foolishly declared her love for the man who'd just destroyed her life.

Her breath caught on a sob. How was she to live with the knowledge that she'd been the one to bring David's Wolf to their door?

Beatrice fought back the tremors rippling down her spine. She needed to learn how to be a warrior as cold and heartless as the one she'd wed. Otherwise it would be impossible to face the coming days.

Her mother stood inside the doorway, waiting for the men from Roul to leave, before storming across the chamber to smack her husband's shoulder.

'Damn, woman! That hurt. I am injured after all.'

'I will injure you. Get off of that bed so I can remove your armour.'

Beatrice stood unmoving by the door through this incomprehensible conversation.

'Come, child, help your mother.' Her father drew her over to him.

Her mind in a whirl, unable to make sense of what her eyes had seen and were now seeing, she helped remove his mail silently. She had no words. Too many thoughts were crowding her mind at once.

Beneath the mail was a padded shirt soaked with blood that still dripped from high on his shoulder. Her mother pulled a knife from her father's scabbard and attacked the drenched garment.

'You have lost the ability to reason completely.' She cut away at least three inches of additional padding from the shoulders of his shirt, then withdrew a small bag that she threw to the floor. She rested her head against her husband's forehead, asking, 'Pig, sheep, or goat?'

'Chicken.' Her father shrugged. 'It was all we could get without being seen.'

Beatrice looked from her parents to the bag on the floor. Picking it up, she realised it was nothing more than a blood-filled bag made from the intestines of an animal.

Rage made her stagger before she caught her footing and threw the bag at her father. 'This was a ruse? A jest played out at my expense?'

Her mother grabbed her arm and pulled her to the bed. Pushing her down on the edge of the mattress, she said, 'Not now, Beatrice. Do not make an issue of this now. Wait.'

'Wait?' She drew in a deep breath. 'Wait? I sent my husband away because I thought he'd killed my father. I chose Warehaven over Roul. That is not something I can simply take back with an apology. And you wish me to wait?'

She turned on her mother. 'You were in on this, too?' Beatrice sprang off the bed, unable to sit still. 'Am I the only one who was made to appear the fool?'

Her father's reddening face warned her that he was losing patience. She didn't care. He had just helped to successfully destroy any chance she had for happiness. He could be as angry as he wished.

'Girl, sit down and listen.'

She took a seat on the small stool near the alcove.

'King David wanted bloodshed. Matilda knew that, since in a fit of anger over ships I refused to give her, she'd put him up to making the request. He issued the order to Gregor, one of his Wolves, knowing it would be carried out without question. He hadn't expected this interference of Matilda.'

Her mother chimed in, saying, 'You know your aunt. Her temper may catch fire at times, but when it comes to your father, it eventually cools. It was too late to call a halt to David's order. However, she suggested perhaps Gregor and your father put their heads together. So they did.'

'But we couldn't let anyone else, especially those who will return to David, suspect anything was afoot. They had to believe all was real. The only other thing Matilda demanded was that blood was shed.'

'I never said what kind of blood.' Matilda entered the chamber and looked down at the bag on the floor, adding, 'But once it was done, I handed the signed documents transferring Warehaven to Gregor over.'

Beatrice's father asked, 'They were signed by everyone?'

Matilda nodded. 'Yes, they were. Even Stephen.'

Her father breathed a sigh of relief. 'Thank you.'

Beatrice knew that Warehaven had not been entailed to the crown since King William had worn the crown. But when her father had taken control of Warehaven and after his father had died, he had convinced Stephen and Matilda both to honour and reconfirm his right to Warehaven.

Beatrice rose and looked at all of them. 'None of this was even necessary. Gregor placed his future, and the futures of his brothers at risk for nothing. You could have simply betrothed me to him and the outcome would have been simpler, cleaner, but in the end the same.'

'No.' Matilda stepped forward. 'Your precious Gregor ruined the marriage between Lady Emelina and Comte Souhomme, by rescuing her from something that had been none of his concern. He cost me much gold and many men that I needed for this war with Stephen—gold and men that I still need desperately. I was angry and demanded revenge through my uncle. Gregor had no choice but to accept this mission. You marrying the man, keeping Warehaven in the family, was not my doing.'

Beatrice sat heavily back down on the stool, uncertain her legs could keep her upright.

'Randall, you are cut!'

Her mother's voice broke through the panic settling in Beatrice's chest.

'Should I summon the surgeon?' Matilda asked.

Her mother bathed her father's neck and shoulder with a clean cloth. 'No. Thankfully it is little more than a deep scratch. It will require cleaning and a stitch or two, but I can manage that much.'

Matilda sighed. 'It is barely noon and already this day has been too long. Perhaps everyone should rest a while.'

Beatrice rose on her still-shaking legs. 'No. I need to find my husband.'

At Matilda's frown, she closed her eyes, asking, 'What?'

'From what I was told, he walked off the battlefield and straight on to a ship.'

She'd told him to leave and he had. Beatrice felt ill with guilt and shame. She had hurt him, terribly.

Even though he'd never said the words, she knew her husband cared for her. It had been evident in the shaking of his hands when she'd been injured in the caves. More evident in the patience he'd had with her these last few nights when he'd not left her to face the terrors of the night, or those lurking behind her closed eyelids, alone.

Beatrice gasped in pain. She had to find him.

Had to go after him. Had to somehow find a way to explain, to make this right.

'Father, may I have a ship?'

'For what?'

Unwilling to discuss what she'd done, she said, 'I must go after him. This was to have been his last mission for King David. If the King discovers this ruse, it places not just Gregor's life in danger, but his brothers' lives also. I cannot let him believe he faces that alone.'

Matilda offered, 'I will see that nothing happens to him and his brothers because of this. Since this whole ruse and mission were partly my fault, I will speak to my uncle and set things to rights.'

She appreciated her aunt's help, but right now, Beatrice's main goal was to find her husband. She repeated her request, 'Father, may I have a ship?'

He laughed softly. 'How quickly you forget. They are not mine to give. They belong to your husband, so they are also yours.'

'If you are going to Roul take one of mine,' Matilda offered, adding, 'One of my ships will raise fewer questions upon arrival.'

'I would suggest taking his men and Sir Brent.'

'Yes, Father, that had already been my thought, too.'

Her mother placed a hand on her arm. 'We will be gone when you return.'

'I guessed as much.' She leaned over to hug her mother. 'I will miss you.'

'No, you won't.' Her father touched her cheek. 'You will be far too busy to notice if we are here or not, at least for a while. But when you do find yourself longing for our company, we will be...' He looked at his wife.

She supplied the locations. 'Either at Dunstan, Montreau or in Wales. If winter has set in, we will be in Wales.'

'I will find you and no matter how busy I am I will miss you.' She kissed each of them and then turned to her aunt. 'Thank you for your help. It was good seeing you again.'

Matilda hugged her. 'You could come to court.'

'Ah, yes, I could.' They all knew that was the last place she wanted to go, but thankfully nobody questioned her response.

She left the bedchamber to find Sir Simon. The older man was seated in a corner of the Great Hall.

She sat down on the bench next to him. 'Did you know that they'd planned this?'

He shook his head. 'No. Not until they started fighting. Then it quickly became obvious.' He slid her an accusing glance. 'I thought you had realised it, too.'

'I did. At first I knew it in my gut. I was so certain they were mock fighting. But at the end, when Gregor raised his sword and sent it straight towards my father's throat, I was positive I'd once again wrongly placed trust in my gut.'

'Do you know what you did, girl?'

She hung her head. 'Yes, I do. I hurt him badly. I don't know how I will ever make that up to him, but I have to try.'

'He is no longer here.'

'I know. I am taking one of the ships and heading for Roul.'

'With his lordship gone, you need to tell me what you wish me to do.'

'As much as I would welcome and appreciate a familiar, even though angry at the moment, face about the ship, I think you should remain here. Someone needs to be in charge, Sir Simon, and I would rather it be you than any other. Hold Warehaven safe for Gregor.'

'Consider it done, my lady.'

'Thank you, Simon,' she said softly.

He clasped her hand. 'You have a long road ahead of you.'

'I know.' She squeezed his fingers. 'But I love him too dearly to walk away without trying.'

Chapter Nineteen

The journey had taken longer because of a storm that kept them at Warehaven and headwinds that slowed them down. Nearly twenty agonising days later, Beatrice walked through the main gates at Roul Keep.

The keep was lightly guarded, the gates open and few guards milled about the bailey. Beatrice entered the Great Hall, wondering how she was going to find Gregor or his brothers.

A dark-haired man approached. 'And you might be?'

It was so obvious that this was one of Gregor's siblings. Same height, same build, his dark hair laced with silver—minus the larger swathe in the front—just a younger version of her husband.

'I am Lady Roul of Warehaven and you are either Rory or Edan.'

'Ah, the elusive bride does exist. I am Rory.' He turned and called out over his shoulder, 'Edan!'

Another younger version of Gregor appeared at his brother's side. 'You called?'

'The men didn't lie. He does have a wife. This is Gregor's bride. Although why he would leave such a pretty thing behind is baffling.'

Edan put his arm around her shoulders and

drew her further into the keep. 'My lady, forgive my brother here, he was raised by dogs. Would you care for refreshments or food? How was your journey?'

'Nothing, thank you. The journey was fine. Where is Gregor?'

'Oh, yes, this is most definitely Gregor's wife. Straight to the point.'

At her look of impatience, he raised his hands as if in surrender. 'I will torment you no more. If it is still daylight, he is at the shipyard. If the sun is about to set, then he is holed up in that unfurnished storage shed he calls a cottage.'

'There are yet a few hours of daylight, so where might I find the shipyard?'

Edan chuckled. The sound reminded her so much of Gregor that it hurt. 'There is a path beyond the postern gate that will take you past that pitiful shed. A short distance beyond is where you'll find Gregor working by himself just off to the side of the main shipyard.'

'We haven't actually seen him yet,' Rory said, explaining, 'Since his return he's yet to venture here.'

'And the one time I went to see him he nearly tore my head off,' Edan added.

She sighed. 'Does he have food there? Clothing? Bedding? Heat?'

In unison they said, 'No.'

'Can I obtain supplies to take with me?'

'Certainly. We'll gather the things and help carry them down.'

Rory warned, 'But after that you're on your own.'

'Could I also have a broom and some rags? A bucket?'

Edan blinked, asking, 'You aren't seriously going to try to clean that place, are you?'

'The cobwebs mostly if it's as bad as you say it is.'

'I'm sure we have a few of those things about.' Rory motioned a maid over. 'Could you help Lady Beatrice gather some cleaning supplies?'

At the woman's questioning look, he said, 'She wants to clean Gregor's shed.'

The woman's surprise slid into a smile. 'And you must be Gregor's lady. Welcome.'

By the time they finished gathering everything she wanted, they needed a small handcart to load it into. The two men pulled the cart behind them as they led her to the shed, their running conversation making the short journey pass quickly.

Once everything had been unloaded, they left, taking the cart with them.

Before she started doing anything in the cottage, she walked the rest of the distance to the shipyard. She wanted to see him. Just to reassure herself that he was indeed here.

Hiding behind a large tree, she watched him work. It was all she could do not to run over and stroke the ragged frown from his face. Regardless of what his brothers thought, he wasn't surly, he was sad and looked so tired and drawn. When was the last time he'd slept? Or eaten a decent meal?

He ran a calloused hand slowly down the length of wood he'd been shaping, his unwavering gaze intent, his touch certain and sensuous. She closed her eyes, imagining him touching her in the same manner. The thought left her shaking with need and longing to be that single piece of wood.

Not wanting to be seen, she left him to his work. From the brief glance she'd had of his cottage, she had plenty of her own work to do before he returned.

His brothers had been right. This was more of a shed than a cottage, but with a little hard work it would do.

There was a well and a fire pit behind the building, and the surrounding woods supplied plenty of dried fodder for the fire. She quickly had a pot of water hanging over the fire. It wouldn't be enough for a bath, but there wasn't a tub to begin with, so it would provide warm water for him to wash up.

She turned and fluffed as best she could the stuffed pallet on the floor in the corner of the shed. Making a small slit in the fabric, she was able to add some sprigs of dried lavender and rosemary to the stuffing, before covering it with the sheets, pillow and cover they'd brought from the keep. She placed a clean set of clothes on the pallet for him to don after washing up.

One leg of the table was broken, so she found a fallen log just about the right height to finish propping up the table. It was sturdy enough to hold the food she'd brought along, which wasn't much, nothing that required cooking, just some bread, cheese, fruit, smoked fish and some sweets the cook swore Gregor liked.

The scraped-skin covering over the single window had seen better days, but she managed to straighten it and, using a rock, put the nails back into place.

Thankfully she'd let his brothers talk her into bringing a brazier and coals, because there was no heat source in the cottage. It didn't matter how warm the day was, at night it would be cool and the heat welcome. Additionally, once the coals had warmed up and she'd sprinkled some of the herbs on top, it lent a sweet smell to the cottage.

A good sweeping of the ceiling, walls and floor assured her that she would not walk into any spiderwebs during the night.

By the time she'd finished, the water was warm enough to bring inside and set on the floor next to a stool where she'd put soap, a towel and a comb.

She used the corner of another towel to dip in the water and cleaned herself up before combing and braiding her hair.

Beatrice then took a seat on the armless chair

in the corner and waited. And paced. And then sat down to wait a little longer.

Each passing minute made her more nervous. And every heartbeat made her more anxious.

Would he send her away? Would he hear her apology? Would he understand her distress at that moment? How could he ever forgive her? These same questions had plagued her since the moment she'd learned of their ruse.

When her mind wasn't tossing those questions and fears at her, it was her body providing the be-devilment.

It had only been a matter of weeks since she'd shared his bed, but she felt as if she'd not seen or touched Gregor in years. Her arms ached to hold him. She ached more to be held, to be pulled close against his chest and embraced just one more time before he set her aside.

Finally, when she thought she couldn't possibly wait a moment longer, the door opened.

He stopped the second he stepped inside, his gaze sweeping the cottage to settle on her. 'What are you doing here?'

This was the welcome she'd expected and she refused to let it upset her. 'My husband is here, where else would I be?'

'You can leave the same way you came, Bea-trice.'

'Gregor, don't send me away. Please, I beg you, let me speak.'

'Don't waste your time begging me for anything, you'll not get it.'

He hadn't yet left. He was still standing in the doorway and as long as she could see him, Beatrice had to believe there was hope.

'Gregor, I wronged you. I know that. And I know nothing I say now will ease the harsh cruelty of those words.'

The cold darkness of his eyes spoke of rage, of the anger she'd caused him. But the line of his mouth was soft instead of hard. Instead of cutting straight across his face, it angled down at the corners. She'd been right, she had hurt him. Deeply. For that she would never forgive herself.

'Gregor, I am sorry I hurt you so.'

'You worry for nothing. I would have had to care for you to hurt me.'

Beatrice ignored the stabbing of her heart. It was no less than what she deserved.

And again she realised, he was still standing there.

'I know there is no forgiveness for what I said. I meant none of it. Oh, Gregor, I don't know how to explain my behaviour. I thought you'd killed my father and when I should have stood by your side regardless of what had happened, I didn't. I chose him over you, even though you are the one I love more than life itself. I cannot find a way to make up for the awful things I said, or for the way I hurt you.'

He just stared at her, not moving, not blinking. She wasn't certain he breathed until he said, 'You did nothing that wasn't expected. He is your father, Beatrice, of course at the moment of your greatest fear you chose him. I could have expected no less.'

'But I sent you away without giving you a chance to explain.'

'I would have left without your order.'

Confusion settled heavy around her. 'Why?'

'I did as I was ordered. I took Warehaven and married its lady. My task was completed.'

'But...' She let her words trail off, uncertain of what she wanted to ask.

'What do you want from me, Beatrice?'

His forgiveness. His love. That's what she wanted from him. But his voice was so flat, so expressionless that the cold web of defeat settled in her belly. She glanced down at the floor. This was her own fault. It would be easier to bear his anger, or even his hate than this...this...nothing, as if they were strangers.

He deserved more than that.

She lifted her head, not at all surprised to feel the heat of tears on her cheeks. 'Gregor, I will leave you in peace. Just know that I am truly sorry for any pain I have caused you. And that you were loved, dearly.'

Beatrice headed to the door. She edged around him, wishing he would do something. Anything.

Say something. Anything. She longed so much for just one more simple touch of his fingertips.

As she crossed the threshold, he pulled her back inside and slammed the door closed.

He stood before her, his arms crossed against his chest and asked, 'Are you finished wallowing in guilt yet?'

At her silence, he said, 'You don't trust me, you don't love me, you hate me and you never want to see me again. Isn't that what you said?'

She nodded. Yes, she had said all of that and more. 'I didn't mean—'

'No.' He shook his head. 'You had your say. It is my turn.'

Beatrice closed her mouth.

'I am fairly certain you even screamed just to be sure I heard you.'

She couldn't disagree, she had screamed at him.

'And I'm also fairly certain that I told you on more than one occasion that I could live with your hatred, did I not?'

She nodded again. Yes, he had said that.

'Not once have I lied to you.'

She couldn't disagree, because he hadn't.

'Never have I raised a hand to harm you.'

Again, she knew he was right.

'Yet those were the reasons you used to order me out of your life and then you come here dripping in the stench of guilt and self-pity to reason with me, to apologise? What do you expect me to do?'

'I… I don't know.' To her horror her tears fell harder. 'I just don't want you to leave me.'

'Stop this.' He wiped at her tears before resting his hands on her shoulders. 'I told you that this was not some fanciful tale of love sung about by the troubadours. Ours is a marriage between two warriors and will rarely be easy, but I will leave you only one way, Beatrice, and that is the day I die.'

He reached into the pouch hanging from his belt, lifted her left hand and slipped her ring back on her finger. 'Do not take this off again.'

'But I thought…'

'And I thought you would have seen through our ruse.'

She hesitantly leaned forward, wanting to rest against him, but held back, uncertain of his reaction. Gregor growled softly, then pulled her hard against his chest.

'I am sorry for the words I spoke, Gregor. I know they must have hurt.'

'Beatrice, they did sting, but I understood them. That was not the reason I left. I knew by the look in your eyes that I had caused you so much pain, so much heartache that I couldn't stay and risk causing you any more. Eventually it would only tear us apart, leaving both of us filled with unbearable rage and heartbreak.'

'My heart wouldn't have ached so had I not

cared for you. When I said I loved you, I meant that sincerely. There is no other man who would be better for me than you. Gregor, my life would be empty without you.'

He sighed heavily. 'To be honest, I would have come back. No matter how many times I've vowed to hold you at arm's length, I've never been able to do so. I'd have probably returned sooner rather than later, considering how much I have missed you at night.'

'Only at night?'

'Yes.'

She flinched at his brutal honesty.

He added, 'And in the morning, during the afternoon and lately in the evening, too.'

He led her over to the chair in the corner, took a seat and pulled her down on to his lap.

'Yes, your words hurt. But even had I killed your father, I still would have kept my vow, I would have shouldered your hatred, had I thought for one heartbeat that I wouldn't cause you any more pain.'

She leaned her cheek against his shoulder. 'Can you forgive me for being so weak?'

'Weak?' He rolled his eyes. 'That is something you will never be. There is nothing to forgive you for, Beatrice.' He shuddered in mock horror. 'And don't beg me for anything. All I am, all I possess is always yours for the asking.'

'There is one thing I would like to beg you for.'

'What is that?'

'I want to be a piece of your wood.'

He pushed her away to look at her in question.

She explained, 'I saw you today, working with your wood. I've never seen anything as sensuous as the way you stroked your palm down that piece of lumber. For a minute, I was lost in lust and jealousy.'

'Jealousy?'

'You were so intent, so focused and passionate, that I felt as if I were watching something that shouldn't be done in public.'

He reached beneath her gown and slowly, almost reverently brushed his palm up the side of her leg. Beatrice sighed and let her head fall back against his arm. 'Oh, yes. Just like that.'

He nuzzled her neck. 'Is there anything else we need to discuss before I haul you over to that freshly made pallet?'

'Yes, I do have one question, may be two.'

He leaned his back against the chair. 'What?'

'Do you have any particular names you prefer for a child?'

He frowned at her. 'Is this your way of telling me you are pregnant?'

'Yes, it is.'

'Perfect.'

'Are you displeased?'

'Not in the least. Just upset that you found it needful to haul my child off on a seagoing vessel. What were you thinking?'

'That I needed to apologise to you before he or she was born.'

'Don't do that again.'

'I won't.'

He stripped off her soft boots and stockings, then rose to set her on her feet. Grasping the hem of her gown, he asked, 'Is there anything else? Are we finished talking?'

'I think we're finished.'

The moment he placed her naked on the pallet, Beatrice said, 'Oh, I forgot, what will King David say?'

She laughed at his glare. He was fully aware that she was tormenting him on purpose.

'I have already spoken to David and it seems David's Wolf is yet bound by chains.'

'So he didn't consider your mission a success?'

'No.'

'But you have Warehaven.'

Gregor stripped off his clothing and knelt between her legs. 'He feels it was given as a bride gift.'

'Why would he believe that?' She tried to ignore the sudden racing of her heart as he stroked his hands up the inside of her thighs ever so slowly.

'While I didn't tell him the fight had been a ruse, I did explain why I failed to kill FitzHenry.'

She tried to focus on his words, but the fingers sliding up her legs had met at the juncture of her thighs and were teasingly muddling her concentration. 'What did you tell him?'

Gregor leaned over her, resting his weight on his forearms, and lowered his head to cover her lips with his.

Whatever concentration she'd possessed fled beneath the warmth of his kiss. Anything she'd planned on saying melted into a fog of need.

'I explained that Warehaven's Warrior possesses a tender heart.' His whisper brushed against her ear. 'Too tender a heart for me to break in such a cruel manner.'

Beatrice moaned at the heat entering her. She pushed her hips up, savouring the warmth slowly filling her, yet wanting something more.

He held her so tightly in his embrace that she felt his heart pounding.

'I told him I could not do so, because I love her far too much.'

His words filled her with more joy than she could bear. Her eyes filled with tears as she stared up at him and cupped his cheek. 'Oh, Gregor, I love you, too.'

Chapter Twenty

Warehaven Keep—Spring 1146

Gregor leaned against the rail on the deck of the forecastle. Warehaven's harbour was in sight and from the line of men standing watch, he feared he'd tarried too long. This rounding up of Beatrice's family and delivering them to Warehaven had been the Wolf's last mission for King David, at least this particular Wolf's last mission, and it had required more time at sea than he would have preferred considering how close Beatrice was to birthing their child.

The task hadn't been hard. Nor had it required the shedding of any blood. In fact, he was certain it had come from the Empress.

He'd basically served as a transport for the entire Warehaven family. Matilda had come aboard in Montreau with Beatrice's brother Jared, his wife and their two babies. The rest of the family had boarded in Dunstan—FitzHenry and his wife, Beatrice's sister Isabella, her husband and their two babies.

At times he'd felt as if this mission had been his final punishment—trapped aboard a small ship with his family-by-marriage and four babies who seemed to cry in unison as if on cue.

It had been the longest two weeks of his entire life.

Now, from the looks on the faces of his men at the docks, it wasn't going to end any better.

He didn't wait for the ship to tie off, instead leaping to land the second they were close enough.

A grim-faced Simon handed him the reins to a waiting horse. 'You need to hurry.'

He didn't wait for the family—they all knew their way to the keep. His man kept pace as the two of them raced ahead.

'Has the baby been born?'

'If not yet, then any minute, my lord.'

'How has Beatrice been?'

'Teary.'

Gregor grinned wryly. 'How many times would you like me to apologise, Simon?'

'Not necessary. Just reminds me why I'll never marry again.'

As they neared the keep, Simon shouted for the guards to open the gate, explaining, 'I had it closed behind me when I headed for the docks this morning.'

'Any reason for the added caution?'

'No. Nothing has occurred, just wanted to be safe.'

Gregor entered the Great Hall to the sound of his wife's scream ripping down the stairwell. Suddenly his legs almost gave out and he took the stairs two at time, slammed through their chamber door and froze. One of his brothers-by-marriage had claimed childbirth was a beautiful thing, the other had solemnly shaken his head and agreed.

They'd both lied.

Three women turned to him at the same time, making it feel oddly like an assault.

Almedha glowered.

Helena, the midwife, pointed at the door. 'If you can't be of any help, leave.'

Beatrice, drenched in sweat, her face red, gasped and reached a hand out to him. 'Don't leave me.'

Without hesitation he crossed the room and took her hand, ignoring the midwife's complaints about him being present at the birth. He couldn't leave her now after he'd repeatedly promised to be here.

She grimaced and curled her fingers tighter around his hand, repeating, 'Don't leave me.'

'I won't.' Although he'd really rather lead a charge into battle on foot and naked than see his wife in such pain.

'Promise.'

'I swear. I will not leave your side.'

'If anything should happen to me—'

'Beatrice, stop. Don't speak nonsense. Nothing is going to happen.' He shot a worried glance at the midwife, who did nothing more than roll her eyes before motioning him to get behind Beatrice on the bed.

He rubbed her back and shoulders between contractions and acted as her support wall during them.

Finally, when he was certain his wife could bear no more, the midwife said, 'This will be it.'

Beatrice cried, 'I can't.'

Gregor reached around her and gripped both of her hands. 'There is no choice here, Beatrice. Push.'

Suddenly everything happened in a blur. Beatrice pushed, screamed, pushed, and then someone claimed, 'It's a girl!'

The next thing he knew the two older women were cleaning, washing, moving, changing, until finally he and his wife were on clean bedding, she was in a fresh shift and the baby was wrapped and laying in her arms.

Then, blessedly, the door to the chamber closed, leaving them alone on the bed.

He stretched out alongside her, his back propped up against the pillows, Beatrice resting in the crook of his arm, her head on his chest, the baby sleeping on her mother's chest.

'Were you hoping for a boy?'

Gregor smiled and stroked her cheek. She sounded so tired, yet so very happy.

'Not really. I was simply hoping for whatever would make you happiest.'

Beatrice sighed. 'You are too good to me.'

'Would you prefer I be cruel? I can be if you would like.'

She laughed. 'No, you couldn't. Besides, I love you just the way you are.'

'And I you, my love. I'd not change a thing.'

* * * * *

If you enjoyed this story, discover more
great reads from Denise Lynn

THE WARRIOR'S WINTER BRIDE
BEDDED BY THE WARRIOR
PREGNANT BY THE WARRIOR
FALCON'S LOVE
FALCON'S HEART

MILLS & BOON®

HISTORICAL

AWAKEN THE ROMANCE OF THE PAST

A sneak peek at next month's titles...

In stores from 23rd March 2017:

- **Claiming His Desert Princess** – Marguerite Kaye
- **Bound by Their Secret Passion** – Diane Gaston
- **The Wallflower Duchess** – Liz Tyner
- **Captive of the Viking** – Juliet Landon
- **The Spaniard's Innocent Maiden** – Greta Gilbert
- **The Cowboy's Orphan Bride** – Lauri Robinson

Just can't wait?
Buy our books online before they hit the shops!
www.millsandboon.co.uk

Also available as eBooks.

MILLS & BOON®

EXCLUSIVE EXTRACT

The Earl of Penford knows his passion for Lorene Summerfield is scandalous, but when he's accused of her husband's murder, he must clear his name—and win her hand!

Read on for a sneak preview of
BOUND BY THEIR SECRET PASSION

Her old romantic dreams burst forth. Why hold back? Dell's kiss was even more than she could have imagined. Why not give herself to it?

She pulled off her bonnet and threw her arms around his neck, answering the press of his lips with eagerness. He urged her mouth open and she readily complied, surprised and delighted that his warm tongue touched hers.

He tasted wonderful.

She plunged her fingers into his hair, loving its softness and its curls. She liked his hair best when it looked tousled by a breeze. Or mussed by her hands.

He pressed her body against his and the thrill intensified. How marvelous to feel his muscles, so firm against her. And more. One hand slid down from his hair to his arm to his hip. How wanton was that?

But she was a widow, was she not? Was not everyone telling her she had license to do as she pleased? It pleased her to touch him. Although she was not quite brazen enough to touch that hard part of him that thrilled her most of all.

'Lorene,' he groaned as his hands pressed against her derriere, intensifying the sensations in all sorts of ways. 'We should stop.'

She did not want to stop. 'Why?' She kissed his neck. 'I am a widow. Are not widows permitted?'

'Do not tempt me,' he said, though his hands caressed her.

She moved away, just enough that he could see her face. 'If you do not want this, then, yes, we should stop, but I do desire it, Dell.'

For a long time, she realized. Since she first met him. He was the man she had dreamed about in her youth, a good man, kind, honorable, handsome. But something more, something that made her want to bed him.

Don't miss
BOUND BY THEIR SECRET PASSION
By Diane Gaston

Available April 2017
www.millsandboon.co.uk